Fool's Gold

Julie Harris

Fool's Gold copyright © Julie Harris 2013, 2015
First published as *Anna's Gold*, 1992 by Arrow Books, Sydney.

Fool's Gold is a work of fiction, and any resemblance to any person, living or dead, or to any actual events, is purely coincidental. All rights reserved.

ISBN 13: 978-0-9873456-9-1
ISBN 10: 0-9873456-9-9

Chapter One

THIRTEEN MONTHS OF FOLLOWING MICHAEL'S dream two hundred miles across the Great Divide came to a relieved finale. The baby in Anna's arms cried and the cries became impatient, angry wails. Her mother was oblivious. Oh, my God, she thought. Is this all there is?

Scattered over a vast section of cleared hillside below were thirty or more calico tents, the occasional tin shack, lean-to and humpy.

Bitter Creek.

Where the making of a fortune or the shatter of a dream waited patiently amid dust, mud and sweat.

Tears welled in Anna's eyes.

At the start, Michael's excited anticipation may have been contagious. She looked at him now and wiped her dirty face on her dirty sleeve. If he noticed her desolation he said nothing. His bright eyes were alive with silent joy. Anna's stung from bitter disappointment.

'Ssh, baby,' she whispered, knowing any attempt to placate Susan was futile.

'Come on, Anna.'

The final few hundred yards was taken on foot.

It was too much to hope for, of course, that the rough, ravaged miners wouldn't notice their arrival. All around, perfunctory curses and noise of machinery began to dwindle and eventually, it faded. The Hall's welcome came in hushed stares, silent perusal and stony wonder at the sight of a woman. A young, pretty one at that.

Again, if Michael noticed there was no reaction. He'd found his Paradise and from it, he'd pull a fortune. Nothing else mattered.

Anna could almost hear the thoughts. Exhaustion was too intense, there was no room for fear. She ached, totally. Make the best of it, her thoughts whirled. Someone whistled. It was instinct to trace its source—a wild, unshaven face, curiosity behind the eyes. Anna clasped her angry baby tighter and watched as her feet trod the uncertain way down the rocky, dusty incline.

1

We are finally here. Tonight I cannot find words to describe the nothing I feel.

Anna tickled her chin with the quill feather and sighed. Her mind, always so eager to translate thoughts to paper, failed. The lamplight cast eerie shadows and demonic silhouettes against the tent side. She tried not to see, tried to force her tired thoughts to recall the events of the day and of the two before, but travelling so far with an unhappy baby and a silent husband was only conducive to despair. If she lay down to sleep now, Susan would wake, crying. Michael was restless enough in his sleep, but he always was. For three years now, she'd watched him toss and turn and his incessant snoring was lately becoming more than annoying. Anna dipped her pen into her ink bottle.

The baby will wake if I settle to sleep. She seems to read my mind and she knows how to frustrate me. She refused the breast twice today and screamed when I offered her water. Michael says she will feed when she is hungry and the more I worry, the worse she will get. Fine for him, I have never felt...

'Anna, I canna sleep with that bloody scratching!'

She bit her lip. He was snoring only a moment ago. 'I'm almost finished,' she said quietly.

He'd heard that before, too. Michael reached over, grabbed his wife's diary and flung it across the tent. 'And you'll put the lamp out this time.'

'But I was waiting for Susan to wake.'

'And I need to sleep!'

'But I need to do this, it's the only time I can!'

She was about to say more until she heard the angry intake of breath and sealed both her lips and her ink bottle. Best not to cause trouble when he was tired. The back of his hand was always heavy and stinging.

Anna retrieved her book, read what she'd written and found she'd have to add a "ness" to the "nothing". It would have to wait until daylight. In daylight, she wouldn't have time. Anna extinguished the lamp and settled down beside her husband.

Shadows from a nearby campfire danced against the calico. Anna drew the covers high, so she wouldn't be frightened by what her imagination saw. Michael kicked the covers off. 'It's too hot, damn you,' he grumbled while she watched the shapes within shadows and heard a stranger's high pitched cackle of laughter. Anna cuddled closer to her husband and felt him flinch away.

2

All was silent again, except for the night sounds of the bush—sounds she doubted she could ever become acquainted with. The light wind whistled through distant treetops.

Her eyes closed involuntarily. More monsters lurked behind the darkness of her eyelids, more fearsome in fact than those she could see in the distorted silhouettes. Slowly, her arm, with a will of its own, found refuge against Michael's strong, muscular side. The rest of her body followed until she was curled safely against him. Here was comfort; nothing could claim her. Nothing.

'Anna, no, I said I was tired.' He flung her arm off and moved so far against the edge of the cot he almost fell out.

She was used to this by now, even if her pride stung. This had been happening almost every night since Susan had been born. Five months was a long, long time.

Another laugh echoed around the Bitter Creek diggings. Anna strained to listen to the distant conversations. Young voices, old voices, and all were men's voices.

'Tis Rose herself for me.'

'Rose is too bloody old, man. Now, Ginger-Lee, that's a woman…'

Woman? Where?

The wind changed direction and she heard no more than garbled voices and the onset of Michael's snores. She couldn't take any more. Anna nudged him fiercely—it was usually enough to quiet the rumblings which, if not stopped, gradually became thunderous.

A laughing obscenity split the night.

'Do ye not know there's a lady among us now?'

Anna waited for the reply.

'If she chose to live here, Billy Squire, she'll have to be getting used to it.'

A lot of voices seemed to agree.

As if on cue, the baby began to squeak. Squeaks always preceded angry cries. Anna scrambled to the baby, and a familiar pungent odour wafted to meet her. Michael stirred. If he woke now, hell's fury itself would only be a joyful promise. Anna whispered to the baby. A mistake. The voice was recognised and immediate attention demanded. On hands and knees, Anna threw the soiled nappy outside. She'd see to it in the morning. All she could hope for was someone's foot not finding it first. If she ventured out into the night now, she'd probably fall down a mine shaft and never be forgiven.

Forgotten? Perhaps. Missed? Doubtful. Forgiven? Never.

3

'Jee-ee-ziz!' someone cried and the echo rebounded around the entire camp. 'We're trying to sleep here!'

Anxiety hit. Everyone was joining in now, the baby's objections becoming fiercer while Michael snored on, unawares. Anna fumbled for the ties on her nightdress and made herself as comfortable as possible, as far as possible from Michael. He hated the sounds the baby made as she fed.

Strangers' voices were unappreciative of a small baby's midnight screams; the baby unappreciative of her mother's nipple at any time. Anna knew that if Susan didn't feed soon, her breasts would explode. Anxiety became tears. A soft plea escaped her lips as she fought a losing battle with the baby. 'Please, baby, stop this crying, please. I'm doing the best I can...'

And suddenly, one voice could take no more. 'Let the girlie be!'

The hush that followed was extremely loud. Michael stirred, mumbled and rolled over. Susan condescended to feed. Anna's panic ebbed.

I have an ally, she thought and then wondered who the voice belonged to. A tiny smile touched her face. In this wilderness, there was someone who cared?

Anna touched the soft wisps of fine hair on her child's head. She knew two huge dark eyes were staring up at her face in the stygian gloom and after a little while, the strong sucking stopped. She felt the child's smile and for a moment lost in time, everything was devoid of futility.

Perhaps it wouldn't be as horrendous as she'd first thought. Perhaps miracles did occur.

The Hall's claim on the southern end of the muddy, stagnant, leech infested waterhole yielded nothing but anger and impatience for the first few days.

Anna's aversion to the horrible place quickly turned to indifference. The days were long and joyless; and although she was surrounded by people, she was terribly alone. Hadn't it always been that way?

The novelty of having a woman and child amongst them was short-lived. The diggers soon accepted her presence and acknowledged it with a smile even though there was rarely any conversation. Her shyness was mistaken for aloofness. One or two would ask after the baby but that was all. They tried and mostly failed to hold tongues when The Lady was about. She was not Anna, nor was she Mrs Hall. She was The Lady. And although The Lady wanted to curse like a Clyde shipbuilder, she did not.

4

Day by day, she sat on the creek bank and silently watched her husband at work. Displaced, bored, Michael's old hat shielded more than a saddened expression. She hoped to hear the call, *Anna! Quick!* which never seemed to come. He was just like the rest of them working for hours at a time under the scorching sun, cursing at splinters from new pick handles, cursing misfortune, cursing the Lord for his indifference to their dreams.

Michael cursed at her when he'd exhausted his targets for profanity. But the afternoon he swore at the baby for being such a screaming, complaining little bastard, no wonder it was a female, Anna attacked. The argument caused some idle curiosity amongst the men—boredom was a terrible thing to endure and a fight between man and wife rather refreshing. Michael's hand quickly silenced the fishwife ravings and pride stinging, Anna retreated. He was congratulated of course.

Never let them win. Never.

Michael was rewarded, his initiation at the site now complete. Each night after supper he'd join the male socializing ritual of drink, talk of gold, talk of women. The gold and the women were each scarce commodities.

Anna stayed away and used the time alone to sketch the images she often saw in her mind's eye—huge elegant hats only ladies of society would dare wear. Mostly, the hats were amusing designs and belonged where they stayed—in dreams. After a few hours, Michael would stumble home, drunk and tired. Which was good, really, because when he was drunk he slept heavily and the scratching of the quill went unheeded deep into the early hours.

To keep him somewhat pacified, she cooked his meals, watched him at work, fetched this and that and tried to quell his antagonism and not add to it by breathing too loud. When he began to find gold, all would change for the better.

It had to.

Her genuine offers to assist him were laughed away and the days stretched to infinity and back again. Uselessness soon became boredom.

Anna began to watch for the old man who would go by the tent in the mornings and evenings. He'd never say much except, 'Howdy', in his rough American voice. Sometimes he'd nod and try to smile. He was always too quick for someone his age and by the time she'd found the courage to ask if he'd stay and have some tea with her, he was too far away and too deaf to hear.

Or perhaps Tom Manning was just like any man, only willing to hear relevant things, not wanting to listen to a lonely woman who lived in dreams while she slowly drowned in the mire of a man's dirty world.

5

On the eleventh morning, two things occurred:

Tom Manning became a friend and Michael found gold.

Anna didn't know which was more valuable.

Tom ambled by the tent with more than a 'Howdy' on his lips that morning. 'How's your eyes, girlie?' he barked.

'My eyes?'

He thrust his wrinkled, spotty hand very close to Anna's face. Her eyesight was fine. She dug the huge splinter from the base of his thumb using the small pocket knife he offered. 'There you are, as good as new,' she said with a smile.

'Don't I wish,' he mumbled, and ambled away.

Anna called out did he want a mug of tea, but her invitation fell on deaf ears.

Later that very morning, she was painstakingly drawing an apple depending from the brim of a hat when Michael's bellowing yell thundered up to meet her. The baby woke screaming and for a moment, Anna didn't know what to do. Ignore both? Keep sketching before the vision faded? Feed the baby? Feign deafness or let them both scream as both were prone to do anyway?

Michael came running to her, gold pan in hand. Anna rose and took the baby from the cradle. Susan stopped crying when Anna gave her a finger to suck on. All problems solved. 'Look!' The gold pan was duly thrust under her nose. Did everyone think she was blind? In the bottom groove of the tin dish sat five flakes of gold, neither small nor large, barely a quarter inch wide and coarse to touch. Anna looked up into Michael's eyes and the brilliance of the gold was of no comparison to what she saw there. Her heart lifted—a lifelong dream achieved. Even if it was his dream.

'Say something!'

'Is it a fortune?'

'No, of course not. It's the beginning, Anna.'

She had never seen elation this severe and she didn't know what to do or say. Michael kissed her forehead and traipsed back to the creek. Anna watched him walk away and one thought echoed around her mind:

Find a lot of gold, Michael.

Tom Manning spat a lump of chewed tobacco at the piece of tin which substituted as a door. It kept some of the cold out in winter. He looked down at the stiff, decaying photograph, so old now he only regarded it

6

once a week, fearing more regular perusal would fade the image completely.

Catherine.

His Katie.

The only surviving memory he could still trust these days lay in that one photograph. Twenty-two when she died, thirty-two years ago. She never got over the birth of the boy. Took her a year to die. April 24, 1835. A cold spring day that took his heart, too.

Katie. Large, dark eyes that could core his soul. Everyone was surprised when the boy's eyes were his father's summer blue.

He's you, Tom, she used to say and try to smile.

Just like the girl across the creek there, trying her best to smile when the eyes said something else. Women were good at that. So much like Katie, she was, her hands, too. Not the touch though—no, that was nothing but an old man's hope of sliding back into a dead yesterday.

Tom was lost in the nice ways, never comfortable playing anyone but himself. The role came with age and wisdom. 'How's your eyes, girl?' he'd asked while his heart ached to hear Katie's voice again. She wasn't Katie of course, but the mirror image deluded his tired old mind into believing it was. It wouldn't have been hard to get the girl talking. He'd seen loneliness, tasted it for most of his life. God knew what she was doing at Bitter Creek in the first place. Little girls and babies didn't belong here. This wasn't Ballarat. There were no women to gossip with, no children. There was nothing. Just Bitter Creek.

He'd heard her all right. 'Would you like a cup of tea?' she'd called, nice and loud. Dreams had been a lie. He'd used the excuse of old age not to hear, not to respond. She'd only go breaking his heart again. But now, as he sat staring at the image of a dead wife he still loved more than life itself, he felt a trifle lost. He'd gone and missed the damned chance.

Tom put the photograph back between two pieces of yellowed, fragile silk and carefully slipped it into the tattered Bible. Hers, not his. He'd never needed no God. God never helped the pain when Katie was dying, so Tom never bothered praying after that.

The old man emerged into the late afternoon sun, glad of the escape from his sweltering tin shelter. His back was aching again, his limp more pronounced. He told everyone it was from a fight at Sutter's Mill—it was only lumbago, an affliction which had haunted him for the last twenty years. Twenty years that felt like fifty.

Anna was drawing some more of her pretties until the husband appeared. Always the way. Tom watched them have their lunch, watched Mick return to his claim and waited for the girl to take out her pretties

7

again. She took up the axe instead. And as he watched, he wished he was young and good looking but that was forty years ago when thoughts cooperated with the body, when memories were still too shiny to rust.

Tom watched and Tom winced.

She'd never split that lump of ironbark. Never. She didn't have the strength or the knowing. It wasn't called ironbark for nothing. Her damned lazy, good for nothing man needed a kick in the ass for letting her do this.

Fortified with another wad of tobacco and knowing that soon he'd have to ask Sam to get more, the old man approached, cautiously. Anna didn't see him coming and he heard her soft curses. 'Bloody thing, you're tougher than a witch's-' Tom pretended he was deaf again. Amusement touched his eyes.

'Howdy,' he said.

She jumped in fright and any exasperated anger faded into a sudden, welcoming smile. 'Oh, hello.' Tom's heart kicked against his ribs as he heard, 'How's your hand?' The crisp English accent made her sound like a schoolmarm. Well educated, this one. If she was educated, what the hell was she doing out here?

'Hand's fine,' he lied. It was swollen, he could barely move his thumb. She wouldn't see, though, because he kept his hand buried in his pocket. The girl had that unmistakeable light in her eye—same one Katie would get. She was wondering what he wanted. Tom spat the tobacco and it curved in a glorious arc before splattering the ground. 'Do that all day, girlie, won't make no difference. You'll just wear yourself out.'

'We'll see. I'm not about to let a block of wood defeat me, too.'

She had Katie's ways, all right. The same defiance in the voice, in the eyes. Only this one caught the back of a husband's hand for her troubles. Tom had seen it and heard it too often. But a man could do what he liked with his woman and although Tom didn't necessarily approve of hitting them—he knew there were other ways to quell spirit without breaking it—he couldn't do much about it. It was none of his business. Could be she enjoyed it. Could be the only way to get noticed. If she didn't like it, she'd soon learn how to avoid it unless she was stupid.

The more he watched, the more he realised she wasn't stupid. Just stubborn. She raised the axe high and brought it down heavily. Tom didn't move away—he knew the axe would bounce again. Bounce right out of her hands, soon. She didn't curse this time. She tried to be ladylike about it all and she mumbled.

'Tom's the name,' he said.

'Yes, I know.'

8

'Oh.'

Anna rested the axe on her weary shoulder and wiped sweat from her forehead before it stung her eyes. 'Billy Squire lives there, Joshua McPherson there, Dinny Masterson over there... I know of everyone and everyone knows of me but Tom Manning happens to be the only man courageous enough to talk to me. I must be an ogre.'

Nope, Tom thought. No one wants to get beat up by Mick Hall, the mad Scotsman. Tom sent her a short, curdled grin and wished his heart would behave itself because she smiled back.

'Would you care for a mug of tea, Mr Manning?'

'Tom's the name,' was all he said.

'Tom, would you like a...'

'Yep. Don't mind if I do.'

The grins were contagious now. Tom settled on a log near the campfire and held the pint mug between his hands. He sipped the bitter, strong brew. Only one thing he knew of could add some taste. The small flask was withdrawn from his tattered coat and he glanced up at Anna. 'Whiskey. No offence, girl, but tea needs a helpin' hand.'

Anna threw a cursory glance to the creek. Michael wasn't looking. She accepted the dash of whiskey from the old man. After a few more sips, her smile was very large.

'How long have you been here?' Anna asked, more for something to say than a genuine inquiry.

'Sometimes too long. Nowhere else to go, nothing else to do.'

To Anna, the words seemed an echo. It was how she felt most of the time. Duty to her husband had brought her here. Michael was all the family she had left. Michael and Susan.

The old man heard the squeaks of the wakening baby. For weeks now, he'd been wanting to have a good look at the little one and here was his opportunity. It was there in its cradle, something like muslin covering it to keep the flies off. Plenty of flies, here, mosquitoes, too. Damn things. Bloodsuckers everywhere. Leeches on your ankles and hands when you panned, mosquitoes trying to carry you off alive while you tried to sleep off a hard day's work...

He lifted the muslin and looked down at the baby. Big dark eyes studied him intently. Apart from the eyes it looked just like an ordinary baby to him, nothing special. 'Girl ain't it?'

'Yes.'

'Looks like you.'

9

'I suppose she does.'

Something was wrong here, Tom felt he'd said the wrong thing again. Silence reigned for a little while.

'He's doing it wrong.'

'Excuse me?'

'He's doing it wrong.'

'Doing what wrong, Tom?'

'He's tippin' it all out his dish, girl. He's got thirty ounces of flake sittin' in his tailings. I see it happening.'

Anna chewed on her thumbnail and dark eyes flickered at him. Tom had seen that look before, many times. In Katie's eyes it meant she was considering a truth. Just took him to find it for her. His old heart pounded again. It hurt.

'Are you sure?' she asked. He knew she would.

'I been prospecting for fifty years and he's doing it wrong. Could be I might teach you the proper way, seeing that Mick of yours got no ears to listen and no eyes to see and no brain wanting to learn.' Strong words, he knew. But this one could tolerate honesty without having to hide from it. He could see that in her eyes. He continued. 'He's stubborn. Sometimes being stubborn's good, but with him, not so good. You know that anyways. He don't have the touch, but you, maybe you do.'

'The touch?'

'I been watching you. You wanna learn. You been itchin' to try.'

'I don't follow you, Mr Manning.'

'You want me to teach you how to pan for gold or not?'

'Of course I do!'

As swiftly as it came, her eagerness departed. The eyes clouded and she looked down into her whiskey flavoured tea. It was as dark as the abyss she'd suddenly fallen into. 'Michael won't approve.'

'Michael won't know till you show him how good you are and then he won't care. All that matters to him is finding gold, and no amount'll ever be enough. Well?'

'Well what?'

'When do you wanna start?'

'Now?' Anna asked, afraid he'd change his mind.

'Yeah, why not? Yesterday's no damned good to me no more and tomorrow might not get here.'

'But Susan…'

10

'I don't think she'd mind comin' along,' Tom said and a gnarled, stiff, tobacco-stained finger tickled the baby's foot. The old man received his reward—a mountainous grin.

And if anyone from Bitter Creek noticed the regular absences and the smiling faces on the crazy old American and the pretty Englishwoman, no one spoke aloud.

I began on the tailings heap whilst Susan slept. At first, Michael was too busy to notice what I was about. I found nothing in the first half hour and began to wonder if what Tom had said that day had been true. Perhaps Michael did know what he was about after all. He surprised me as he usually does when I'm concentrating.

'What's all this, then?' he asked.

'I'm going to pan.'

Michael thought it was amusing. 'That's the tailings, Anna. Do you know what the tailings are?'

'What you've thrown away, of course.'

'Anna, if there was any gold to be found would it be there?'

'I want to practise. Perhaps you missed some.'

'You're wasting your time.'

Wasting my time, she thought and anger rose. I'm always wasting my time. Whenever I'm doing something you feel is odd, you explain it as a waste of time. Her spark of anger threatened to strike into a flame.

'Isn't there something else you could be doing?'

'Such as?'

'Don't speak to me in that tone.'

'There's nothing for me to do, Michael. The baby is asleep, I've hardly any ink left and it's too hot for a walk. I'm doing no harm, I'm not nagging you. Please let me do this?'

Michael rolled his eyes and walked off. 'It's your back. Don't come to me complaining.'

Anna pulled a face at his retreating figure.

'You can sit there all day as far as I care. It'll do you no good. But you never listen to a man, you never have, you never will...'

Anna returned to her panning and mimicked his grumbles as he took his woeful complaints with him to the shaker. She took her sieve, put it on top of her goldpan, scooped a hefty amount of Tom's decreed goldbearing wash from the tailings heap on the sieve. Even if she did have a sore back she'd keep it secret. Michael's incessant, "I told you so" were far worse than her grandmother's ever had been. With a sigh, Anna immersed pan and all in the creek and began the underwater shake.

Tom had taught her "The Art" by salting coarse sand with shotgun pellets. In theory, the pellets, being heavy like gold, would drop through the sieve into the pan. Then came the ritual of washing the lighter sand and dirt away by gentle swirlings and tippings of the dish. Tom made it appear quite easy. Her arms ached, her back ached, her hands and fingers grew stiff and sore. Dish after dish after dish and Tom wasn't satisfied until nothing remained except the pellets. All of them. He'd tap her head and huff if she shook too savagely. He sighed if she got the angle wrong and the water lapped too hard against the dish. He only raised his voice occasionally. Now she was on her own without so much as a shotgun pellet to find.

The dish was put aside, the sieve studied. There were no nuggets caught in the mesh but a leech was attached to her wrist. Anna pulled it off, ignored the blood and began to pan. In the bottom of her third dish lay a sliver of gold a quarter inch wide and when she picked it out, it was as long as her little fingernail. She forgot her aches and grumbles. Anna began to smile again.

I panned for three hours until Susan woke. The flakes I found in Michael's tailings now cover the bottom of my tiny bottle. When dried and separated from the black sand as Tom showed me how, I suppose the flakes would fit neatly into my palm. Dare I say it, but I have recovered more gold than Michael has in eight long weeks of work. It is a satisfying feeling. I do not care that it is not a fortune. I have promised myself not to show Michael until he asks to see my bottle. Then, he may realise how useful I can be other than for cooking his meals and catching mosquitoes at night.

Michael shook the bottle and the gold flakes cascaded and settled. It was rather heavy, the collected gold reaching up to a quarter inch from the bottom. 'Who showed you how to pan?'

'Tom Manning.'

'The American?'

'Yes.'

'When?'

'Oh, recently,' Anna replied quietly and studied her hands.

'All this came from my tailings heap?' Michael asked, shaking the bottle again, watching the flakes cascade to the bottom. The water in the bottle made them seem a lot larger than they really were. 'All this from

12

my tailings?' he asked again and Anna thought silence her best reply in this situation. 'Why didn't you tell me you knew how to pan?'

'I didn't know what you would do. You said it was to be our fortune and I do need to help. There's little else for me to do here.'

Michael, a man of few words at the best of times, was momentarily lost. He let the bottle drop into Anna's lap. 'Remember what you are. Wife. Mother.'

A conciliatory remark with a bottomless warning. Anna saw it in his eyes when he looked down at her. 'And all this? Wearing my clothes?'

'I can't do a man's work in women's clothes.'

Michael was about to speak when a scream of agony hushed the entire diggings. Anna scrambled to her feet.

Dinny Masterson's partner, Bert, was dragging his screaming offsider from their shaft and even from a distance, Anna could see the pick embedded in Dinny's boot.

She was running before she realised it and pushed her way through the curious, shocked crowd.

'Someone hold him down!'

'No, Bert! You mustn't panic.' Heart in mouth, Anna couldn't believe her own words. She sank to her knees and her touch to Dinny's face helped to ease his yells and curses. 'Ease the pick out gently, Bert. Someone get clean cloth, quickly! Don't stand here staring, help us!'

Dinny didn't scream when the pick was removed. He lay on the ground, face covered by arm.

'Ease his boot off very slowly, Bert.'

Bert's face was as white as a wedding gown. He couldn't move. All he could do was stare, helpless.

Tom pushed him out of the way and knelt beside Anna.

When the boot was pulled off, the big toe and two others spewed to the ground in a wash of blood.

Dinny's screams could be heard for miles.

13

For endless days, Dinny knew he was dying and simply refused the many offers to transport him to town and to the doctor there. A drunk, they say; not many people in their right minds would let him tend a sick dog. There was nothing I could do to help Dinny. I have seen lockjaw take its slow hold too many times in my life. We all waited quietly for the release of death.

Today, it came.

I shall remember Dinny as a huge, smiling man. His friends will remember him as a glutton for food, drink and women. With me though, when he was ill, Dinny was no more than a quiet child who knew death was near and he certainly was no less a man because of his quiet agony.

He wanted to see his children again. Most of all, he wanted to be held by his wife—a wife, who, as far as I knew, was still in Ireland, awaiting his return, a rich man.

We buried him this day, September 4, 1867. Jokingly, with unhidden tears, Bert said, "Here the place be, boys. 'Tis too far to ride to have him stuffed and mounted above the bar at Rosie's." They all laughed because jest can hide the ache in the heart. There were few tears for Dinny and life, such as it is, goes on.

The troopers are expected soon. I suppose they will be notified of Dinny's passing when they check the licenses. I wonder who will tell his wife?

The wake continued late into the night and died in the early hours. As the bottles emptied in lieu of Dinny's passing, Joshua's fiddle became louder and so did the stories.

Of Dinny.

Anna stayed in the tent and listened. She dared not venture out into the man's night, not even to look at the night rider whose horse had cantered by. She listened though to the voice. It spoke to Tom and held the same accent and pitch; a hint of gravel, deep yet melodic. Light-hearted until he heard the news about Dinny. *What'd you say, Dad?*

Tom had a son?

Why hadn't he told her?

14

Sam Manning took his hat off and drew it across his sweating face. He squinted into the blinding sun that seemed to envelop the tiny town in a blanket of gold mist.

The police station was unattended as he knew it would be. A smile creased his face and he fixed his attentions to the pub opposite where loud roars and screams of laughter echoed up to meet him. For a little while, Sam wondered what the celebration was for. Sitting up here all day, he'd never find out. He walked his grey mare down to the park where two boys were playing cricket with a lump of wood and a green lemon.

'Hello, Sam.'

'Boys,' he replied as he went by.

'Traps ain't here, they gone to Bitter Creek. Left last night they did, the sergeant and Daniel and Billy.'

'Yes, I know,' Sam said with a smile. The boy's grins were conspiratorial. Sam's presence soon forgotten, they returned to their game. Sam tied his horse behind the stables of Rose Keller's Establishment.

Ginger-Lee, the short, plump blonde who today wore red, abandoned her hopeful customer the instant Sam walked in. Curiosity forgotten, Sam let his body decide immediate course of action. A couple of whiskeys could wait. He swept Ginger-Lee into his arms. He knew the way to her boudoir blindfolded and like always, he was blinded by Ginger-Lee.

'I was worried the traps had you,' she said as he put her down and locked the door.

'I think you'd hear if they had,' Sam said quietly. It was dark in there, sparsely furnished apart from a wash stand and a squeaky iron bed. The faint, musky odour of sex lingered in the stuffy air. 'It's so good to see you,' Sam whispered and nibbled on her ear while deft fingers parted the ties on her red dress. She sighed. Not for the first time Sam wondered if she sighed like this for every man, or if she rested her head back against any man's shoulder and played at relishing the touch.

'I worry about you, Sam. At times you're all I think of. Lucas won't rest until he has a rope around your neck.'

Sam turned her and lifted her face. 'He's not quick enough,' Sam whispered.

'And don't you be so quick, either.'

The bed protested, the two bodies did not. Before long, she'd forgotten her fears and despair. Sam Manning could make her forget everything. When he'd finally done, there was none of this dressing and leaving. He stayed for a change, holding her in the crook of his arm. Ginger-Lee

15

listened to the strong beat of his heart, the tired sigh, and wished he would never go, ever. Wishes were lies and always would be where Sam was concerned.

'Was it you who knocked off the coach from Warwick?'

'Would I do that?'

'You're costing me hard earned money,' she whined, rising on elbow, sweeping a stray wisp of brown hair from his bright blue eyes; eyes that were watching her now with a mixture of caution and dying lust. His fingertips drew invisible spirals on her skin and he touched her face with the same intricate gentleness.

'I don't like the thought of you sleepin' with Luke Hannaford.'

'You'd rather I starved? I've no choice, Sam.' Marry me, the eyes pleaded. You said you would. You said you loved me...

Sam drew her down once more and his sigh this time was huge and almost sad. Or was it resigned? 'Tell me where the Sub-Inspector's gone, Ginger-Lee.'

She groaned. Each time it was the same! He'd have his fill, he never paid, and he wanted information. Each damned time and it wasn't right. Ginger-Lee tried to move. Sam held her fast. 'Come on, girl, it's important.'

'And I'm not? What's my life worth if Lucas finds out I'm telling you things I hear? Things I know?'

'Please?' His eyes were as hungry as a starving child's.

'Inspector Ritchie's gone to Brisbane. He'll be away six weeks or more or so is the whisper. Daniel told Nelly as much.'

'So Luke's in charge, right?'

'God help us all, yes.'

A tiny smile crossed Sam's face as he lay back once more. The smile lingered in his eyes as he stared at the ceiling. It was a smile she recognised as trouble. 'What are you planning this time, Sam Manning?'

'I might take myself a bath,' he replied.

She tugged at the few hairs growing on his chest. 'The day you take a bath is the day a toff gentleman walks me down the aisle.'

The talk of wedded bliss sent Sam bouncing off the bed to dress in his usual hurry.

Ginger-Lee realised he was serious about taking the bath when an hour later, Nelly happened to notice the bushranger dragging a tub down the main street of the small town. 'Oh, Sam, the devil's got you,' Ginger-Lee whispered to the pane of glass at her lips.

16

And as if he'd heard, he turned in his saddle and looked up to her window. Sam grinned and lifted his tattered hat in farewell.

'He never asks for me,' Nelly said with a pout on her face. Ginger-Lee walked away, happy.

And as always when the traps were away, no one would see a thing.

Anna rarely liked to judge people on first impressions. Not only was it unfair, sometimes first impressions could be wrong. But when the two troopers rode in to the Bitter Creek diggings early that morning, her skin began to crawl. It was a feeling she couldn't ignore.

Accompanying them was a black man—they called them Native Mounted Police, a fancy name for an Aboriginal in a uniform. Anna took little notice of the young constable, barely nineteen. It was the sergeant who held her attention far too long.

She did not join the queues for the licenses to be perused—she kept panning, mindful of the talk she overheard from a distance. The sergeant asked Michael where he was from. Brisbane, came the reply. The conversation seemed quite ordinary and she didn't look up when her name was mentioned in passing. Some time later, the hair on her nape prickled as it tended to do whenever there were spiders nearby. With the approaching footsteps came the smells: leather, horse, unwashed male body. She looked up from where she sat on the creek bank with her legs immersed to the knees in the dirty water. She caught the sergeant's coring gaze and her skin crawled yet again. She shivered despite the heat.

'Mrs Hall, is it?' The voice was grating, authoritarian, demanding of attention and used to receiving it, immediately.

'Sergeant?' she asked, recognising the rank from the uniform coat hanging over his wide shoulder. The man would have been handsome were it not for the expression in his eyes. Behind him a young constable kicked at the dusty ground. He was bored, hot and tired. His eyes were dark and kind if not very intelligent. He looked directly at Anna and smiled, shyly. 'Constable,' she greeted, quietly.

The lad whispered, 'Ma'am' and filled his lungs with air.

Anna clasped Michael's shirt tightly to her neck and didn't particularly want to look at the sergeant again.

'I'm told you were with Dennis Masterson when he died, is that not so?'

'Yes.'

'And how did he die?'

'Slowly and painfully, Sergeant. It was lockjaw.'

While Anna recounted the tale in as few words as possible, the man squatted and picked up her bottle of gold. He swirled it about, mesmerized by its glitter. 'And how do you know it was lockjaw, Mrs Hall? Or may I call you Anna?'

Thoughts reflected in both's eyes. The boy seemed surprised at the sergeant's boldness. He smiled to himself when he heard:

'To you and everyone here I am Mrs Hall, thank you, Sergeant. And I know it was lockjaw for I used to work in a London hospital before we emigrated.' She emphasized the final word.

He took no notice. 'Ah, London hospital. You'd be a handy one to have about then, Mrs Hall?'

Anna said nothing. He hadn't specified what she'd be handy for. He didn't have to. The silence was uncomfortable, perhaps more unsettling than the way the man's gaze crusted her skin. He left her feeling as if she'd been coated in mud and now it was peeling and cracking, thick, uncomfortable. 'His death was accidental and unfortunate.'

'Frankly, Mrs Hall, I don't care. It only means one less to me. You have a baby, is that correct?'

'Yes.'

'How old?'

'Seven months.'

'And has the birth been registered?'

'Registered? No, I haven't had the opportunity.'

'Ignorance is no excuse, Madam.'

'And if you'd let me finish what I was about to say, you would have known that in any of the towns we passed through, the local constabulary were never there or if they were, there were no registration papers available. Now if you'll excuse me, I'm rather busy.'

Anna noticed the lad's quick smile the instant he turned away to wipe off his offending expression. Although the sergeant smiled, no humour touched his eyes. Despite the innocuous sunshine filtering through the eucalypts, Anna grew suddenly cold.

'I suggest when you're in town next, you call in to see me and register your daughter's birth. Good day.' The man loped off with the constable following him and came to a sudden standstill. The boy crashed into his back and was clipped on the ear for his trouble. 'Your husband's license doesn't include you. I suggest you refrain from prospecting until you acquire your own permit.'

'Then shouldn't we attend to it now while you're here?'

'I don't have the relevant papers with me.'

Liar, she thought. The boy was about to speak on the contrary and even reached into his coat. But something was whispered and the boy was led away. She couldn't hear the argument.

The threesome finally rode away, the brooding, silent Aboriginal the last to mount his horse.

'Bastards,' and Joshua spat into the dirt.

More sooner than later, the diggings fell into its normal, punishing routine. Illegal or not, Anna went back to her panning.

Michael had said there was no need to waste days travelling to town when Harry Ryan's wagon made three monthly trips to Bitter Creek. How was she to register the birth and obtain her permit if her husband wouldn't take her to town?

Sergeant Lucas Hannaford was lost amid his own thoughts as he crossed Mitchell's Hill. He'd heard about the woman at Bitter creek and had finally seen her for himself. A beauty sure enough, with one flaw. The delicate face hid a will of iron. If he hadn't been so tired, he'd have seen the spark of intelligence in the eyes and would have played it into a full symphony. She was well spoken. A nurse by God. A healer of the ill and tender of the dying indeed.

Police never about when needed? What in hell's name did these people expect of him? Miracles? One hundred square miles of mountainous territory to police. One snotty nosed constable too honest for his own good, and a half caste with eager mates easily led astray with promises of alcoholic rewards. Such was his help.

Never available when needed indeed. His pride stung.

The finds at Bitter Creek only added to his workload. God knew what trouble would be at foot when the Chinese from Thane or Liston caught a whiff of the gold and converged.

Those yellow bastards could smell it.

The only trouble Luke wanted was the kind he could anticipate, incite and prosper from.

'Sarge?' Billy Dingo asked cautiously, aware of the reverie he was interrupting. 'Down there, looks like a bloke dragging a bathtub to me.'

19

Daniel Brannigan saw it too. 'It's Manning, sir!'

Hannaford couldn't see a bloody thing. His eyesight at a distance was fading but the twist of his gut affirmed Daniel's statement. It was Manning. Sam Bloody Manning, at it again.

Daniel's echoing call reverberated down through the thick bush, giving the outlaw plenty of time to cut the rope on the tub and canter off up the creek.

A three hundred yard lead may well have been three hundred miles.

Luke wished it was.

While Dingo and Brannigan were in futile pursuit, the sergeant guided his mount down the precarious, boulder ridden slope.

The bath tub was damming up the clear, bubbling creek.

Too tired to curse, Luke rubbed his face, sighed and reached for his tobacco. All he could do now was wait for the troopers' return and their inevitable:

Lost him, sir, sorry.

He'd heard it a hundred times too often.

Sometimes he thought they did this on purpose.

Sam watched sadly from the relative safety of his hiding place, high above. Luke was down there, bored, smoking. Idle. The other two finally managed to secure the bath and drag it away.

Damn, he thought. They're stealing my tub.

Gone now, the visual impact of imagining Inspector Petrie's wife heading for her weekly bath and finding her tub gone.

At the first yelp, Harry would think she was stuck.

I say Harry, someone has stolen our bath tub!

Now all the magic was gone, dammit.

From far away, Daniel was being cursed at. Sam enjoyed listening to Luke's echoing shouts of stupidity, what was the world coming to, surrounded by fools … It reminded Sam of the sergeant they'd both been unfortunate enough to serve under. Back then, it had always been Luke in trouble. How the past always repeated and lived to haunt the future.

Once the best of friends, now…

Sam fell asleep in the afternoon shade. It had been a long, tiring day. The grey picked at grass, tail swishing at flies.

20

He'd get his tub back, though.

He wouldn't let them win, not now, not ever.

Chapter Two

ANNA EMERGED FROM THE TENT eager to see what was causing all the din. Once in the fresh air, she was enveloped in a dark cloud of hatred which was directed at the rattling wagon making its slow way past the camp. She didn't understand the fuss until she saw the Chinese girl walking steadily behind the wagon.

Chinese.

In the battle for gold they were nothing but the yellow enemy.

All Anna could see was the young woman leading the tired pack horse. Her head was lowered throughout the tirade of abuse.

Anna ran farther up the slope to get as close as she dared. She discarded her hat. The mane of long dark hair suddenly free captured the Chinese girl's attention and for a brief moment, gazes locked.

Anna smiled, inspired by hope but the gesture wasn't returned.

Michael was calling her back. She turned. Why was he so upset? When she looked to the wagon again, the Chinese girl was studying her feet as she walked. She couldn't get her attention back now.

'What in God's name do you think you're doing!'

Anna winced from the sudden, tight grip on her arm. 'I was trying to attract her attention.'

'What the hell for?' Michael yelled, eyes wide, disbelieving.

'What for?' Anna couldn't believe he could be so inane, so insensitive. 'She's the first woman I've seen in months! And months seem like years out here!'

'She's not a woman, she's Chinese!' he yelled back, pure disgust in his voice. He pushed Anna away with the warning, 'Don't even think it. You hear me?'

'Think what?' Anna snapped at his retreating figure. Michael marched off, muttering something that sounded awfully like, Why me? Rage welled. Why you indeed! Anna kicked the ground and now her foot hurt as much as her arm did. Damn him, the bruises were already showing. Anna snatched at the hat that lay in the dirt and pulled it on her head. 'They are only people!' she cried and didn't expect her voice to carry quite as far as it did. Every face turned to her and she realised her mistake. She mustn't take sides with the enemy—it would be a quick, certain way to be tarred and feathered. But she refused to let these men

22

win. 'If you hate it comes back to you! Don't you know that yet?' she called. Disgusted faces turned away, dismissing her stupidity, her insane logic.

And Tom simply watched and sighed. He could feel the beginning of the end. It was as close as a thunderstorm in December. Close, and all was pin-drop quiet now. Tom understood her anger and confusion—he'd been the only one who hadn't left his claim to hurl abuse and he was all too understanding of the thoughts whirling through the girlie's head. But it all culminated in another weary sigh. He picked the small, round nugget from the gravel in his pan and rolled it between his fingers.

Females, damn them all, longed for each other's company and it didn't matter what colour they were, female was female. But this union surely meant trouble. Tom began the routine shake and swirl in the patch of muddy water he called his own.

Another mistake, thinking that, because he knew that nothing of this earth really belonged to anyone: just borrowing it for a little while. Too bad the others didn't realise it, too.

'Nothin' but trouble,' he mumbled.

Supper cooks. I hope it burns. Michael is away drinking rum.

'I hope he drowns in it,' Anna whispered but didn't write that down. Her anger had intensified during the long day. There was so much anger inside that all she wanted to do was take a long walk and scream at the surrounding mountains. But leaving the camp so suddenly would only make Michael angry and suspicious.

She stared at the words she'd written and tried not to listen to the talk of the murdering, robbing yellow-skins. The pivot of conversation lately was, 'Slanty-eyed bastards, hanging's too good.'

'Aye and too quick.'

How dare they. How *dare* they.

And the plan slowly formed in her devious mind. Didn't she have to fetch drinking water each day? Didn't she have to wash the baby's clothes and didn't she have to walk a full mile to the waterhole and then back again? Perhaps she would find the Chinese campsite by mistake?

Yes, perhaps, if she searched long enough.

And what Michael never knew could never hurt her.

How dare they...

23

Sam dismounted, dropped the reins and kept his hand on his hat. The horse followed him as he searched the diggings for his father. It was late afternoon and there he was, sipping tea like he was at the Governor's garden party. Sam whistled. When the old man turned, he saw who Tom was sitting with. Too pretty to be a man but sometimes it was hard to tell. The horse rubbed her itchy face up and down Sam's back and put him off balance.

'Here comes trouble,' Tom mumbled as Sam took his hat off and chased the horse with it. Alas the horse would not be parted from the one she loved. She followed anyway.

Anna watched the stranger approach. He was perhaps the most handsome being she'd ever seen in her life, and she thought her heart would explode when he smiled at her, impishly, unsurely. Somewhat confused, too, no doubt. Had she been wearing a dress, there would be no confusion at all but she was dressed in Michael's huge pants and shirt and her hair was tucked up under the old hat.

'Did you bring me tobacco?' Tom demanded.

'Course I did.'

It was the same voice she'd heard a few weeks ago. Tom's son. Yes, it had to be. He had the old man's eyes and was making a show of searching his many pockets for the precious tobacco. The tins were duly found and slapped into Tom's outstretched hand. Tom pocketed the gifts with a grunt.

She couldn't just sit there and say nothing. 'Would you like to join us?' she asked politely.

'No. He don't want no tea. He's leaving, right now, he's leaving. Git. Go on, git.'

The impolite farewell of father to son was ignored, of course, and Anna was glad of it. 'I'd love a cup of tea, Ma'am. It's been a long ride.' Sam was happy now. Yes, this was female and a very pretty one at that. 'Call me Sam, Ma'am,' he added politely.

'Sam,' Anna whispered. Her hands shook and her face deepened in hue when she caught his smile again. It was the way he watched her—curious, interested. No man had ever gazed at her like that before, not that she noticed anyway.

'Thank you, Ma'am.' His words were soft, his actions almost shy as he took the offered pint mug but Anna saw no such shyness in his eyes. He was melting her and he knew it.

'My name is Anna.'

'No, it ain't. Her name's Mrs Hall. Hear that? Missus. She's married to that grizzly bear over there.'

24

Sam smiled again and Anna wondered if Michael was watching. As she turned to look, a gust of wind blew her hat off. Sam moved quickly and killed the flight long before the hat landed in the muddy water. He noted the flash of dark eyes, the mane of dark, shining hair set free and he stooped to retrieve the hat. So did Anna. Heads collided. She took two stumbling steps backwards and sat flat on her behind. 'You right there, Ma'am?' he asked, rubbing his forehead. Then with the hat in one hand, her hand in the other, his powerful grip eased her back to her feet. Anna swayed. Vision blurred. 'You have a very hard head, Mr Manning.'

'Here, let me see.' Rough fingers touched her forehead and swept hair from her eyes. Anna looked up into his face. He was too close, just too close. He stepped away as if realising it too and stared down at the hat. Muddied, squashed. 'Sorry, Anna-ma'am. I'll get you a new one.'

'No! I mean, no, it's not necessary. Accidents happen.'

'I'm a walking accident, Ma'am.'

She couldn't tear away from his teasing gaze. She felt her face blushing again and her head was pounding almost as hard as her heart.

Tom closed his eyes. *If Hannaford don't hang you, son, Mick Hall will. If I don't get you first.*

Tom could see it happening for the hundredth time. The boy had some magnetism that attracted ladies like bugs fly to light. Tom didn't know where it came from and even at his age, he'd have joined a queue of a thousand men just to get a little thrown his way.

Anna had been hit by a ton of it. Trouble, nothing but trouble. She'll be full of questions now, dammit.

Jealousy prompted Tom to sweep the mug of tea from his son's hand, grab him by the collar and drag him off for a little chat that essentially was a waste of time and energy. Too late, the interest was rising. Tom saw its full bloom as Sam rearranged his pants before getting on his horse and riding away. And he looked back at Anna and nodded. Smiled. She had her thumb in her mouth. Chewing her nail, thinking things she shouldn't have been thinking. Tom read the eyes. 'He's not what you think, girlie.'

Anna turned to him absently. She hadn't heard. No use repeating himself, she still wouldn't hear. 'What was that you just said, Tom?'

'Mick won't like it, Anna.'

'Don't be silly, Tom. I'm married.'

'Yeah? Coulda fooled me.'

25

Coulda fooled me.

The words haunted her that night as she curled into Michael and tried not to hear his snores. She ran her hand over his chest, his stomach and hips, hoping the feel of her breasts squashing into his back might prompt a little attention. Even being held close for a little while would sometimes suffice, but he rolled over and squashed her. Michael woke and mumbling, he was abusive, telling her to put some clothes on. He was tired.

Anna rolled away, fumbled for her nightgown and felt tears stinging behind her eyes. Tears of shame. It wasn't Michael she wanted.

The mail coach drew to a rattling, grinding stop in the middle of Mitchell's Crossing. For a change, it wasn't muddy. There'd been no rain for weeks and the danger of bogging to the axle was slim.

The bushranger stood with arms casually folded and Colt pistol tapping the shoulder of his coat. A fearsome sight to anyone who was unsuspecting or unknowing. Sam Manning was easily recognised by the sparkling blue of his eyes even though he wore the appropriate black scarf across his nose and mouth. 'Just the mail today, Sam. Nothing here of importance.'

The eyes narrowed from the hidden grin. 'Depends what you think's important, Lionel. Where's Bill?'

'Broke a leg last Friday, Sam,' Lionel replied as he heaved the mail bag from the rack behind him. It landed with a thud near Manning's grey mare.

Sam thanked him with the normal nod of head and walked to the window of the coach. The canvas was down. Sam peered in anyway. Bert Whipps, the town's Postmaster sat quietly shaking while his new young wife cringed in his arms. Sam knew of the union—he'd read most of their love letters. 'Morning, Bert. Ma'am. Out you get, Bert.'

'My wife's ill.'

'My wife's ill,' Sam imitated in matching falsetto. He wasn't entirely stupid. If she looked sick, he was the Queen of France. 'Out.' Sam opened the door and stood aside as Bert emerged. The old fart had put on at least twenty pounds during his honeymoon—he probably couldn't do much else but eat, anyway. 'No, I'll help the lady out.' Adding insult, Sam slapped Bert's hand from his wife's arm and gallantly assisted the lovely Mrs Whipps to the rocky ground.

Two beautiful women within twenty-four hours. Sam felt elated just to touch her hand. Nice legs. He noticed them when she hoisted skirts to disembark. Nice everything. Lionel was looking and he had a better view from where he sat.

Bert watched, humiliated to the core. Sam had a pistol in one hand and Rebecca in the other. She wasn't trying to get away and now Bert regretted asking her to wear the collarless dress he'd bought in Sydney. Too much bosom showed, not to mention the gold plated locket half hiding within.

'What's your name?' Sam asked, eyes sparkling.

'Rebecca,' she squeaked.

'Rebecca. Nice name. Can I?'

Rebecca turned to her husband the moment Sam let go of her hand and reached to grope for the locket. Bert was so angry he was studying the ground. Rebecca felt the warm fingers glide over her shoulder, her breasts. Goosebumps followed. Then came the tug as the delicate chain snapped.

'Don't take my locket, please!'

Sam slipped it into his pocket and took her left hand. A beautiful hand. He told her so and smiled at her. Her face turned crimson. On her third finger was a wide gold band and next to it, a huge array of... Sam looked closer. Rebecca tried to pull her hand away. It was more a gesture of propriety than anything meaningful. Sam clung tighter. 'Nice ring, Bert. What's it worth?'

'To you, nothing.'

'Nothing to anyone I think. What'd it cost you, Bert?'

'Leave them be, Sam. You have the mail.'

'Quiet, Lionel. I asked Bert here a question. Didn't I, Bert.'

'Twenty pounds,' came the hoarse, quick whisper.

'Come again?'

'I said, twenty pounds!'

Rebecca was aghast. She pulled her hand from Sam's and turned to her husband. 'You said they were real diamonds and they cost you a bloody fortune!'

Sam winced from the sudden Cockney outburst. She was no lady.

'Now, Bert,' Sam gently chided. 'You been married enough times to know you can't start off by lying. Don't you know that yet?'

'What's he saying, Bertie?'

27

'Rebecca please, now is not the time.'

'Now's as good as any,' Sam said, scratching his chin.

Even Lionel was interested in Bert's excuses but nothing more would come from the silent man—his mouth was snapped tight as a rabbit trap. Sam slipped the worthless locket back into its soft, warm nest. His fingers stayed a moment too long for Bert's liking.

'Touch my wife again, Manning and I swear, I… I'll…'

'Why don't you shut up and take your boots off, Bert?'

'What?'

'You heard me. Your ears are pretty good hearing gossip and spreading it around, especially about me, so you know all the stories about what I do to folks who don't cooperate. If I was you I'd take your boots off. Now.'

'I will not.' The little enraged man stamped his foot like an angry ram.

'For God's sake, Bertie, do as he says!'

Bert took his boots off.

'Socks, too.'

Humiliated to the core, Bert discarded his socks and stood barefooted on rocky, hard ground.

'Pants now.'

'I object!'

'Take his pants off, Rebecca.'

She did.

Lionel looked away although he didn't want to. It served Whipps right. The uppity little wombat had it coming. He'd often said nuisances like Manning should be hung from the nearest tree and not necessarily by the neck, either. Somehow, like always, Sam had heard.

Finally, the lovely new wife dropped her husband's boots, socks and pants unceremoniously into the creek. Four pairs of eyes watched expressionlessly as the items floated in a tumble for a little way. One boot sank with a gulping, final pop of despair.

And Sam cantered off into his hills with the Royal Mail bag dragging along behind the horse.

As Rebecca searched the luggage for trousers, Bert screamed, 'I'll see you hang for this, Manning!'

Lionel thought, not bloody likely, but he kept his opinions to himself. It was still a long haul into town.

28

The sergeant watched as the coach rattled to a stop outside Ryan's General Merchandise Store across the street. Lionel Jeffries, the regular driver and alone today, jumped down. Children appeared from nowhere, all eager to know if Sam had held up the coach again.

The sergeant saw the nodding head and sighed.

More bloody paperwork. No doubt it was the mail again.

A barefooted Bert Whipps emerged from the coach. One hand was holding up beltless trousers, the other was gesturing wildly. The sergeant opened the nearest book and appeared to be busy, looking up only when Whipps, followed by beautiful young woman, burst in.

With great difficulty, the sergeant kept his smile hidden. He had prayed for this moment a long, long time. After two years of: Something must be done! whilst safely seated behind his postmaster's desk, Bert had finally been confronted with the elusive enemy of the postal system, Sam Manning.

The woman looked bored by it all. They usually did.

'I demand immediate action!'

'Sit down, Bert.'

The little man wilted. He sat and the woman, who Luke discovered was the New Wife, remained standing, gazing about the charmless, somewhat distasteful room. No doubt she would find the town charmless and distasteful, too. Most women did.

'What happened?' It was always the question he need not bother to ask.

'I've been robbed of my dignity and physically assaulted by that... that...'

'By what, Bert?'

'You know who I'm referring to!'

'If, indeed, I knew, I would not ask.'

'His name is Sam Manning,' Rebecca Whipps said and picked at her fingernails. They were long. Women with long nails rarely did any work. Luke knew as much because Jane had talons and produced them daily. He averted his gaze back to Bert.

'We were assaulted by that... that... and I demand satisfaction. Hang him!'

'For robbing you of your dignity?'

'Well, he stole my locket but he gave it back,' Rebecca said.

From a cell in the depths of the lock-up, Daniel Brannigan chuckled.

'You have something else to do, Brannigan?'

After a moment, the back door closed.

'You're saying he stole your locket and he gave it back?'

'Here, I'll show you.' The girl's right hand disappeared into the depths of her green dress. Her face was alight with intense concentration for a moment before the locket was found and withdrawn.

He sighed. 'Perhaps if we start from the beginning?'

The tale was recounted and whenever Bert began to exaggerate the facts, the new wife countered with basic truth. She ruined Bert's story completely.

'Bert, I can't hang a man for wounding your pride. It wasn't Manning who tossed your clothing into the creek and as the locket wasn't stolen there's little I can do.'

'He stole the bloody mail!'

'I realise that, Bert. Lionel will give me his usual statement in due course. And as always, the mail will show up on your doorstep in two day's time.'

'What's he going to do?' Rebecca asked.

'Nothing. Bloody nothing!'

'Take me home, Bertie. I'm tired.' She led him away, full of promises of how she'd make him feel better, very quickly.

She left her locket. It wasn't heavy enough to be pure gold so Luke slipped it into the desk drawer and hoped she'd be back to reclaim it.

Alone of course.

Manning. Why did he persist? Wasn't he tired yet? Stealing mail for God's sake. The only things he ever opened were objects bearing governmental seals and, Luke had to admit, anything which looked interesting. Keeping his hand in, Luke supposed. Quietly persistent, extremely annoying.

On a number of occasions, Luke had ordered a police escort for the mail coach. On those occasions, there was never any sign of Manning. An attempt or two to place troopers in civilian clothing on board the coach was futile, too. It seemed as though Manning was a fly on the wall and Luke needed these annoying antics as much as he needed a broken leg. He soon discovered it was almost impossible to bushwack a bushwacker. Especially Manning.

Take, for instance, the bathtub that sat outside the stables. No one had reported a tub missing. Surely to God people knew whether their tubs were there or not? There was only one answer to the problem. Manning was going slowly insane. Unfortunately, he was endeavouring to take Luke along on the journey as well.

Damn him. There was more pressing business to attend to. The arrival of Chinese at Bitter Creek was more than rumour now. Give them a month at the most. Yes, a month. Dingo can organize his half caste friends, offer them a few pounds, a supply of grog. And the Chinese can be persuaded to move on.

'Dingo! Where the hell are you!'

The call was answered by Billy's dark face cautiously peering around a corner. 'Get the boys together. Send up your smoke signals or whatever the hell it is you lot do.'

'But Sarge,' Billy said quietly, 'Unless you pay them for last time they won't help you out no more.'

The last time. A family of squatters with the wrong attitudes. A gallon of rum. Yeah, we'll scare em out for you, Sarge, no worries there.

'Tell them there'll be gold this time.'

'Okay, boss.'

Luke took out a bottle of rum from the empty boot under the desk, uncorked it and took a huge mouthful. It burnt and his upper lip broke into a cold sweat. 'Get going.'

Billy Dingo, otherwise known as Dingo, lingered. 'What's happening this time, Sarge?'

'We'll have to move a few Chinese on, that's all.'

'The ones at Bitter Creek?'

'Yes. I don't want any riots. Not now. I've had enough of Chinese to last me a lifetime.'

'Lambing Flat?'

'Yes.'

Billy accepted it as fact and walked out.

The Chinese.

Easy enough targets providing they don't set up camp too close to the whites at Bitter Creek. Give the Chinas a couple of weeks and they'd be doubling any European finds—they could smell gold a hundred yards underground. Wherever there was a Chinese camp there was wealth for the taking.

The weapons required could be lost in transit, stolen perhaps. Refreshments for the boys supplied thanks to Rose Keller's reluctance to officially license her brothel.

Yellow blood meant nothing. It hadn't at Lambing Flat when he'd had the lawful excuse to shoot a dozen of them in as many minutes. It certainly didn't matter now.

Anna dipped the bucket into the creek and withdrew the day's supply of clean drinking water. She was close to the Chinese campsite because over the next hill she could hear the rattles and bangs of the shakers and blowers; now and then a foreigner's impatient call. How she wished she had the courage to find that Chinese girl. Talk to her. It was ludicrous, of course. Michael just wouldn't approve. He'd beat her for certain. Hadn't she already been warned?

Damn Michael. He'll never know.

Anna put the bucket down in a patch of shade and heaving the baby to her hip, she began the trek up the wearying incline.

The baby gabbled to herself and slobbered on Anna's neck. She was ignored. Anna looked down on tents, wagons, men and machinery. The Chinese camp was perhaps no different from Bitter Creek.

Bent over a huge iron crock like a grey-clothed witch from a fairytale was the object of Anna's latest obsession. The Chinese girl. Her hair was so black, it was almost blue in the sunlight. She was small, thin. She looked so fragile and tired.

Anna's courage rose and faltered with each alternate heartbeat. But she'd come this far, it would only take a few steps more. 'Should I, Baby?' she whispered but there was no answer. Anna took a few tentative steps down the hillside.

All work suddenly ceased, all heads turned after one jabbering shout. It sounded alarmed.

Anna froze. Michael's terrible stories of the Chinese and what they did to white women leapt at her in a thousand tangled forms. Anna tried to smile and held Susan tighter, hoping the baby's warmth and innocence would calm her frantic heart. The Chinese girl turned to her, studied her for a moment and continued with her cooking.

So this is all she will do? I should have expected as much, Anna thought. One glance, weeks ago and I expect a cure for my loneliness. Michael was right and I have no right being here. No right at all. I may need a friend but she doesn't. That is obvious.

Dejected, Anna turned and saw the man blocking her way. Anna looked into an aged, oriental face framed by thin, white hair. She stepped back, he stepped forward. He said something, not to her but at her and she glanced down at what he held in his hand.

Her water bucket.

Oh, no, she thought. They've laid claim to the only drinking water for miles. I've stolen his water. I'm dead. Dear God, he's going to murder me because I stole his water.

The old man gabbled at her again. He sounded annoyed, impatient. Demanding. She started to shake and tears filled her eyes. Anna tried to explain. Her words were lost because he couldn't understand her any more than she could understand him. But tears were universal language and fright heralded their fall. Anna screamed when he touched her shoulder. She took a frightened step backwards and the old man saved both her and the baby from tumbling down the hill.

His voice was angrier than ever now.

Anna's mouth ran like an overfilled glass of water. On and on and on:

'I didn't know it was your water, I don't know why I'm here, I'm so sorry...'

The old man stared at her as if she was some kind of life he'd never seen before.

'My father say you leave this.'

Anna spun. The Chinese girl was coming up the steep incline towards her. In an instant, she seemed a saviour. 'But I can't leave it. It's the only bucket we have.'

'No, no, he say you leave, you... forget.'

That would be a good idea, Anna thought. But she couldn't go without her bucket. How would she explain it to Michael? I'm sorry, but I had no choice? The old Chinese man stole it? She didn't know which fate was worse. 'Leave? Forget I came?'

'No, no!' The girl was more impatient than the old man. 'This is yours. Do not forget. Father say clean water precious!'

'Oh, is *that* what he was saying?' A smile lit her eyes before it touched her face. She'd never felt relief quite as intense and only now was she aware of her stinging eyes and blurred vision.

'Why you cry? Father see you coming and he follow. He just curious. We see many... many...' The girl gestured with her arms. Anna was never very good at charades.

'Snakes?' she offered.

'Yes, exact. Snake. Ignore him and come. Please. I expect you long ago.' The Chinese girl took the bucket from the old man and beckoned Anna to follow her down to the camp.

Anna couldn't refuse. Although her knees still shook, there was no turning back. Not now. She was glad. Nothing was ever quite as bad as her imagination consistently led her to believe. These people would not cut her throat and drink her blood. In fact, they took no notice of her.

'I am Lu Sun.'

'Anna Hall.'

Anna was allowed to sit in the shade and she watched while the men, all of whom looked the same to her, were fed rice in a thick broth. Lu Sun attended to all of them. She didn't speak to Anna until the food had been eaten and the men had dispersed. No one took any notice except for the old man who watched the baby with the intensity of an eagle after prey. 'A girl?' Lu Sun asked. Anna nodded and Lu Sun said something in Chinese to the old man. He grunted in much the same way Tom grunted. 'Father say it look like boy to him. I once had boy. Dead. In here.' She patted her belly.

'I'm so sorry.'

Lu Sun walked off and scraped the bowls out to the waiting magpies. She came back, smiled at Anna and patted her stomach again. 'This one live. I know. I feel.'

She didn't look pregnant to Anna. 'Congratulations.'

Lu Sun didn't know what the word meant.

'I'm happy for you, Lu Sun.'

'So is Lu Sun husband.' She pointed him out amid the tangle of lookalikes at the other end of the dry gully. He was digging around the base of a huge gum tree. Anna couldn't even guess his age. 'Eat?' Lu Sun offered. There was a lot of rice left, so Anna had lunch with her new friend and all the while, the girl's eyes feasted on Susan. 'You can hold her if you wish.'

The offer was declined. 'I must work now.'

Anna could tell by the sun's position in the sky and the short shadows that time was passing too quickly. Already it was nearing midday. 'I'd better be going, too. Thank you for the rice and the tea.'

'You come every day here?' Lu Sun asked.

Anna didn't want to lie. She picked up her bucket and steeled herself for the long, hot walk back to Bitter Creek. 'Yes. I do this every day.'

'Good. You see me when you come for water, yes?'

'Oh, yes!'

Michael was very curious. I can't hide happiness very well and nor can I lie effectively, so I told him I'd been walking and had forgotten the time. It is not quite a lie, nor is it quite the truth. I do need to tell someone about Lu Sun...

'Hello, Anna-ma'am.'

The nib Anna was dipping into the ink pot slipped and ink spread like a black bloodstain across the diary page before the entire bottle tipped down her shirt. Her sins of meeting Lu Sun were thereby obliterated forever. She almost swore and looked up into Sam's eyes. He was full of clumsy apologies. 'Sorry, Ma'am. I didn't mean to scare you, I thought you saw me coming.'

'That was all the ink I had left,' she moaned.

'Oh. I can get you some more if you want.'

Anna closed her eyes in despair. 'No, it's not necessary.' What had Michael said? When it was all gone, there would be no more? All this writing and drawing hats was a waste of time and money. He was forever buying ink. No more, not now.

'But I made you knock it over.'

Her gaze wandered to his face again as he crouched down beside her.

'I ruined your shirt, too.'

She looked down at the stained shirt. What would she say to Michael? *I fell over?* What does it matter what I say, he'll be happy that the ink is gone. Anna looked across the diggings and saw Michael working at the creek.

'I'm real sorry, Anna-ma'am.'

Anna said nothing. She closed the diary and slid it into the tent, out of sight, out of mind, until she had another vision, or an idea, and what good would that do her now?

Sam scratched his nose. 'I really did it this time.'

Anna didn't argue with that.

'I came to apologise for squashing your hat that day, Ma'am. Brought you these as my way of saying sorry. Looks like I shoulda brought the whole tree.' As he spoke he withdrew a multitude of oranges from the depths of his coat and he thrust them at her, one by one until her arms were crowded and she was juggling fruit.

'But Sam, there's no need for this.'

'Maybe. But I've got a tree full of them. Nothing grows out here except wild limes and prickly pears and they're no good. All you get's a mouthful of prickles.'

'Are you sure you don't want them?'

Pleasure lit his eyes. 'I'm sure, Ma'am.' With the Ma'am came a smile. Innocence belied the intelligent knowing in his eyes. A stranger was stealing her heart and the stranger was all too aware of it.

'Thank you, Mr Manning.'

'Mister?' He laughed. 'Call me Sam, all right?'

Anna purposely let her gaze wander to the creek. Sam looked over that way, too. He'd heard about her bearded, giant of a Scottish husband. 'You sure I can't get you more ink? Pop says you draw a lot.'

'Perhaps your Pop says too much. No, thank you, my husband won't allow me to have any more ink.'

'Why?'

'Please, Mr Manning, it's best if you leave, now.'

'Oh,' he said quietly, and for a moment he looked like a hurt child. Anna felt awful for turning him away like that but all she could do was watch him leave. One of the oranges fell from her arms. How on earth would she explain these?

Hide them. Yes. Hide them.

'Got a cuppa for an old man?'

Anna threw the oranges into the tent and innocently turned to Tom.

'Stealin' oranges now is he? That's what he is. A thief.'

'Sam?'

'I told you he was trouble. What's all that?' Tom pointed at her clothing.

'I spilled the last of my ink. Michael won't be pleased I've ruined his shirt.'

'It's not right for women to wear a man's clothes, anyway.'

'I can't pan in a dress, Tom. You know that.'

He huffed. It was his idea she wore long pants. 'And how much did you recover today?'

'I ... I didn't. I went for a walk instead.'

'You went to meet with that China girl.'

'You know?'

36

Tom laughed away the shock in her eyes. 'Girlie, girlie, you can make trouble for yourself without even trying. Ah, it's all right, I won't tell nobody but what you tell Michael is this. You say it was him what kicked the bottle of ink over when he was drunk. That way you might get another one.'

'But that's a lie.'

Tom grinned. 'What he don't know can't hurt. But you be careful with them Chinas, girl. You be careful for me. They're not like us. They're different.'

'They seem very nice people.'

'Girlie, everyone seems very nice to you. Just be careful is all I say. Chinas come and trouble follows.'

'Yes, Tom.'

And as he walked away, he knew his warning had fallen upon deaf ears.

'I thought you wanted some tea!' she called.

Tom Manning had selective hearing.

All he had to do now was drag the tub just another hundred yards up the treacherous slope and hope like hell either it or he didn't slip. Sam stopped for a rest.

He needed something to keep his wood dry and leaving the tub here would save him a busted back, too. Or maybe he was just getting lazier each day.

The mare lovingly rubbed her face up and down Sam's back and made a quick lunge for his hat. Sam ripped the hat out of her mouth before she ate this one too. She snorted full in his face. A sure sign of love. Sam wiped it all off. 'Leave the hat alone. I won't tell you again.'

She probably understood the words, too. She rubbed her itchy face against his back once more. With hat firmly in hand, Sam surveyed the decaying miner's hut otherwise known as home. It was bare of anything decorative, littered with bits and pieces he'd collected over the past couple of years of living alone. A couple of years which were the longest he'd stayed anywhere, including prison. He'd lied about the oranges, there was no tree but she would never know that. No one would except for a couple of trusted friends who knew where he lived. It was safer that way, safer for others.

The only times he saw his father were during his infrequent trips to Bitter Creek. He didn't know why he bothered. Tom ran off when Sam was fifteen and meeting up with each other eighteen years on and halfway across the world came as a shock to them both. More so to Tom to discover his only son was destined to hang for murder. After all those years apart, some fragile, invisible bond remained. A few visits, help from a few friends in uniform, and Sam was free again. Free, but still hunted and definitely not forgotten. Tom moved north to Queensland and settled in Warwick for a while until the finds were made at Thane and then Bitter Creek. Too late, he discovered Luke Hannaford was in Queensland, too. Same area.

The troopers annoyed the hell out of the old man. He disappeared for a week one time and reappeared again, broken and bruised. Luke was no wiser, though. He quit the harassment and almost believed there was no family tie because of the name, the eyes. He almost believed.

Sam had told Tom to move on. For his own safety, get away.

Tom had told Sam to move on. He had his claim at Bitter Creek and the only way he'd leave was to be carted out, dead.

So neither father nor son moved on. Tom had his home at Bitter Creek and Sam's home was wherever Luke Hannaford was posted. From Lambing Flat where it had all begun, to Muswellbrook, to Brisbane. Now here. Girraween. Ah, yes, the haunting was planned to continue until one of them died.

Sam wanted to live forever and take his revenge one lazy, idle day at a time. Sam would never forget and while Sam lived, Luke would not be allowed to forget either. Sam could forgive almost anything except the betrayal, its causes, its effects.

'Damn,' he said and yawned. He left the tub where it lay between the hut and the outhouse. Too tired to care now. He unsaddled the grey and set her free. The horse tried to follow him inside but with her in there it was too crowded. 'Get out, there ain't no room.' The horse backed out and a squawking, speckled hen followed.

Sam appeared with a Winchester rifle and a pocket full of bullets. The hen bided her time before slipping back to her full nest under his bed.

Singing a parodied sea shanty about drunk sailors, Sam loped off towards the creek and the flats beyond. It was his own private piece of peace here, a little hut nestled below, and protected by, the mountains, with a good supply of water, rabbits, the occasional scrub turkey. He even tried to grow his own vegetables after he put up a fence to keep the horse out.

He had all a man could need, except a woman. But he couldn't share his life with one, not now. Not again.

38

When he brought down the rabbit, he wished he had a dog because he had to walk fifty yards to find his dinner and as he skinned and gutted the rabbit, he remembered the ink.

And Anna.

He had a box of stationery, the useless booty from one of his earlier robberies. Where it was in his cave stash remained a mystery he'd solve later, after he ate. And first he had to cook. Sam hated cooking. Women's work this.

Anna. Thoughts always returned to her. He wasn't used to ladies being scared of him. Shy maybe but scared? Maybe she had her reasons, maybe not. But eyes never lied. Best to forget about her. Women were nothing but trouble.

Yet he did have ink and he also had some paper. It was all going to waste where it was and she'd be able to use it. It looked like she didn't have much at all.

Sam looked at the rabbit dangling from his hand. The thought of eating stew again turned his stomach. Next time he was in town, he'd go to Harry's and get some tinned bully beef. 'Yeah, something decent to eat,' he whispered to himself.

And as he sat, listening to his supper boiling, he fondled the bottle of ink he'd found quicker than he'd expected. He fantasized about the ink being Anna Hall's face. It was smooth, pretty, soft. Then he threw the fantasy aside and put the ink bottle down on the table.

Fantasies too, caused trouble.

There was a sheaf of old paper he'd found for her to draw on. A great heap of it, yellow with age. Dusty. Brittle. He wanted to see her again even if it would be from a distance, even if it meant giving the ink and paper to Tom to pass on to her.

Sam wanted her to have it. She reminded him of someone and he didn't know who. That was the worst of it. He liked her, she was married. Funny how it never mattered before.

When he finally slept around midnight, his last thought was to avoid the lady completely. But she came to him in his dream and even in his dreams she was bright, alive, smiling. And she was there the next day, too, more alive than in any fantasy his mind could have created.

Chapter Three

SAM WAS SET TO FILL his small waterbag and rest the horse when he heard the sounds which took him by surprise because they were unsuited to the bush stillness and unheard once away from Rosie's Establishment.

Female laughter.

For a moment he wondered if he was awake. The horse heard it, too. The light breeze was an ally for a change because the laughter was coming from the waterhole.

Sam got off his horse, tied it and slunk through the undergrowth, circling the mass of blackberry, stealing carefully and quietly up the granite outcrop that enfolded the creek.

He'd dreamed of seeing things like this—spying on a bevy of naked females, stripping down to nothing and diving in with them. Daydreams made no sense. Not only did he hate water, but only girls like Ginger-Lee would think it funny. It was all wishful thinking. No girl like Ginger-Lee would be this far away from civilization.

So he lay on his belly and watched.

One was Chinese. The other, Anna. The baby was there, too, in the shallows with its mother, happily obstructing Sam's view of nakedness. If they knew or sensed the voyeur there would be no show to watch. So far, so good. He tried to hear what they were saying but the voices faded to the breeze.

He had all the time he wanted.

The tall Chinese took hold of the baby and Anna stood. From a distance there wasn't much to see. He blinked at the wrong time and next she was swimming. Graceful, quiet. Hardly a splash. He wanted to reach out and touch until sense returned. She was another man's wife. Someone else got her first. Shouldn't be here watching. Not her, not like this.

Sam slid down the rockface as quietly as he'd climbed it. Heart pounding, body aching, he retraced his path to the horse and went in search of another waterhole to fill his bag and wash her out of his system.

Water wasn't that strong.

'What's wrong?' Anna asked. Lu Sun had a strange, lost expression in her dark eyes, as if she wasn't really there. Something was wrong. Anna could feel it. She swam back to where Lu Sun sat in the shallows, her long fingered hands wrapped around the baby. 'Are you feeling unwell?' Anna asked.

Lu Sun couldn't voice her feelings in any language that either of them could understand. Whatever had prompted the sudden oddness was gone now. She no longer felt vulnerable, simply lost for explanation. 'Sun hot. Skin burn.' And with those curt words, she rose and stepped out of the water. Although Anna didn't want to leave so soon, she followed and reached for her rag of a towel. What was happening? Had she said something amiss? Or was it her lack of conversation again? Somehow, there was no need to talk in Lu Sun's presence. One day they'd be full of frustrated chatter and laughter, the next both would be thoughtful and silent. The silences were mostly enjoyable. Not now. Anna had the feeling something was being hidden. How she hated secrets.

'Lu Sun? Please tell me what's on your mind?'

There was confusion and indecision for a moment. 'Feels how you say, bad?'

'What feels bad?'

'Feels this be last time.'

'Last time for what?'

'Last time we meet. Talk. Laugh. Be fun.' Tears welled in her eyes.

'Don't be so silly. What could stop us from having fun?' Anna didn't wait for Lu Sun to answer. She pulled her dress over her head and fastened it together.

'Lu Sun not be silly. Anna feels it, too. Anna does not lie good.'

Even if it was the truth, Anna couldn't admit it, not even in her thoughts. Perhaps she's been drinking too much of that strange tea. 'I'd better be going. I'll see you tomorrow.'

Half a mile to go to Bitter Creek. Sam was in no hurry, walking the grey along the goat track of a weaving trail. He heard singing. It wasn't very good singing. It made him wince. *Molly Malone.* He'd never liked that song.

The voice faded as he drew nearer and for that he was pleased.

It was Anna again. She put the bucket of water down, heaved the baby to the other hip and continued her song. She didn't know he was there. Other things on her mind, Sam guessed.

'Morning, Ma'am. Nice day.'

Anna squealed in fright and almost dropped the bucket. She spun and there he was, studying her from his seat on his huge grey horse. He was smiling.

'Sam Manning, are you trying to scare me to death?'

'Who, me?' Sam knew he really should ride on but he sat there for awhile, looking at her, smiling. Her hair was dry now and pulled back and she wore a dress, too. A colourless grey thing that must have been hot as hell. There were sweat marks down her back, under her arms. And the baby was squinting up at him and jabbering something until it stuck its fist in its mouth and grinned at him. The grin made him uncomfortable—it was as if the baby knew something he didn't. Not only that, she'd called him by his name instead of "Mr Manning". He was pleased, his heart lifted. 'Would you like a ride to Bitter Creek, Ma'am?' he asked.

'No, thank you. I'm fine.'

It was his cue to ride on of course, but his feet wouldn't tap the horse and his brain had gone numb. For the first time in years, Sam Manning was lost for words.

'I hope you have a pleasant day, Mr Manning,' Anna said in her little girl voice. She tried to smile as she picked up the bucket. Sam watched her walk off. He was dejected. First Sam, then Mr Manning. He didn't have a chance. Or did he? If anything he was known for persistence even if the odds were against it.

'I'll take that if you like.'

'No, I do this every day. Really.'

Sam moved the horse on, pacing it with the woman.

'Looks heavy.'

She glanced up at him, shook her head and kept walking.

'I found some ink for you, Ma'am. Some paper too.'

Anna stopped walking again and when she looked up this time, he saw an immeasurable amount of sadness in her eyes. 'I thought I told you my husband wouldn't allow it.'

'Why not?'

'He just won't. But thank you for thinking of me.'

Thinking of you? He wanted to laugh. Sam dismounted and took the sheaf of paper and the ink bottle from his saddlebag. 'Here, I'll swap you. Which is heavier?' he asked, glancing from the bucket to the baby. Without giving her time to decide or object, Sam took the bucket and

42

started walking. The protests soon came. He ignored them all. The horse followed lazily behind. 'What's his name?' Sam asked.

'I beg your pardon?'

'The kid. What's his name?'

'Susan Louise.'

'Oh. Nice name. Watch the horse or she'll eat your hat, there.'

Anna promptly moved away from the horse. The horse followed. It was interested in the baby and the baby was interested in the horse.

'I suppose Tom's told you all about me?' Sam asked. He was walking too fast, so he slowed.

'He did mention something about you being a thief.'

'Is that all?'

'That's enough, isn't it?'

Sam changed hands. The bucket was heavy all right. 'You really lug this two miles a day, Ma'am?'

'How do you know I carry it two miles a day?'

'Pop told me,' he lied. She seemed to accept it. The last thing he needed her to know was how he'd been watching her and her Chinese friend. How he knew almost every move she made. The walk continued in silence for a little way until Anna had to rest. Sam sat too, but not too close in case she got the wrong idea. Getting the wrong idea was probably a good idea, though. Another fantasy, ruined when the baby grabbed a fistful of Anna's nose. Sam winced in sympathy. She didn't seem to mind. She didn't seem to feel it. 'Ma'am?' he asked.

She turned to him and couldn't meet his gaze for long. A lot of women couldn't. He often wondered why. 'Are you happy out here?'

'I don't think that's any of your business, Mr...'

'Would you call me, Sam? I like it when you call me Sam.'

'I shouldn't call you anything.'

'Cos I'm a thief?'

'Amongst other things, yes.'

'Other things? What else you heard about me?'

'Please, Sam. Just give me my bucket. If anyone should see us...'

'There's one!' he suddenly cried, changing the subject and surprising her again. He grabbed her hand, heaved her to her feet and darted off into the bush beside the track. Numerous nightmares leapt into her mind until she saw what he was reaching for—a small green fruit from a bushy tree. 'Take it, it won't bite you. It's the prickly pears that bite.' He was smiling at her.

Anna dared not read the signals behind his eyes. 'Please let go of my hand?'

Sam looked down to see and feel his tight grip on her small fingers and he let go quickly. And over her shoulder he saw the horse with its head buried in her water bucket. He cursed and darted off.

Anna closed her eyes and tried not to listen to his apologies. 'It's all right, I'll get more!'

Before she could protest, he was on his horse, bucket in hand, and cantering back towards the waterhole.

Michael saw his wife return to the diggings. Sam Manning was walking with her. She was exceptionally quiet at lunch, too quiet. With Anna, quiet was synonymous with guilt.

'Enjoy your walk?' Michael asked. She looked up but said nothing. Her attention went back to the dancing flames of the open fire. Her mind wasn't on meat and damper, that much he knew. 'I think I'll be fetching our water from now on, Anna.' She sent him an alarmed look. Michael sipped at his tea. She'd sweetened it too much and for a moment he was tempted to throw it into her face and ask if Manning liked tea this bloody sweet. The urges soon passed. 'I thought you said you'd spilled the last of your ink.'

'Yes.'

'Where'd that bottle come from?'

Silence. She was trying to think of a reasonable lie and wasn't quick enough.

'Anna!'

She jumped and tensed and when she tensed he was tempted to hit. When she cowered like a dog he hated her.

'I asked you a question.'

'Tom's son gave me a bottle. Some paper, too. I said I didn't want it.'

'Tom's son? So you're friendly with a bushranger?'

'A bushranger?' she asked, all eyes now.

And he hated her dull innocence, too. 'I see he carries our water these days?'

44

'Michael, you don't understand. His horse drank it and he fetched more to save me the long walk. That is all.'

'When was this? Where?'

'I was coming back from the waterhole. He rode by and he stopped and...' She faltered. Michael suspected it was to fabricate a little more. He'd heard of Manning and how irresistible he was. But he remained calm. A disquieting harbinger of the inevitable.

'And? Go on, lass. Dare ye not stop now.'

'He talked.'

'He talked? You didn't?'

'Michael, I've done nothing wrong!'

Tears in her eyes now. Face trembling.

'He seems to visit the diggings a lot of late. Everyone's commenting.'

'I've heard nothing.'

'You'd never be here!'

'That's not true!'

'You're meeting him, aren't you? Every bloody morning you saunter off with the baby. Fetchin' water's just a bloody excuse! You're meeting him.'

'No!'

'You're supposed to be my wife, can you not act like one!'

'I do! It's you who's not a proper husband!'

The back of his hand struck her mouth, splitting lip. The force sent her backwards to the ground. On his feet and towering over her, Michael felt like kicking. He resisted. 'Nae more, you hear me! Nae more! Be only so much a man can take!'

Anna covered her face with her arms as he stepped over her, throwing his pannikin mug to the ground. He cursed all the way back to his claim.

Anna lay there quite still but shaking inside from fear. And she cried because it wasn't over. It had barely begun. He'd get drunk and he'd never let her forget, never.

Blood was warm and salty and filling her mouth. This time he'd loosened a tooth.

Anna struggled to sit up. Her back hurt from the rock she'd fallen on. Head swam from pain, sobs came from the depths to scour her lungs. She touched the back of her head and had to wipe her eyes to see her fingertips.

Blood.

Hate welled. It was pure and deep.

She squinted at the diggings, at the men who had seen and pretended otherwise and her blurred gaze fell on Tom. He made no move toward her yet the message that passed was silent. After a moment, Tom wiped his nose on his shirtsleeve and returned to his work.

And she heard the baby crying—angry demands she hadn't noticed before. She crawled into the tent and drew the flaps to a close. While Susan fed and quiet tears continued, Anna could barely discern the colour of the one orange that remained. She wouldn't be able to eat it now. It would go rotten.

Like this place. Rotten.

And she'd never see Lu Sun again.

That hurt most of all.

Lu Sun had been right. She'd said it would be the last time.

When Michael came home it was very late and he was very drunk. He hadn't returned for any tea, the food had been wasted. He'd been drinking rum for hours with the mad Yugoslav and all her fears were realised when Michael blustered in. Apprehension tickled her spine. It was hard if not impossible to judge his moods when he'd been drinking. She pretended she was sleeping. If she was lucky, he'd simply fall over and lay there until morning. And in the morning he'd be unaware of anything that had happened.

'Where is it!'

The words were slurred, incomprehensible. Angry.

'What?' she asked, sleepy, innocent. Anna did the best she could under the circumstances.

'Where's it gone. Where is it!'

He began demolishing everything he could find in Anna's trunk.

'Michael!'

'Find it, I want to see it!'

'What!'

'That diary thing of yours! I wanna know what you been writing about him!'

'About who for God's sake!'

Too late, he found her diary and started to tear at its pages, throwing them about, trying to read, swaying on his feet.

'Michael, that's mine, don't!'

46

But it was more than just hers, it was her life's dreams, everything she was or had ever aspired to be, recorded in her infinitely neat handwriting, forever. And he was destroying it. He was destroying her very soul. Despite the paining back and blistering headache, she attacked.

He pushed her away as if she were made of paper. By the time she scrambled to her feet once more, Michael had flung the book outside and into the fire. She tried to go after it, to save it but he held her fast. She punched at him, screaming out her hate, trying to hurt him. It was futile until she bit. She drew blood on his forearm. His elbow caught her in the chest and she fell, winded. Michael stared down at her and touched his arm. He looked at the blood. Amazement was in his eyes. Shock had sobered him and Anna's sudden, overwhelming anger was replaced with terror.

'Not a proper husband?'

She couldn't breathe let alone speak to defend herself. But words never helped.

'Not a proper husband? You're nothing but a whore! It's not me you want, it's him! You think I don't know!'

Hate was in his eyes. He reached down and fisting his hand in the front of her nightgown, he heaved her to her feet. 'Does he bed you? Or is it you beddin' him!' Anna closed her eyes. His breath was fouled by rum. She wanted to vomit but all she could do was shake her head. 'And you're a lyin' whore, too!'

Anna tried to get away, as far from his Scottish temper as she could.

Futile.

'I'll show you what proper husbands do!'

Tom said nothing. Nor did any of the others who had heard the commotion and the screams of the night before. From the moment she appeared in the blinding sunlight, faces turned to her, and away just as quickly. Anna pretended she hadn't seen the looks. It was the best way.

Michael was nowhere in sight. His rifle and the tin bucket were gone. There was no kindling for the fire and all that remained of her diary was the brass clip amid the smouldering ashes. He'd have forgotten. In a few days, he would probably ask why she hadn't touched her piddling book.

Anna sat down slowly, wincing. It hurt to walk. She ached all over and was covered in bruises. Inside, there was nothing left to feel.

She knew where he'd gone and why he'd taken the rifle. She'd be in for another hiding if by chance Lu Sun was waiting at the waterhole but no, it was far too early. Even Lu Sun had work to do, and by now she'd know to hide from Michael Hall. Lu Sun had inquired about a bruise or two and ordinarily Anna would have lied quite convincingly. Lying became easier with practise, especially where her marriage was concerned, but there'd been no reason to lie to Lu Sun. If she'd tried she'd have been transparent. 'He hits you? What you do?' she'd ask. Anna found it difficult to explain impossibilities. Michael never needed a reason to do anything.

He duly returned with rifle over shoulder and water bucket in hand. There was barely a flicker of emotion. She winced when he walked by. He rarely hit when her face was this swollen and tortured. Anna stabbed at the fire with a long stick and pretended the coals were Michael's soft, hairy belly. She could still feel it sloshing against her body. And he never bathed. It wasn't fair that her Chinese friend had a husband who loved her and cared for her as best he could. Why, the woman who'd lived in the house next door in Brisbane had determinedly refused to let her husband touch her unless he bathed first. Worse, her husband was a meek little creature, always saying, 'Yes, Millie, yes, whatever you say,' and venturing off to wash. Once, Millie had laughed about her new dress and had given Anna all the details of how she'd acquired it.

Michael mumbled something. Anna was deaf. He went away and returned with an armload of kindling. The fire was soon a blaze.

'Make some tea for me.'

Anna made some tea. When he'd finally gone off to work, she dipped her handkerchief into the water pail and held it to her closed eye, then to her split lip. The coolness seemed to help.

Tom almost stopped his way past. He would have if she'd looked up. Shame or anger, she didn't know which, prevented it.

Two days passed into infinity. Michael, never the one to apologise, spent otherwise valuable time with his sullen wife. Anna had seen him do this once before—to a dog he had. He'd punished it severely and later had discovered it wasn't his dog that had killed every hen in Blackburn's chicken enclosure. So he tried in his own way to make amends. The dog cowered away, wanting to approach but fearful of more pain. Not understanding why. And it slunk to Anna instead because it trusted her. She was then blamed for turning his own dog against him.

Anna was fearful of nothing now. She wanted him to suffer for his sins. It was simple.

48

The afternoon when he gently touched her hand, she looked at him as if he were a dead cockroach found in the flour tin. He didn't say he was sorry. He never would. To him, sorry was an admittance of defeat yet she always waited to hear it.

'Are you going to pan, today?' he asked instead.

'No.'

'I see.' With a sigh, he walked off a little way and turned back. Something vague on his lips, too. It never emerged. He kicked a rock down into the muddy creek.

Sam Manning rode in a few days later. Anna watched him in conversation with his father. She didn't need to hear the words being exchanged. Sam even attempted to walk to where Michael was working, unawares. Tom stopped him. In anger, Sam rode away.

However innocently Sam had caused this latest drama, Anna wasn't pleased to see him go. She hoped he'd have the courage to walk up to her in full view of everybody.

She lived in hope most of her life.

Later, Tom came to speak.

'Girlie.'

'Tom.'

'Can't stay like this forever.'

Anna's gaze slowly met his. Tom could have chipped the ice off her eyeballs. He honestly thought she'd gone and accepted Bitter Creek and its unending futility as her inevitable destiny. Life would never get better and if she kept this up, it damn well wouldn't. She couldn't sulk forever. Nor could Kate. 'You know,' he said and spat his tobacco into the fire. 'If they said to me, Tom, you're dyin and you got one week to live, do you know where I'd wanna go?'

Anna shook her head.

'Nowhere at all. I'd stay right here, girl, cos one week sure feels like two.'

A faint smile touched her face. Tom wiped his nose on his sleeve and began to cough. Eventually he had to sit down and when he did, he touched her hand. She tried to pull away, he held tighter. 'Me and the boys been ignoring him but enough's enough. I think he knows he did wrong. Some men just can't say it, girlie.'

49

'Say what?'

'Sorry. He is, you know. In his own stupid way, he does love you.'

Anna looked into Tom's eyes. Yes, he meant it. No lie was present. Her eyes stung. Tom reached for some more tobacco to chew on. 'The sooner you get to smiling again, the sooner things'll be like they used to. Took us a while to get used to havin' a lady about but we're used to it now. We don't like too much change, girlie, so you best start smiling again.'

'There's nothing to smile about.' Anna expected him to say something. There was no sympathy from Tom Manning and there never would be. But his presence was a strange sort of comfort and it always had been. She held his hand a little tighter. 'Nothing will ever be the same, Tom. Nothing.'

'And where'd we all be if things never changed? Still be wearing fur coats and gruntin' at each other, that's where we'd be.'

'I hate this place, Tom!'

'Watch it don't start hatin' you, girlie.' He reached into his pocket and withdrew a doll which was carved roughly from wood. Crude, misshapen. He studied it before handing it to her. 'It's all right. You tell him it was a present from me.' Anna took it. She knew who had made it. The carved face was smiling. Best she study it now before she gave it to the teething baby. 'I never figured you was a quitter. Suppose I been wrong before.' With another squeeze to her knee this time, he rose to his feet, turned and walked away.

'I'm not a quitter!'

Tom was deaf yet again.

'How dare you say I'm a quitter!' She'd never quit at anything in her twenty-two years of life.

Was he right? Was she really wallowing in self pity or was it deep anger she felt? She wanted to pick up a shovel and hit Michael with it. She didn't really understand why. Revenge perhaps, for his lies at the beginning. The wily ways he employed when he was ill and in the hospital. Marry me, Annabelle? The bright eyes implored her. We'll have a new life together... Oh, all those promises, indeed.

She watched him work for his piddling gold, not that gold would ever make him happy. She wished he'd die the same slow, painful way poor Dinny had. The wish became a desperate urgency until common sense reared. Death was no answer. I'll be a widow, she thought. An outcast, forgotten and left to manage alone. With a baby, too. Then I would have to make his imaginings a reality, just to survive. I would be the whore he thinks I am.

'I am not a quitter, Tom Manning!'

50

A few surprised faces turned to her. No one had heard the lady's yell from across the diggings for weeks now. Some of the faces grinned. Nudges and whispers abounded.

Anna poked savagely at the fire coals. Blue flame licked at the breezeless air. Her brass clip was still in the ashes. Burnt dreams. But dreams and visions were still complete in her mind's eye. There were always new ones appearing.

Anna searched the tent for the sheaf of yellowed, brittle paper. The pages were loose and there were hundreds of them. Two sketches to a page, perhaps?

What remained in yesterday anyway? Nothing that couldn't be recreated new and fresh with a new perspective, devoid of depression. Yesterdays were filled to overflowing with written memories which only inspired more recollections of tedium, of heat, of weariness and achings for something she could never have.

Now she was pleased the diary lay in ash. It couldn't hurt her any more. Nor could Michael.

Anna searched for something hard and smooth so the nib wouldn't tear the paper. To get what she wanted, what she'd dreamed of most of her life, would be a sole endeavour. She'd need no husband to help her reach her goals. He'd only laughed anyway. Wasting time again? he'd said more often than not.

Hope fluttered until its presence became a reality. She began the drawing in stolen ink on stolen paper, on the metal trunk containing everything she owned.

And it wasn't a hat she drew, it was her dream. The sign above the doorway bore the shop's name:

Annabelle's Millinery.

Then came the shop front.

She could see it now as clearly as it had appeared in her child's mind. Oh, these dreams of yours, her Grandmother would scoff. But it was here again—clear, sharp and bathed in sunlight.

Where the shop would be remained a mystery but she knew it was a lifetime from Bitter Creek.

Annabelle's Millinery...

Cobblestones on the footpath outside. Three stairs. A bell near the door. A bell which jingled when a customer entered. The smell would be of lavender, the walls a pale lavender, too. Hats of all kinds, for all purposes and occasions, would be arranged attractively in the window.

51

And outside, a gas lamplight would illuminate her dream for all to see, even at night.

This is mine, she thought and the thought brought tears to her eyes. One day, this will be mine.

Anna looked down at her sleeping child. And one day it will be yours, and your daughter's … 'I am not a quitter, Tom Manning,' she whispered as she found a safe nest for her future, a nest Michael would never chance upon—under the flour and tea tins.

He'd ruined enough of her life already.

That same afternoon, she filled her ten ounce bottle with flakes of gold. She hadn't touched a pan for three weeks and three weeks felt like years.

Bitter Creek had returned to its normal pace and the men's cursings filled her with a comfortable warmth. She even smiled at Michael.

And God help him, he smiled back.

A huge weight had finally lifted.

Sam kicked the same rock in an ever-widening circle until his anger finally unleashed. The rock curved high into the air and came down heavily in the creek. And now it felt like two toes were broken.

For over a week now, it lingered in the back of his mind and surfaced too easily, the slightest thing its inspiration:

His only satisfaction would come from beating the crap out of Michael Hall. There was no other way. And Sam didn't care if the man was six feet three and weighed sixteen stone.

He'd stewed long enough and kept away long enough.

Quiet. Too quiet. A tingle he knew as fear rose and ebbed. Tom felt the flutter of unreasonable panic as an itching ache in his chest. He wondered where the girl was. Anna. The baby. That's right. Lately, she'd been taking off to meet the China again. Asking for trouble. But what he felt now was a different kind of trouble.

No one else seemed to feel it.

52

Tom tried to discern the movement in the distance. Maybe it was the girlie coming back? No, he saw men. A couple of men. With black, painted skins.

There was no time to voice a thing.

Joshua was the first to fall. Tom saw the spearhead strike, Joshua's hands claw at his belly. The wide eyes. The surprise. Then he fell to his knees and an agile, young black was there, kicking Joshua to his back and pulling the spear out to use it again on someone else. And a crazy thought ran through Tom's mind:

He's no more than a kid. What's the world comin' to?

Chaos. Shouts as the diggers ran for some kind of weapon. Screams of outrage blistering into screams of agony. Before he felt the searing heat, Tom saw the white man on the horse. He looked familiar until he realised that what Sam had said all along was true. Dammit, he'd never believed him. Never. Then the bullet tore into his chest and it had come from the white man's rifle.

Anna heaved the baby to her hip and traipsed up the hill. Lu Sun had definitely said Thursday. Something must have happened. The Chinese camp was without a sound at all except for a squeaking of a tree limb. Anna made it to the top of the hill and was swept away into a nightmare.

Lu Sun's father was making that branch squeak—the old man was tied by his ankles and swinging. Dead. Face covered in blood. It had pooled, drying now, on the ground. His throat was cut. His long white plait was almost black from blood.

No sound would come although she wanted to scream.

She didn't remember very much of what happened, how she sidestepped around the body, how her eyes gazed on even more horrors. Had she screamed for Lu Sun, hoping against hope she'd somehow been spared? But her friend's body floated face down in the muddy, bloodied water.

Only then was she aware of the noise.

Shooting. Distant. Coming from the south.

From Bitter Creek.

Anna ran for a full mile and felt nothing except terror, disbelief.

Again, she was too late. She stood atop the hill near Dinny's grave and looked down at another sight her mind steadfastly refused to believe.

53

'Michael! Tom!'

She set the baby down heavily and ran, skimming the campfires, leaping overturned machinery, bodies of people she knew. Tom's shack was nothing more than a few bent pieces of tin and splintered wood. But she couldn't find him. She was still screaming for Michael.

Luke watched, amused for a little while before he dismounted from his nervous horse. He took the rifle from the saddle.

She was still calling.

Keep screaming, Anna Hall. They won't hear you now.

Luke walked towards her.

Only the dead could tell no lies.

Anna slid down the creek bank and landed on her face in the fouled water. She scrambled to get to her feet and her husband.

Luke thought it was touching. He stepped over the crawling, crying baby—he'd see to it later. Perhaps, perhaps not. And there she was, her husband's brains goring her dripping shirt. Blood on her face and in her hair as she held his limp, heavy body, hoping no doubt her anguish would bring him back to life. No woman had that power.

Silly girl. This was no place for a woman, anyway. Certainly no place for miracles.

Anna heard the rifle cock and looked up into the blinding ten o'clock sun. Just a silhouette of a man but she knew the stance and she knew who it was without having to see his face.

The sergeant slid down into the creek. 'I'm afraid he's dead.'

Anna held tighter. The man reached down, grabbed a handful of Michael's shirt and heaved the body into the water. Anna tried to scramble up the muddy incline but her booted feet had no hold and she kept slipping.

She grabbed for a handful of mud and threw it wildly at his face. He only laughed and swung the rifle down. It ceased her blind attempts to scramble free. The hard barrel crushing into her chest defied her to breathe.

'Do you want your baby to live?'

Any reply she may have had was frozen.

'Billy!' he called. 'Bring me the baby!'

54

And when she tried to move, the barrel of the rifle crushed again. The aboriginal she'd seen in uniform was now semi-naked and covered in body paint. And she saw him lift Susan by the leg. Her baby screamed. Anna tried to move, the rifle wouldn't allow it. But her thoughts weren't on the rifle, or the sergeant or the death that surrounded her—her terror was for her child. As the black man walked towards them, Anna could see the knife in his hand. It glistened in the sun. It was bloody.

'Don't hurt my baby...'

At first it was a whisper. Then it became a screamed plea, over and over.

'What sort of monster do you think I am, Anna?' the sergeant asked with a humourless smile. 'Whether your child here survives or not is entirely up to you. Right, Billy?'

'Whatever you say, boss,' was the reply.

And more came—a small army of them. Here and there, they held their wounds, blood shining on slick, dark skins.

'And what do you say, Anna?' he asked.

'Just don't hurt my baby!'

'Anna, Anna, I have a daughter of my own. So you see, we have something in common.' The rifle lifted and she scrambled away again, this time to her child. But the aboriginal holding the baby stepped back. He was smiling. Anna counted four of them. She looked back to the sergeant.

'Please don't hurt my baby.'

The silence hit first. Under any other circumstance, Sam would have looked to the sky to see the approaching storm. There wasn't a sound, just a loud silence. Eerie, foreboding. His rehearsed words for Michael Hall filtered away into the sunset hush.

As he drew closer, faint wisps of smoke tickled his nose. Beyond lay something else he sensed.

Death.

He knew it well. He'd carried it in his pocket for so long now he was too familiar with its presence. And death was there, twenty yards away, over the rise at Bitter Creek.

Nearly everything once standing was demolished; burnt, or still smouldering.

Sam's first thought was for Tom. And with the thought came a feeling of hope. Hope that it'd been quick. He searched for his father. One of two places—Anna's, or his claim. He was at the claim, and he was dead. Shot. Most of the others had caught spears or axes.

Jesus.

Sam sat hard on the ground and checked the bile that rose. He swallowed his nausea so many times that in the end he had to turn his head and throw up. And he sat amid the dead in the still dusk silence, the only sounds the steady hum of flies and the quick pounding of his heart. He didn't know he was holding his father's body until he heard the noise.

Faint, like a baby crying. The cries obliterated his echoing silent questions and he couldn't ignore the cries; he wasn't that strong. It was Anna's baby.

He was on his feet and tracking the source before he realised it. How the hell it got over to the other side of the creek, he'd never know and he couldn't remember its name, either. Names weren't important now. It was crawling over a body. Joshua's body. Crying. Sobbing. 'Jesus Christ,' he whispered and the baby looked up at Sam and chewed on its fist. It's face was covered in blood and mud and snot and flies. How it could cry in those long, deep, choking sobs and chew its hand at the same time, he'd never know. Sam's eyes clouded for the second time and he tasted the salt of his own tears when the baby lifted its arms to him. It didn't have to talk to communicate.

Sam ran a shaking hand over his face and turned away from the sight.

Jesus Christ.

But he couldn't walk away from it, either. He turned back. It still had its arms in the air, it was still sobbing. Long breaths ending in a hiccup.

He kept watching, frozen now, unable to move. It was trying to climb up his leg.

Jesus, what'll I do?

He bent to pick the baby up. It stopped sobbing and for that he was glad, but it reeked of piss and buried its fat little snotty face against his neck and started sobbing again. So he held it tighter. 'Be all right,' he whispered. 'Be okay, little Susie.'

Sam was surprised that he suddenly remembered her name.

The baby took a fistful of shirt and chest hair and started chewing on his neck.

The images in his mind reappeared. He didn't want to look too far because he knew what he'd see if he did. Anna either strung up or staked out but whatever, she'd be dead and it wouldn't have been quick. It rarely

56

was for a woman in these circumstances. But he had her kid in his arms now and he had to make sure. For the kid's sake. He didn't want to, but there was no other choice.

This time it was easier because he had something to hold on to and he wasn't so alone. The baby sucked at his buttons now and took no notice of its mother lying at the man's feet. Sam crouched and turned her over. There was a very faint moan.

'Holy shit,' he whispered and put the baby on the ground. It squealed. He didn't hear a thing. He couldn't believe what he was seeing and touching. There was a half inch hole high on her chest where she'd been shot, and she was still alive. 'Ma'am?' he asked softly, voice shaking. So did his fingers when he touched her muddied face. 'Ma'am? Can you hear me?'

Her eyes opened for a fleeting second, rolled and closed again.

Chapter Four

'OH, YOU'RE BACK,' DANIEL SAID and quickly removed his boots from the sergeant's desk.

'Get off home, Brannigan.'

'Archie McMorrow's sleeping off and...'

'I said get home!'

'Yes, sir.' Brannigan couldn't move fast enough. He wondered what had upset the sarge this time. Whatever it was, he wasn't staying around to be within kicking distance.

Once the door had closed, Luke pulled off his boots and stretched his aching feet. He was about to reach for the rum bottle when Rose Keller flounced in. The perfume she wore was potent.

'What the hell do you want?' he asked, trying to stifle the sneeze he felt coming.

'Fifty pounds should do.'

'What?'

'Playing deaf now? You'll be paying me fifty pounds. It should cover the damages your black friends have caused me.'

'Rose, go away. I'm in no mood for your games.' Luke caressed his aching feet. 'And you're in no position to be demanding money from me. One word, Rose, I can close you down.'

'And one word from me, Lucas dear, and I can watch you hang.'

He turned to her slowly. She was leaning over his desk, light amusement there in her eyes. She was still a striking, if not hard-faced woman for her late forties and Luke knew she was quite serious. Threats were never light where Miss Keller was concerned.

'One of Dingo's friends let something slip before he passed out. Billy was quite upset. The poor boy almost turned white. What was said was something I'm sure Inspector Ritchie would like to hear when he gets back. But of course, I could keep my mouth shut if I wanted to. I could pretend it was just the talk of drunks. Not to be taken seriously if you know what I mean.'

An intelligent calmness strengthened her stare. There was no amusement now. She straightened and stretched her spine, reminiscent of the dancer she'd once been. There was no grace in her eyes when she

58

turned her head and caught the sergeant's gaze. What lay there was a simple warning. 'Thirty people if you include Chinese? Sorry Lucas, shall we make that fourteen only? Chinese aren't people, are they? Come now, Lucas, my old friend, why aren't you talking?'

His huge hands fisted and his heart pounded, not from fright but from anger.

Rose moved away and studied the Wanted Posters as if she were interested. 'And of course, should anything happen to me, my solicitor in Melbourne will be forced to open the letter I've already sent him. It would be a shame to miss your hanging. Perhaps we could discuss my license application while I'm here?'

The silence was thick.

'Fifty, you said?'

Rose thought carefully. 'Seventy. Seems fair, does it not?'

She watched as he unlocked a large metal cashbox. Rose enjoyed the sight of his eyes closing as he touched the money inside. Had she asked him to cut off his very arm there'd not be as much pain visible.

Rose took the money and stuffed it down her dress. 'And the license?'

Luke closed his eyes. 'See me tomorrow.'

She touched his face. 'That's a nasty scratch on your cheek, Lucas love. Mind you get it seen to before it turns septic.'

And she left with money she had taken from a murdering thief.

Sam upended the packing crate, heaved a blanket from his bed and stuffed it in. The baby was deposited next. She could wail as much as she liked, his first priority was Anna, still outside, draped over the horse. She was probably dead by now. If the bullet hadn't killed her, the six mile ride from Bitter Creek should have.

Sam pulled her off the horse as gently as he could. She weighed as much as a full sack of wheat and was about as helpful. She was still alive—he could feel her warm breath against his shoulder as he carried her into his shack and put her down as gently as possible on his narrow, creaking bed.

Sam took three steps back and looked down at her, a little terrified because for the first time in his life, he wasn't sure what to do.

There was no jagged exit wound on her back which meant the bullet was still in her. He didn't fancy leaving it there, nor did he think digging into her chest was a good idea, but her breathing was rattly and strained, not to mention the fine trickle of frothy blood escaping from her mouth.

It was night. No moon. Sam could make it to Cormac's though, and Cormac would do what he could, which wouldn't be much more than what Sam could do here and now. The sooner the better.

The baby climbed out of the packing crate and headed for the open door. Sam swooped on her and her squeal of delight punctured the silence. He closed the door and cursed himself for not bringing in any wood. But he'd been in too much of a hurry to get to Bitter Creek that morning. With baby under arm, he somehow managed to add to the limited wood supply in front of his fireplace.

There was chicken shit everywhere. It had never worried him before but he'd never had company either. The baby tried to kick out of his grip—it was like holding a live fish. Sam supposed he could tie it up so it couldn't crawl into the fire. Times like this he wished he had five hands. The kid's here five minutes and my whole life's rearranged.

The tin bucket was empty. Sam cursed again and with the cackling baby under his left arm, he ventured to the creek for clean drinking water. A short time later he gave the baby a spoon to chew on and hoped it would keep her entertained. The little squirmer should be asleep. It was night. 'Why aren't you asleep?' he asked.

She grinned at him and kept gnawing the silver spoon.

Sam turned back to Anna. He'd postponed the inevitable long enough. He reached for a bottle of spirits, washed his hands and then the knife. Small cuts on his fingers stung like hell. He was furiously blowing on them when the spoon fell on the baby's nose and she started screaming. He turned and there she was, climbing out of the crate again.

'Jesus, Suzie.'

She crawled to him and grabbing his leg, she started to chew on his pants. Sam put the knife down and replaced the baby in the crate. 'You asked for this.' He took a loop of thin rope from the hook on the door and tied the baby's hands to her feet—not tight, she could still move about, she just couldn't go anywhere. 'Stay. Okay?'

Sam brought the lamp closer and unbuttoned the coat he'd covered Anna with. She was still unconscious.

The white skin surrounding the bullet hole was burnt. God knew how far in or even where the bullet was. Sam rubbed more alcohol on his hands, picked up the knife and leaned across her. Knifepoint touched her chest and indecision rose in a tidal wave. His stomach churned, his knees turned to jelly. He was about to tell himself he couldn't do it when as if

60

from nowhere, he thought he heard Tom's voice. *Not like that, you idiot.* Suddenly Sam was calm. Very calm. His hands weren't shaking any more.

Sam put the knife down again and eased Anna to her right side. He put his fingers on her back and he could feel the bullet just below her shoulderblade. It was caught in the muscle there. Now, he knew what to do.

When he'd washed the blood from his hands, padded the wounds and bandaged her securely, he sat back and admired his handiwork. The misshapen bullet lay bloodied on the table. He picked it up and looked at the woman once more. She was still alive, breathing with difficulty. There was nothing else he could do—she alone had to decide whether to live or die. The next couple of days would tell, if she lasted that long. Sam didn't think she would. He rubbed at his face. He needed a shave, his three day growth was itching.

She looked peaceful. Innocent. She'd lost none of the loveliness that had first captured him. She'd lost nothing except maybe, her life. The baby wasn't too happy about her latest situation but Sam hadn't yet finished. He used some water and a cloth to wipe the mud and blood from Anna's face, arms and body before he covered her.

Then he turned to his other problem.

Susan.

She was chewing on the rope. 'You can't eat your way outa those knots.'

Big dark eyes peered up at him and she grinned.

Her smile was contagious. 'Think you're smart, don't you, kid.'

The question filtered in from the edges of a haze. Gone now the comfort of hands, the echoes of a heart not her own. Now, there was warmth to quell the cold; a tickle in her throat kinder than the burning, bottomless ache in her chest. The voice again. Her eyes wouldn't open. The voice seemed familiar and there was no fear to associate with it. But just when she almost broke the surface, Anna felt herself falling into the grey depths once more. Here there was no pain. There was nothing at all.

The smell hit him first. It was a smell that couldn't be ignored or mistaken. Fear hit. Pure fear. God was pulling some kind of joke on him. It wasn't damned well fair. The kid grinned on. What to do now? He didn't know how to put a diaper on or what he'd use for one. He found his only towel and sighed. It had to be sacrificed. He tore it in half and

61

pondered the problem. What next? 'Yeah, yeah, I'm new at this. Stop laughing at me.'

The kid kicked and wriggled, and laughed some more. No sooner had she stopped laughing, she was crying. 'Be kind, kid. Please. I've had a bad day.'

Somehow, he managed to secure the fabric. She didn't appreciate that. Sam picked her up. Didn't appreciate that, either. The screams ceased when mouth found buttons, then she started again.

She's hungry, he thought. She probably hasn't had a feed all day. He knew the feeling well. He hadn't either. Sam looked around his shack. There was some leftover stew in the pot. He tipped some into a dish and found the spoon. He took the first mouthful, not hot, not cold. Certainly not appetizing either. He balanced Susan on his knee. 'Here, try it. You'll hate it.'

She wouldn't shut up. The screams were really disturbing him. Spoon touched mouth. Mouth opened. Sam shovelled some stew in. He knew his cooking was bad but hell, it hadn't killed him yet. The face told him exactly what he didn't want to know. The baby let the stew dribble out and she choked on her next lungful of revenge. Obviously, she'd never had this sort of stuff before. All Sam knew about babies was where they came from and that was it to a certain extent.

Milk.

No cow for miles. Twelve miles to be precise—Lonnigan had a Jersey house cow. Twelve miles was twelve miles. There was no cow at the diggings. He'd have remembered if he'd seen one there.

Jesus.

Sam looked at Anna. She was either sleeping or unconscious, he didn't know which. He had no other choice. The spoon clattered into the bowl and a hot warmth melted through the leg of his pants. 'Why didn't you do that before?' He could barely hear his own voice over her angry screams.

Sam took the baby to Anna and drew the covers back. He rolled the mother to her side and put the baby down close, hoping it'd know what to do.

It did.

And that was all it had wanted right from the start.

The sergeant walked the short way home and was hit with a full recitation of how the neighbour's dog had finally killed mother's prized rose. Maddy, his sixteen year old daughter, greeted him with this news and a smile as she placed a small glass of rum into his hand. Luke looked down at Maddy and something in her eyes made him think about the baby. It would have been kinder to cut its throat. Billy though, wouldn't be convinced. He must have had a couple of children himself. Luke smiled at Maddy and looked away from her innocent eyes.

'You look tired, Papa.'

His smile was forced. 'Show me this rose, girl,' he said and was led away into the backyard where Maddy was attempting to grow vegetables with brackish artesian water. Her efforts at gardening were failures, too. The rose didn't look dead. It looked as it always had, ill. A dose of ratshot would cure Bartlett's pissing dog. 'Do we have any ratshot left, girl?'

'I used the last of it today, Papa,' Maddy said proudly. 'I don't think he'll come back or sit down for a long time.'

'Caught him in the act, did you?'

'Got him fair up the…'

'Maddy, remember you're a lady.'

'Sorry, Papa.'

'Where's your mother?'

'Asleep. She has one of her headaches again.'

'Oh. I see.'

'What happened to your face?'

'Oh,' he said, touching the scratch. 'The horse bolted. It was a tree branch, I think.' He finished his rum quickly, gave her the glass and walked off for the house.

'I made an apple pie for supper.'

'Not hungry, girl. Maybe tomorrow.'

The back door squeaked to a close.

'I suppose you won't eat my apple pie, either,' Maddy said to the sleeping hens in the chook house. With a sigh she traipsed up the stairs. He'd been away a long time and it was always good to see him again, even if he was tired and cranky. It was light relief really to mother's never ending headaches and complaints about the heat. It wasn't even summer yet.

63

The sound of the bubbling water was enough. Sam dropped the bundle of shitty and bloody clothing and relieved his aching bladder. He looked up to the starlit sky. Different stars here, closer somehow. The clouds rolled in, his stomach began to roar from emptiness. Even the thought of his leftover stew was enticing. Anything but this. Boots off and barefooted, he limped downstream from where he normally fetched drinking water and after taking a bar of soap from his pocket, he washed the clothing.

Woman's work this.

He only washed his own clothes just before they walked to the creek by themselves. He didn't want to change his ways. He hated having no choices.

It would take his coat a couple of days to dry. All the frantic scrubbing hadn't got rid of the bloodstains. As for the rest of it, Sam did the best he could. With any luck it wouldn't rain and most of it might dry by morning.

He was thinking like a woman now.

But thinking like a housewife took his mind off the day. If he stopped this train of thought he'd only start to ache. He kept his body busy in the hope the nagging suspicions wouldn't rise again. They'd haunted him like a bad smell all day long.

He wondered if Anna knew what had become of her friend. What they'd done to her. He'd ridden home via the shortcut through the Chinese camp. He'd seen it all. And her friend, the old man, everyone.

Natives. It had to be. But what would natives do with white man's gold? Yellow man's gold for that matter, too? Nothing made sense. Raiding the Chinese camp would have been more fruitful for whites. Blacks couldn't sell it or trade it.

Anxiety began to fade as pure numbness set in. He still had the photo in his pocket. He hadn't taken Tom's Bible. There'd been no time, no inclination. Amid every other thought and feeling, he'd wondered about the silk. His father was dead and there he was, wondering what the hell that piece of silk was for. Even that hadn't made sense. Christ, he didn't even realise his father had a damned photograph of his mother. And to find it like that—discarded. Of no value. At least it hadn't been burnt.

Sam hung the dripping clothes over the porch rail and hesitated before stepping inside. All was quiet though, the baby asleep. Squeaking, but asleep against its mother. She was semi-conscious. The sight alarmed him. She was covered in sweat, her lips were parched and cracked. She couldn't move but her big eyes followed him everywhere. Sam dipped a mug into the drinking water. 'Here,' he said softly and helped her up a little. She choked. Spots of blood appeared as if by magic. Sam took the

64

mug away even though her eyes begged him not to. He found the cloth he'd sponged her with, rinsed it a few times and gave it to her, dripping.

Anna sucked on it feverishly. Then she tried to say, 'Thank you,' and had to take three breaths for the simple word.

Sam smiled at her. 'It's okay, Ma'am, you take it easy.'

'Michael?' she asked next. It was like waiting for a stutterer to say hello.

'Try and sleep, Ma'am. We can talk later.'

Later. If there is a later. Death was surely swinging from the rafters, laughing, watching, waiting to take her.

'Dead. He's dead.'

'Don't talk.'

'Michael's dead,' she whimpered, emphasizing the word.

Sam wondered what he should say. He wasn't good at words so he turned away instead. It was all he could think of to do and when he next glanced at her, her eyes were closed. Relief flooded through him like a cooling wave. Now he wouldn't be able to sleep. He'd lay awake wondering what the hell he'd say to her.

But he was hurting too. It'd been his father out there. An old man with bad lungs, a bad heart and bad teeth and not much time left anyway. It would have been quick, just how the old man would want it to be. One second alive … None of this getting sick or losing your mind. It was over with quick.

Sam leaned against the fireplace and rubbed at his face. With a sigh, he took out the photograph of his mother. He never knew her. She'd died when he was a baby and that was all he knew. Well, almost. He turned to Anna and took his attention back to the photo.

And then he realised a lot of things.

Tom's mysterious friendship with young Anna made awful sense now as did Sam's immediate interest.

The lady in the photo, his mother, had died years before Anna had been born. They seemed to be about the same age, judging from the photo, and they were mirror images of each other: the same dark hair, same eyes. Same everything. But different people. Of course they were. Christ, what am I thinking? he asked himself.

She was alone now. A widow. Husband dead, and with him died any security his name had given her. All she had was the kid. Little Suzie.

Sam balanced the photograph of his mother on the mantelpiece. Next time he was in town, he'd try to remember to get a frame for it.

65

Sam camped on the floor. His hearing was alert to every squeak from the bed, every strained breath Anna took, every gurgle and noise from the baby.

And he surprised himself because in a way, it was a warm feeling to have someone under the same roof.

Anna woke sobbing five times during the long night. The baby woke twice and he had to steer it to a nipple. Then there'd be silence broken by the loud beating of his heart. It didn't take long to discover that Anna didn't whimper as much if he held her hand. She was different now to the pretty girl whose book he'd ruined, whose hat he'd trampled, whose husband beat the crap out of her because a horse drank a bucket of water. Anna was different now because she was here with him when all the odds had decreed she should have been dead. What do I do now, Sam thought and with that, he fell asleep.

Susan woke him at dawn with fresh encores of savagery. Sam sat bolt upright, wondering why he was on the floor and what the hell was the noise, when all memory flooded back, hard, uncompromising.

Baby.

Baby. It was galloping across the bed, Anna vainly trying to reach it before it splattered on the floor. 'Hey, get back here,' and Sam was on his knees, grabbing the child by the scruff of the neck and swinging it high. She laughed and immediately grabbed a fistful of nose. The nails were like razors.

And last night he really believed he could survive this? 'Morning, Ma'am.' He placed the baby back in its usual nest and closed his eyes. 'I'm not looking. I haven't seen a thing,' he lied and pulled the covers high.

Frothy blood was seeping from her mouth again. She was trying not to cough, trying to talk at the same time.

'Higher. Lift me … higher.'

He only had one pillow.

'Drown.'

'What?'

Anna closed her eyes. There was too much pain, inside and out. The baby at her breast didn't help either. 'Lift me higher … or I will drown.'

Sam pulled a chest out from under the bed and rolled a heap of clothing into a ball. A short time later, she was sitting higher and she tried to smile despite the pain.

'Drink?' she asked.

'Water or whiskey, Ma'am?' he offered with a grin and dipped the mug into the water again. She didn't choke this time—he stood by, just in case.

66

'Michael's dead.'

It wasn't a question this time, just a statement of fact. So how much did she see? Sam watched the eyes. 'It would have been quick.'

The dark eyes stared at him. No, not at him, through him. For a moment he thought she'd start crying but no. Not yet, anyway. She held out the mug weakly and he took it in a shaking hand. 'Would you like some tea or something?'

She nodded.

Sam turned away. 'Gotta get some … Jesus,' he mumbled and groped for the door, pushing it open. Escape. He breathed deeply of the cool mountain air but he couldn't shake the feeling that she was still staring at him. He'd never felt anything like it. The air quelled his uneasiness.

Fresh air always helped him think. So what had she seen, apart from her dead husband, and how much would she relate? Sam knew it wouldn't be wise to hold his breath waiting.

Chapter Five

'SERGEANT?'

'What?'

'The bath tub's gone, sir.'

Luke closed his eyes. 'It's been gone since Friday, Brannigan.'

'Oh. Has it?' The tone was surprised. His news was not news at all. Daniel could have sworn it was there yesterday. Or was it the day before? What day was it, anyway?

'You and Dingo get out to Mitchell's Hill. Camp if necessary.'

'What for?'

'Are you questioning me, boy?'

'I'm supposed to have tomorrow off, sir.'

'Would you like permanent days off, Brannigan?'

'Mitchell's Hill, sir. For Manning, I suppose?'

Luke almost stood. He didn't have to. It was perhaps the quickest he'd ever seen Brannigan move. There was a collision with Maddy at the door.

Daniel tried hard to smile and politely dodge the enormous basket she balanced in her arms. 'Would you like a biscuit, Daniel?'

'Sorry, Maddy, I have to go. Maybe another time.'

She beamed, pale eyes effervescing at the age old promise of, 'another time,' which she always held dear. It added to Daniel's torment. He liked her. He'd like her more if she didn't try so bloody hard. Besides, he'd tasted her cooking. Let Luke have it and choke. Tinned meat and open air was healthier.

'What is it, Maddy?'

Reveries shattered. Maddy had to tear away from the window where she'd been watching handsome young Daniel mount his horse. 'I thought you and Daniel may have been hungry, Papa.'

She heard the groan and pretended he was only tired, not cranky or impatient. 'What's in the basket?' he asked, bored, trying to be friendly.

Maddy had felt the invisible barriers before. As he looked through the goodies in the basket, she studied him and wished he could be something else. Anything but a trooper. But he'd always been a trooper and she blamed his job for being the sole cause of her friendless existence. All she

68

ever got was torment—about him, about her mother whom they christened Lady Jane because she never spoke to anyone lower than her regal self and when she did, Maddy shuddered from embarrassment. Boys teased her about her hefty proportions, her red hair, the trouble she had with saying esses—they always came out: 'th' and her head ached from holding it high so much. Then she'd go home and cry and even that she couldn't do very well. Mother cried like a lady. Maddy howled. Her eyes stung, swelled and her whole face blew up...

'Just leave it, Maddy,' was all her father said that morning and he returned to his work. He was writing something official.

'Is there anything you want me to do, Papa?'

'No.'

Useless to even try to talk now. 'Mother asked me to fetch the wash.'

'You know where it is.'

'Yes, Papa.' Maddy went through to the cells where one solitary, smelly drunk was snoring in a straw-lined cell corner. Maddy picked up the heavy drum of evil smelling linen. Someone had sicked. Maddy was fine if she didn't have to see it.

The drum would have beaten most girls her age, even some women. Maddy didn't think it was too heavy at all, but if Daniel was still here, he'd offer to carry it for her, all the way home. He'd done that once or twice, usually when Papa was throwing a tantrum. Maddy pretended it was her company Daniel enjoyed, not any excuse for an escape. She was waiting patiently for an invitation to the dance at Yarrawonga. He'd almost said he would take her.

'Are you right with that, Maddy?'

'Fine, Papa.'

Out she struggled into the morning sun with the drum of dirty linen in her arms. She came to a standstill and watched the long line of people walking behind Harry Ryan's horse-drawn hearse. The coffin inside had a bunch of flowers on it. Maddy wondered who it was lying in that plain box. She turned away after a little while, knowing if she kept staring at a coffin like that, the next might be hers.

A bunch of horrible little boys led by David Stills who had rabbit's teeth, began following her as she crossed the street near Ryan's. Each time she stopped walking, they pretended to be playing marbles.

Cretins, she thought, determined now to make it home and slam the door in their ugly, leering little faces. Mother would shoo them away. Boys playing by her fence always shattered the dark security of her curtained sitting room and made her headaches worse. Lately, even a bottle of sherry a day wasn't helping.

69

'Big bum Hannaford. Big bum Hannaford.'

Maddy kept walking as far as pride allowed until something hit the back of her head and knocked her hat off. Horse dung. Maddy put the drum down and turned to her tormentors. She was hit by another blast. Boys plunged to their knees and scooted marbles over the dusty street. 'Who did that!'

They all looked up, hiding laughter as best they could, all of them feigning innocence. Maddy stamped her feet. Sometimes that was enough to send them running in different directions. A few baulked. David Stills yelled:

'Why don't you send us to jail!'

'I wish I could!'

'Big bum Hannaford! Big bum Hannaford!'

With a scream, Maddy charged at the boys. They scattered. She found a pile of horse dung laying idly on the street and threw it at the squealing retreaters, hitting a few like moving bulls eyes. One on the behind, two on the head. Then she realised it was wet. Warm. 'I hate you! I hate all of you!'

And they laughed.

Nothing ever changed and nothing ever would.

Too angry to cry aloud, but with tears trailing down her face, she walked on with her burden. Maddy had no free hands to wipe her face. The flies loved her more, now.

Mother would have a fit.

Had she been faster, she'd have caught David Stills and beaten him to a pulp. It would have improved his looks. But it was so unladylike to fight. Ladies led extremely dull, boring lives anyway.

Why was I born a girl?

The thought alone made her howls more intense than ever.

The logs in the wall so close to her face were horizontally laid. Within the gaps, spiders had weaved intricate webs. Anna watched a small black spider close in on the frantic flying ant trapped there. Anna watched until the spider wrapped itself around the victim. The spider, hungry and victorious, the flying ant terrified until the end. Could such a tiny thing feel terror?

Anna looked away. She wondered if the tiny thing was able to scream. She hadn't. Or had she? She couldn't remember very much. Perhaps it was for the best.

Alone again, pain her only companion. She could hardly raise her hand; each breath was slow and deliberate in coming and agony to let go.

Where had he gone this time? Come back, Sam, please. Throat parched, mouth felt like fouled sand. Tasted like it, too. But there was no sound at all, save for birds. Birds of the like she'd never heard before. Or had she? There'd been something similar as they climbed the range known as Cunningham's Gap—scores of tiny, bright green parrots. Noisy but delightful. Cheeky things, too. What had happened that night? Hadn't one of the horses died of snake bite? No. Of course not. That night, she'd finally given birth to Susan. The next night the horse had…

Anna closed her eyes. She didn't really want to remember because she kept seeing Michael's face. And still there was nothing to be felt, not even loss. Her heart's most intense wish had been granted. Now he was dead—she was free. But what price?

Surely she'd loved him once?

Anna turned her concentration back to the gap in the wall. The flying ant was dead now and the spider moving away. Hadn't even eaten it. Was keeping it for later.

Her eyes closed. It was so easy to sleep now, so easy to wake, too. She turned to the sudden source of noise—her baby's cackles of laughter, the thumping outside. Anna tried to move, her body felt weighted.

'Ssh,' Sam said from outside. 'Not so loud, kid. Your mother's sleeping.'

He came in as quietly as he could. Susan was hanging upside down under his arm. Anna had never seen her child as dirty. Her newfound playmate was almost as bad. 'Oh,' he said, 'You're awake.'

'Water, please?'

Sam brought her some water, put Susan on the floor and went outside again. So much noise now. Anna could see his one leg holding the door open. The baby crawled towards him and was in the way as he dragged a huge wooden crate inside. Its sides were high. Anna wondered what this thief was up to now and she sipped her water, watching curiously. Sam swooped on the baby like a big bird of prey and in a moment, she was out of sight, deep in the bowels of the wooden crate. 'See if you can get outa that.'

On cue, two dirty, chubby hands gripped the top but nothing else of the baby showed. Sam stood there watching, smiling victoriously. 'Gotcha now.'

71

Susan began to yell and the yells faded to her gabble. The hands disappeared and soon there was silence.

'She needs a bath.'

'She'll only get dirty again,' Sam said and glanced at Anna. 'Oh, okay. I'll take her down to the creek later. That be all right?'

Anna had no choice. She couldn't move to help herself let alone her child. She nodded and looked away from the thief's bright eyes. 'I don't know how to thank you, Mr Manning.'

'You can call me Sam for a start.'

'Not proper.'

'Bullshit,' he whispered with a tiny grin. 'I think she's sleeping. Must have done something right.'

'She won't sleep for long.'

'Funny little thing, ain't she?'

Ain't. Anna hated that word almost as much as Michael's annoying 'cannae.' Ye cannae do this, ye cannae do that …

'How you feeling, Ma'am?'

'Tired. Hungry.'

'Oh. You eat stew?'

Stew. After months of tinned meat he asks if she eats stew? 'Yes. I like it. Very much.'

Sam thought it was funny and scratched his head. Anna wondered if he had lice. 'Some stew coming up.' He retreated to the open air and returned with two potatoes, a few carrots. He threw them on the small rickety table and reached for a rifle over the door.

Anna felt her entire body tense the moment he touched and loaded it. 'You be okay for a while?' she heard him ask. He gave her no time to reply. 'Won't be long.'

Anna was left to wait again, while the pressures in her body intensified and screamed for release. She waited for the shot so long that when it finally came as a crack in the distance, the sound still frightened her. She almost wet herself. And what seemed hours later, Sam returned. He'd shot, skinned and cleaned a rabbit. The carcass dangled from his bloodied hands. 'Hope you like rabbit, Ma'am.'

She nodded.

He prepared his food as he prepared his life. He was not very systematic or hygienic: throwing everything in at once and hoping for a successful outcome.

72

'Sam?'

He turned to her. Again, she had to close her eyes against the artillery of innocence on his face. 'I need to … I need to …' Embarrassment was a huge hurdle.

She thought he may have been a little intelligent—hadn't she seen some kind of spark in his eyes at some stage? He just stood there, regarding her in that same bored way Michael had. Waiting.

'I need to…'

'What?'

'Sam, If I don't go soon, I'll burst!'

'Oh. Why didn't you say so?'

'Please Sam, it's rather urgent.'

At least he wiped his hands on his dirty pants before he lifted her from the bed.

'Let me see if I can walk.'

'No.'

'Put me down.'

'No. Maybe tomorrow.'

'Sam…'

'Sam…' he imitated as he carried her outside. The brilliance of the sunlight stung her eyes and she turned her face into his shoulder. She was dizzy, and glimpses of mountains surrounding her bobbed up and down quickly.

But she managed to focus on, and stare, disbelieving, at the outhouse. It looked neither safe nor usable. Sam put her down after he'd kicked the door open and held her steady. 'Think you can manage?'

'I'm sure I can.'

He guided her in. The door closed in his face. And he waited. He waited forever. For Sam, five minutes with nothing to do was eternity.

'Anna-ma'am?'

'Yes, yes. Must you do that?'

'Do what?'

'Stand there waiting?'

'Just making sure.'

'Sam Manning, if I fall down into this hole, I'm sure you'll hear the scream.'

73

Sam smiled. If she fell in, he wouldn't be fishing her out. He was quiet for a little while and drew abstract designs in the dust with the toe of his boot. A thousand questions were surfacing but would the time ever be right to ask them?

'Sam?'

'Ma'am?'

'I can't open the door.'

'Stand aside. Tell me when.'

After a little while he heard Anna say, 'When.'

Sam kicked the door in. Anna took two steps towards the fresh air and her knees jelled. Sam caught her. 'I tried to say you wouldn't be able to walk.'

'You said no such thing. You just said no.'

'I did not.'

'You did so.'

'You arguing with me?'

'Stating facts.'

'Listen Anna, I know best.'

'You think you do. You need a shave,' she said quietly and shielded her eyes from the bright sunlight as she clung to his neck a little tighter. 'And a bath.'

'You're gonna nag me, aren't you.'

'Just stating fact.'

'Fact is, you won't win.'

Her silence was a loud reply. Once inside, the shack seemed stuffy and the one window looked as if it hadn't been opened for twenty years. 'I don't want to lie down.'

'Sorry,' Sam said and deposited her back into bed.

'You're being unfair.'

'No, its called sense.'

'Being sensible.'

'That, too. You a schoolteacher or something?'

'No.'

'Thank Christ for that,' Sam muttered and went back to the stew. 'You'll never get better if you don't take it easy.'

'I can take it easy and sit up.'

74

'No. You'll only fall over.'

'Let me try?'

Sam carried the pot to the fire. 'Nope. Maybe next week.'

'What happened to tomorrow?'

'Never comes, Ma'am.'

'Please, Sam?'

He sighed. 'You always get your own way?' he asked.

'Eventually,' Anna replied quietly. Sam helped her sit up in a fashion and she sent him a very small smile.

An hour later it was his turn to smile. He wouldn't let her feed herself and proved it by letting her try. She failed. Too weak to even argue now so the thief fed her.

'You really like this?' he asked, amazed at how quickly she was eating his stew.

'Very much. Yes.'

'You sure?'

'Why aren't you eating?'

Sam glanced down at the bowl of stew. He'd ladled most of the meat into the dish for her and what remained now was no more than soup. The sight of it turned his stomach. 'I eat when I'm hungry, Ma'am.'

The eyes watching him seemed too knowing. 'Because you live on your own and you're responsible for no one?'

'Full of questions, aren't you?'

'Curious.'

'Maybe you shouldn't be.'

'You are.'

'I'm what.'

'Curious.'

'Anna?' he whispered and thrust the spoon into her mouth so she couldn't get the last word out. 'You won't win.'

Her smile was both contagious and unsettling. She didn't have to say a thing.

She slept and while she slept she couldn't nag or argue. She'd already said the baby needed a bath. Easy to say. It was true, the kid stank but she didn't seem to mind. Sam couldn't postpone the inevitable now it was midday and hot enough to brave the cold water in the creek. He just

75

hoped the kid didn't hate getting wet as much as he did. But if he did some serious thinking, maybe he wouldn't have to get wet.

Sam pocketed the soap. There wasn't much left. One cake usually lasted half a year. Now with the sudden company, a half year's supply was nearly gone in two days.

The baby grinned at him.

'Don't make this any harder than it has to be, all right?'

She lifted her arms.

'Fungus,' he whispered and lifted her out of her new indestructible prison.

She liked the water. Had no fear of it. Tried to drown a couple of times, too. She came out clean. She talked a lot. Sam didn't know if it was da da or dad dad she kept jabbering but whatever it was supposed to be, it frightened him. With a clean, naked baby under his arm: 'Enough of this dad-dad crap, kid. I'm doing you a favour, no more, no less. So don't get any ideas, right?'

Susan dad-dadded all the way back to the shack.

Anna had thrown up in her sleep. Sam smelt it the moment he stepped inside. He didn't know how much more of this he could take.

This was going too far. If he'd half a brain, he'd have taken her and her adventurous child straight to Cormac and Alice, wiped his hands of all this trouble. Right from the start.

And he shouldn't have let her eat so much in the first place, either. As he cleaned up this latest quagmire and tried not to puke, too, he swore he wouldn't give in to her ever again. The twinkle of a female eye and a soft please and what happened? Every damned time. Well, not again.

I've had enough.

Sam had to change the bedding. One clean sheet left. It'd tear if he breathed on it. He had to dress her in his last shirt. Before long he'd have to change the bandages, too. She probably thought she could do that herself—if she woke up of course. How could someone throw up and not know it?

By the time he'd finished he felt sick and emotionally drained. All he wanted was some peace. The baby started bellowing, right on cue. Sam tiredly recognized the tone. Communication lines were open wide. He did as he'd done for the last couple of days and waited for the yells to subside as they normally did.

But mother sweated and skin glistened. She shivered, remained unconscious. Sam was hit with the truth of the situation. It'd been too

76

good to last. The well had gone dry, evaporated by the fever that had hit so suddenly.

He wanted to walk away from it all. He cursed himself for going to Bitter Creek in the first place. Damn his instincts and to hell with everything.

Why couldn't the world just leave him alone? Was that too much to ask these days?

Maybe it was. He couldn't be left alone, not with some other man's baby screaming from hunger in his arms. Then she started. Was she dreaming? The screams grew intense. There was nothing but pure terror in the voice. Sam's spine chilled and his scalp crawled. Before he'd realised what he'd done, the baby was back in her cot.

Anna, sitting ramrod straight, was screaming so hard she was bleeding again. Her eyes were wide open. It was as if she'd just seen a ghost or three. Lord knew there were enough hanging around to haunt her.

'Anna?'

Nothing. She kept sweating. Coughing blood. Screaming.

This morning she'd been almost... well, good. But that happened to people close to dying. They suddenly got better and happy and bright and a few hours later...

'Anna, don't die. What the hell will I do with the kid? Don't die.' His frantic words frightened him because they felt very real. 'Anna?'

She was screaming one word now: No!

'Anna!'

She heard. Her eyes flickered with recognition.

'It's okay, Ma'am. Nothing's gonna hurt you here,' and other platitudes escaped him quicker than he believed possible. His mouth ran to overflowing and she seemed to drink in his words. The shakings eased but not the shivering or the sweating. 'You're safe here with me.'

'With you?'

The tension eased.

'Yeah. Safe.'

'Dreams?'

'Dreams can't hurt, Ma'am.'

'The sergeant...' Her voice trailed off to nothing.

'The sergeant what?' But her eyes glazed and all the fire died. Sam's grip tightened on her arms. 'The sergeant what?' he asked again, searching her face. 'What about him, Anna?'

'Hurt my baby.'

'Baby's fine, Anna. She's fine.'

The flicker momentarily returned. 'Susan?'

'She's great. Just had a bath. Just what you wanted, remember? The sergeant what, Anna? Tell me.'

No, it was gone. Whatever haunted her mind had dispersed. Anna slumped against him, extremely hot to touch, her teeth chattering from the cold within.

She's dying, he thought. She's gonna die and there's nothing I can do.

Sam held her for a little while and tried to think. He had to get some kind of help even if it was help for himself. He couldn't handle this anymore and he was the first to admit it.

Chapter Six

ALICE WAS PLEASED THAT HER unexpected visitors were Daniel and the quiet Aboriginal who belied his wild dog of a nickname. She had no time for Lucas Hannaford and it was quite mutual. Daniel didn't have the sergeant's hatred of the Irish in his blood.

Long before the riders approached the small stone farmhouse, Alice sent young Leonie on a quest to find Cormac. 'He's off planting by the creek. Go now.' The girl and her huge black dog bounded away, south.

Alice tended to her wilting petunias and waited.

Daniel was pleased to see Alice's smiling face. The last time he was here she'd upended a jug of water over the sergeant's head. The quiet chuckle he'd had then returned now, the memory spurred by Alice's grin. 'Good day to you, Mrs Newberry.'

Billy Dingo said nothing. He dismounted and sat under the shade of a nearby tree.

'I suppose it's a cool drink you'd be needing?'

'If it's no trouble.'

For you? No lad, not for you. 'Come on in out of the sun, now.'

Daniel followed her inside while Billy put his cap over his eyes and tried to doze. The young trooper took off his cap and possession of the cool drink in almost the same movement. He'd been salivating over this drink for the past three miles. 'Thank you, Mrs Newberry.'

'It's high time you called me Alice.'

Daniel hid a smile and downed his lime drink. It was just as he'd expected.

'I suppose it's Sam Manning you'd be after again?'

'Yes, Ma'am." Daniel knew this woman was well acquainted with Manning. His calls to the Newberry farm were routine at the end of any mail coach week.

'He's not been here,' she said, no need to lie this time.

'Would you tell me if he had?'

'Probably not. What's he done this time?' Alice asked and poured another drink for the lad who looked as if he hadn't eaten in a week, too. A few more pounds on the thin frame, a few more years …

'He's stolen a bath tub.'

''Tis a joke, no?'

'No. He's stolen a tub.'

'Not the sergeant's, I hope?'

'Well, we don't know whose it is, yet. No one's reported a missing bath tub.'

'Daniel have you nothing better to do with your time than chase Sam Manning about the hills?'

'Have you seen him, Alice?'

'If only I had.'

Somehow, she meant it. Daniel knew that wishful look. He'd spoken to a number of Manning's victims, most were still starry-eyed two days after their ordeal. 'Let us know if you see him,' was all he said, wasting his words like he usually did when confronting civilians over the disappearing Manning, a legend around here and Daniel's secret hero. But he kept such secrets to himself—it was safer for his masculinity that way. 'Thanks for the drink. I'd better be on my way.'

Alice slipped two scones into his pocket and watched as he walked off into the scorching sun, replacing his cap, taking his reins, and tossing one of the scones to Billy. She knew he would. With a wave, Daniel Brannigan was gone.

And Cormac had been called up from the back block without reason. He'd be wanting a cup of tea to compensate for his long haul.

When he appeared, the afternoon feast was ready and Leonie was sitting on her father's shoulders, the dog circling them.

'What'd the bastard want this time?' Cormac asked and put his daughter to the ground.

'Papa, bad word!'

'Don't hit your father, Leonie. Go and wash up now.'

When the girl was out of sight:

'It was only Daniel. Sam's stolen a bath tub.'

Cormac wasn't surprised. 'Hannaford's, I suppose?'

'Is that all you can say? Don't you wonder he might be going crazy up there in the mountains all on his own?'

'Where's my tea woman?' Cormac grunted. Alice ignored him and continued in her normal way as she always did when she had something new to chew over.

80

'A bath of all things. He hasn't had a bath for years. You can smell him before he's seen.'

'That's because he has no nagging wife to contend with.'

'Don't you go saying that. You'd be lost without me.'

It was cool inside—too long in, he'd not want to go out again.

'Talk to him, Cormac. He listens to you.'

'Ha. He pretends to listen. The head nods, nothing sinks in. He caught the habit from you, wife.'

Alice thumped him, Cormac pretended to fall dead and Leonie watched, smiling, all the while hoping her father would hurry up and take a cake before she starved to death.

'I'm serious now.' She was too. Hands on hips, mouth at full speed. 'Tell him if he let the troopers be, if he didn't cause trouble for himself, he'd be soon forgotten.'

'Mama, what if Sam doesn't want to be forgotten?'

'Mind your business, child. You be seen and not heard.'

'Leonie's right. Hannaford wouldn't see it that way, either. Where's my tea, woman?'

The tea duly came and Leonie ate most of the cakes she'd helped her mother bake. Both husband and daughter switched off from mother's monologue about the bushranger. Leonie's mind was actively planning the rest of the afternoon. She might try a special game with Dog—an adventure about the Indians Sam once told her about, or she may dress Dog in doll's clothes.

And Cormac thought of Sam who sometimes helped him fence or harvest and didn't mind being paid with Alice's food. And what had she said? She'd have fed him whether he'd helped or not?

'May I be excused?' No one was listening. Her mother was still talking, her father in a daydream. 'May I be excused?' Leonie tried four times, excused herself and ran off. Well, she'd been seen and not heard, how could she be in trouble now? As she tried to plan her latest adventure, Dog not cooperating, not sitting or playing dead when he was supposed to, Leonie decided for the ninth time that week she needed a brother or sister to play with.

'Oh, Dog!'

It had no intention of playing dead. He was barking at someone coming. Leonie watched, excited. Two visitors in one day? She couldn't believe it.

Sam?

81

The girl was elated. He'd play a quick game of "cowboys and injins"…

'Papa! Ma! It's Sam! Come and see what he's found!'

Cormac didn't have to see, he could hear it. There was a fight to be out of the door and by the time both emerged into the sunlight, Leonie had her arms full of screaming baby. The grey horse of Sam's foamed with sweat, Sam was shaking, trying to speak, not able to.

'Lord Almighty,' Alice whispered. 'Sam, get inside with you, quickly, there's troopers about.'

'Yes, I know. I've been waiting for them to go. I don't have much time, can you help me? The kid's hungry, I need a cow or something. Anything…'

'Leonie, go and get Marigold, now.'

'But Ma…'

'Now!' Alice gave the girl a smack on the ear and she ran off, mumbling unfairness, she never got to see a real live baby, ever. And just when she'd wished for one, it appeared. Miracles *did* happen, but nothing in life was fair.

Sam looked frightened, hungry. A week's sleep would have done justice.

'Inside, out of the sun.'

Alice was ignored. Sam and Cormac were studying each other, a thousand questions on each's silent lips.

Alice took the baby inside. Cormac didn't know what to say except for:

'What the hell is this?' as he followed Sam's gaze to Leonie, still running in the distance. 'Come in, it'll take the girl half an hour or more to get the goat. Come on, now.'

Cormac didn't notice how Sam settled into his chair. 'Will you be telling me what's happening? Where on earth did you find the child?'

'For heaven's sakes, give the lad time to catch his breath!' Alice called from another room.

It wasn't breath Sam needed, it was the right word to begin with. 'She was the only one left alive at Bitter Creek. The kid, it's mother.'

'She was what?' Alice yelled.

'I need your help. The mother, Anna, she was shot. She's at home. That's why I'm here so if you'd just help me with the kid…'

'She's alive then?'

'If I don't get back to her she won't be much longer!'

82

Cormac flinched from the angry madness in the eyes. No words could calm him, not now.

'Off with you, Sam. Get home, we'll be by tomorrow.'

Sam looked up at Alice, holding the baby like a prized jewel she'd never relinquish. 'You can't have her.'

'Will you let me worry about the baby! Just you get off home!'

Cormac followed Sam outside and grabbed hold of the horse. 'Take one of mine, I'll bring the grey tomorrow.'

Terror and indecision welled. Common sense was displaced for a little while. Sam didn't want to leave the baby with them, how the hell would he explain it to Anna? Maybe he wouldn't have to. Maybe she was already dead and if she was, the baby would have a good life with the Irish couple—the only friends he had.

'You can't be seen with my horse,' was all Sam said, turning the grey and cantering off the way he'd come. The canter became a gallop and as he rode, he already felt as if half of him wasn't there. A couple of days and that damned kid had become a part of him.

Sorry Little Suzie, but I don't know what else to do.

Sam saw the traps first. It was always the way. He could hear Daniel's chatter as they two followed the creek downstream. Sam watched, torn between priorities. If they kept following the stream, it'd take two hours for them to reach Bitter Creek. Across country, fifteen minutes at the most. Sam figured the raid hadn't been reported—Alice hadn't said a thing and she knew everything that happened within a twenty-five mile radius usually before the event occurred.

Luck was with him. It was only Brannigan. Sam had nothing against the lad, mainly because he knew Brannigan didn't shoot first and question after. He'd try to take him alive. He'd tried a dozen times. Nearly had him twice in fact. Nearly. But they'd gazed into each other's eyes, a smile touched each's lips and freedom reigned once more.

If Anna was going to live another half hour wouldn't matter either way. The authorities had to know about the slaughter.

If they didn't already.

No, they couldn't know.

Now was no time to argue with himself. Sam whistled and two heads turned. Brannigan didn't reach for his gun. Dingo did, the movement was stopped. 'No, don't shoot. He's worth more alive,' Daniel probably said.

Bullshit of course and again, Sam wondered why the kid always let him go as he turned his horse and bid them follow.

He made sure he kept in sight during the chase across heavily wooded and steep rocky hills because if they suddenly lost sight of him, they'd stop. Like they always had before.

A few hundred yards from Bitter Creek, Sam was hit with Death. Three times as ferocious now because of the hot days. He didn't want to witness it again. He rode further, hoping the breeze's stench would slow the pursuit. When next Sam glanced behind, the two troopers had come to a complete stop.

Sam circled, his duty done. He was too far away to see the look of terror on Daniel's face yet he was close enough to feel it. 'Sorry, boy,' he whispered to himself and wasted no more time in getting home to Anna.

Home to Anna. Christ, what was he thinking of?

Billy Dingo was spooked and he refused to venture any closer. 'No, they're dead. I'm not going up there, I know that stink. I know what it is.'

Daniel was frightened enough to threaten to shoot Dingo but still he refused to budge. He started some bloody unnerving wailing chant designed to ward off evil spirits or some such rot. But someone had to do it. Someone had to see exactly what was causing the stench. With heart in mouth and a handkerchief over his face, Daniel took the final steps alone.

All thoughts of Manning disappeared. The contents of his stomach emptied over his uniform and his horse.

A speckled hen was staring at her from the mantelpiece. All was quiet, no sound at all. No horse looking in the window at her, just the hen.

'Sam?'

Her voice was no more than a squeak. She tried again, louder this time. Nothing. No plod of heavy feet on the porch outside, no squeak of the door accompanied by the baby's cackle of laughter. 'Sam?'

He's gone, her mind said.

No, he can't have gone. He wouldn't leave me alone.

He's stolen your baby. He's going to sell her. He'll come back with pockets jangling.

84

No!

He's a thief. He'll tell you that just as his father told you.

No.

He's left you alone to die.

Tears came and forfeited the pain, heightened the despair. Anna wiped her face but more tears filled her eyes. He would not leave me alone. He would not, there must be a reason.

Yes, he's off selling your baby.

No!

Anna rubbed at her eyes and saw the gunbelt hanging on the back of the door. There was a rifle near the fireplace and a shotgun on the wall, too.

He's taken Susan for a walk.

She repeated the thought until she believed it.

From the small, cracked, filthy window, Anna could see the grey storm clouds devouring the blue of the sky.

They shall come home wet.

If they come home at all.

She closed her eyes and the sergeant's face flashed into her mind's eye. She caught her fright with the sharp intake of breath and opening her eyes quickly, she saw the hen again. A pretty hen. Quite benign. Still staring at her.

A hen inside his house.

It was almost enough to make her smile.

Almost.

Alone. So alone. Born alone, die alone. No one can share either experience with you. Like pain. No one can share that, either.

Anna pushed the covers aside and focused her mind on the task of movement. It was slow, painful. It made her sweat so much she didn't know if her eyes stung from tears or perspiration. Bare feet touched earthen floor. Determination was winning. Anna rose unsteadily, yet undefeated. her body screamed to be inert once more.

No.

Savage thoughts ruled when she lay helpless and she would not be helpless any more.

She was dizzy. The rickety table kept moving and remained still as she grabbed it. The room undulated, steadied. Not far to the door. Six steps perhaps. Although she wanted to cough and she could taste blood, she ignored it. The door seemed the most important thing in her life. Freedom, perhaps another world was waiting out there. Even though the sun was hiding behind the storm, the glare threw her off balance. Anna hugged the porch upright and either didn't see or misjudged the one step to the ground.

Someone called her name too late to stop the fall.

Sam was off the horse before it had skidded to a halt and he couldn't decide if it was anger stirring him—anger at seeing her out like this—or relief that she was still alive. Both seemed a miracle. He'd thought his emotional reserves had been tapped and completely drained. Until he saw her, touched her.

'Come on, Anna-ma'am. Get you back inside.'

'Where's my baby?' she asked in a tired, child-like voice.

There was a jolt of searing pain as she was lifted and held tight. 'Baby's fine.'

That wasn't the answer she needed. 'Where's my baby?'

All Sam heard was a very tired, aching anger and he didn't blame her. It didn't feel right without little Suzie. It didn't feel right at all. 'Suzie's okay, trust me.'

'Trust you?

'Yeah. It's been known to happen sometimes.'

Anna felt the bed greet her and she tried to protest. Her squeaks were drowned by the sound of the sudden, hard rain.

'Where's my baby? What have you done with her?'

'If you knew how worried I was, you wouldn't be so angry.'

She couldn't hear a word he was saying. He brought her water. Anna knocked it away, tipping it over him. Sam closed his eyes. And he rushed home for this?

'What'd you do that for?'

'Where is my baby!'

'She's okay. I took her to a lady I know.' Calling Alice a lady seemed strangely inappropriate. He should have said friend.

'You gave her away?'

'No, no, she'll be back.'

'You gave my baby away!'

'Anna, calm down, huh?' Huge red flowers were blooming across his last clean shirt. 'I didn't give her away.'

'No, you sold her!'

86

'Why would I do that?'

Tears started. Christ, he thought, why me? He sat close to her and tried to take one of her hands away from her face. 'Anna, listen to me. Suzie was hungry, I had no choice.'

She looked up into his bright bloodshot eyes. He was tired. Upset. She felt his fingers tighten on her hand. The rain lessened its fury and the honesty she felt lessened her fury. 'What do you mean she was hungry?'

'You've got nothing for her no more. I had to take her to someone who knew what to do. But she's coming back. I wouldn't lie to you.' And as if to prove it, he wrapped both his hands around hers.

'She's safe with this ... lady?'

'Probably clean and dressed pretty and fed and you name it by now. But if this storm keeps up, it might take a couple of days for them to bring her home.'

'*Days*?' Anna asked, eyes filling again. Sam had to look away. 'But she's never been away from me, ever!'

'I know how you feel.'

'You don't! You can't know how I feel!'

Sam let go of her hand and stood up. 'I know enough.'

'I need her with me!'

'Well, you can't damn well have her and that's all there is to it! I thought you'd be dead by now, right? Hell, I wasn't gonna risk that kid of yours goin' the same way! I don't like it much either, so can you just shut up and give me a little peace? Is that too much to ask?'

Wide eyes blinked and turned away to study the wall. Sam walked to the fireplace, grabbed the hen and threw her out into the rain. After that, he took off his shirt and hung it on the hook near the door.

'You didn't sell Susan?'

'No. I didn't think of it. Are you happy now?'

Silence ruled for a little while.

'I'm sorry,' she whispered.

Sam turned to her. Now he was feeling guilty.

'Yeah, well, so am I.'

'Don't you get any ideas, wife.'

Alice looked up innocently. Cormac's face was bright red, redder than usual from the shadows of the lamplight. Alice looked down at the baby, at the soft, tiny fingers clasping her hand. There was a towel catching any spills.

She'd taken to the cup. Hunger made the little one adapt quickly. 'She's such a pretty thing. Have you not seen her eyes? So large and so dark. Wise eyes.'

'Was I like her, Ma?' Leonie asked, the jug of warm goat's milk ready just in case more was needed.

'A little,' Alice said quietly.

'I want a brother, Ma.'

'Want all you like, girl, it'll do no good.'

'Don't say that, Cormac. There's always a chance.'

'Do we have to give her back?' Leonie asked.

'Yes,' Cormac said quickly the moment Alice said, 'No.'

Leonie glanced from one to the other. 'If she was a boy, you'd want her, wouldn't you, Pa?'

'Leonie, she belongs to someone else.'

'But if her mother dies, who will she belong to then?'

Cormac looked away from Alice's inquiring eyes. 'Time I was in bed,' he mumbled. 'Kiss me goodnight, Leonie.'

The little girl kissed him hastily and waited until he was out of sight. 'Ma, is it because I'm a girl that Papa doesn't like me?'

'Your father loves you very much and I don't want to hear such nonsense ever again.'

'Was I as pretty when I wore that dress?'

Alice looked up into her daughter's green Irish eyes, the round face covered in freckles, surrounded by curly auburn hair. 'Prettier,' Alice said. 'Now give me a hug and get to bed. It's late.'

The baby smiled at Leonie when the girl touched the pretty, tiny face before walking to her room. Susan then talked to herself and didn't want any more of the cup. Alice put it on the table, turned the child to face her and strong legs kicked against her stomach. The baby smiled and reached for Alice's face. Then her huge eyes searched the room. Alice knew who she was looking for.

She belongs to someone else.

But Alice rocked her to sleep, anyway.

88

Sam wrapped a blanket around his half naked body and lay down near the fire. The air was cool but not cold. All he wanted was to sleep. Anna hadn't spoken for what seemed like hours, she just stared at the wall, sniffed back tears and suffered quietly. And the silence he was accustomed to seemed unnatural now. She was able to sit up without much help, she could even feed herself and that added to his uselessness.

'Are you really a thief?' she asked a few minutes after he extinguished the lamp and ten seconds after he'd found comfort.

'I suppose I am.'

'Tell me why?

'Why what?'

'Why did you bring us here?'

Sam raised himself on elbow and looked at her. She was sitting up, watching him. So she wanted to talk, did she? Good. 'Even a thief wouldn't leave a baby out to die. Or you,' he added.

'Perhaps you should have.'

'I suppose I could have. Easy.'

He knew he hadn't convinced her of that, or himself for that matter. He settled down once more and his eyes closed.

'Do you think you're earning a place in heaven for this?'

Sam's face creased with a smile she wouldn't have seen. Heaven? What in hell was that? 'Sure I am. Yep, a place in heaven...'

'Why won't you talk to me? You were making excuses to talk to me at the diggings.'

'I'm tired, okay?'

'Goodnight, Mr Manning.'

Sam winced at the sound of the 'Mister'. How many times did he have to tell her?

Silence ruled for a little while.

'Sam?'

'Mmm.'

'I'll be needing a bath tomorrow.'

He made a noise that sounded like, sure thing, and then he was asleep. There was nothing there to haunt him.

Not so, Anna. The darkness of the shack was frightening enough but terror waited behind closed eyes—a terror she'd live with for the rest of her life or so it now seemed.

Maddy Hannaford sat on the front verandah and gazed up at the stars while her deaf white cat purred on her lap. She tickled the cat's chin absently until the last tiny space of clear night was obliterated by cloud. She could smell the rain coming and the breeze turned into a wind which after such a hot spring day, was more refreshing than a warm bath.

Woolly hated the wind. It turned him into a lion. She let him go before he scratched to get away. He bounded down the stairs and under the house without so much as a goodbye.

The town was very quiet.

Maddy loved this time of day/night. Mother was asleep, Papa asleep (the best place for him lately, he was so cranky he'd bite her head off for breathing.) The whores were still working, though, and the men were still spending their earnings on drink.

She could never quite understand why, but it was a fact of life. So many smiling faces going into and coming out of the pub. Perhaps it was easier to be bad than good? She never saw too many happy faces at church on Sundays. So if the Devil was alive and well at Rose Keller's ... She didn't understand it. She never heard the whores gossiping about the town ladies. Yet the town ladies gossiped non-stop about the whores, usually over the cups of tea and biscuits after church.

The whores would look at Maddy and smile and say hello and the town ladies never listened to a thing she had to say. Not that she ever said much. Maddy was useful for pouring tea for the circle that circled Mother and urged for more stories about Brisbane society.

Maddy sighed and wished she'd fit in somewhere.

She stood up and decided it was worth trying to sleep again. By now, the goings on behind the wall would have ceased—the grunts and groans and bedsprings squeaking was too much to bear at times but all seemed quiet now.

She heard the sound of the horses as she opened the door. Maddy turned back. It was Daniel, alone. But wasn't he supposed to be camping out at Mitchell's Hill? He wasn't due back until ...

'Maddy, get your father, quickly!' He leaped the low fence and took the stairs three at a time. He was breathless, his eyes wide. She'd never seen him in such a state.

'Quickly!' he almost screamed.

Maddy was knocking on her parent's bedroom door before she realised it. Daniel's heated mood had been contagious. 'Papa!'

'What, what, what!'

'Daniel's here, Papa! Quickly!'

90

She looked back at Daniel, juggling his cap nervously. His face in the light was quite pale and what was that all over his uniform? Pooh, he smelled, too.

Maddy was pushed out of the way by her father's bulk.

'What the hell is it, boy!'

Crankier than ever now at being woken up and Maddy wasn't game to move. All she could do was watch. Frozen.

Daniel couldn't seem to speak and when he finally did, Maddy didn't believe what she'd heard.

'Bitter Creek, sir. Everybody's dead. Everyone is dead.'

Maddy glanced at her father's face, her mouth open in shock. Her father didn't twitch. Only his Adam's apple moved when he swallowed. 'Maddy get to bed. Now.'

'But Papa!'

'Do as I say!'

'Lucas?' Mother called wearily.

'It's fine dear, fine,' her father lied and grabbing Daniel by the collar, hauled him down the hallway and into the kitchen. The door slammed.

Maddy remained glued to the spot. She hadn't even worried about Daniel seeing her in her nightdress, barefooted.

Everyone at Bitter Creek was dead.

What from? Fever? No, a fever wouldn't be so lethal as to wipe out a whole mining camp like that. Why, only recently, Papa had been out there checking licenses. She'd overheard him tell Mother about the young mother and baby out there. Maddy remembered because her mother started nagging, how it was no different than dragging a woman into the wilderness and giving her a house that was hot in summer and freezing in winter and telling her this was home and she should be happy she had a roof over her head and food on the table... The young mother and her baby had caused yet another argument.

Did that mean that the mother and baby were dead, too?

Maddy crept up the hallway and stood at the closed kitchen door. She could hear sounds as such but not words and not clearly enough to fully comprehend, either. But she did hear:

'Would you stop that snivelling and get the rum into you!'

And a moment later:

'Maddy, get to bed before I whip you!'

91

Oh God, she thought, heart in mouth. He can see through walls, too. Or could he? Maddy ignored the warning and stayed.

Another rum, he'd have fallen over. Daniel clutched his cap in one hand, the glass in the other. 'The Chinese, too, sir. Everyone.'

'Blacks, you said?'

'I said most of them were speared.'

'Any sign of gold?'

'Nothing was left. Not a bloody thing. Days ago, it was.' His stomach was turning over again at the memory of the stink that still pervaded the air, his clothes. Daniel wanted to strip off and burn them, scrub himself until he bled. It would be the only way to properly cleanse himself.

'And it was Manning who led you there?'

Daniel nodded.

'I see.'

Two words that chilled the spine. 'Sir, I'm only guessing that he led us there. If he knew what was at Bitter Creek, he couldn't very well ride into town to report it, could he. Sir.'

The sergeant said nothing. Daniel had seen the look in the eye before, countless times when a scapegoat had been found and used accordingly. And how often had Daniel turned his head?

'You can't be serious, Sarge. Manning's not a murderer.'

'He's wanted for murder.'

'That was years ago!'

'Are you defending him?'

'No, but...' Yes, he was defending him. If it had been anyone else leading him to sites of wholesale slaughter, he'd have been filled with questions, certainly.

'Anyone who breathes is capable of murder, Brannigan. You should know that by now.'

'There's no proof it was Manning.'

'Proof?' Lucas almost laughed. 'Go home and try to sleep.'

Daniel wondered if his hearing was now impaired. How in hell could he sleep?

'Take this with you. It's the best company you're likely to have.'

The sergeant handed Daniel the bottle of rum and Daniel took it because he knew he'd never be able to sleep unaided. Not tonight, at least.

92

The movement in the kitchen prompted Maddy to vacate, quickly. She darted into her room and jumped into her bed with the swift agility of a frightened mongoose. Shaking, she huddled deep into the covers.

Daniel had seen all manner of horrors.

So had Maddy, in her head as she'd eavesdropped.

Her father blamed poor Sam Manning.

And now Mother would have her excuse to go back to Aunt Rachel's in Brisbane. Maddy was almost crying when her door opened and there he stood—Papa in his underwear, his arms folded.

'How much did you hear?'

'Papa?' she asked, pretending to be half asleep. He seemed to believe it. After a little while the door closed and darkness fell. Maddy didn't sleep at all that night.

Chapter Seven

HE WANTED TO BE AN enamel mug, the one touching her lips like that. The thought took him unawares and he realised he was staring again. Anna hadn't noticed. She sipped her tea and closed her eyes, sighing. 'What's today?' she asked.

'Sunday.'

'And it would be,' she paused and looked out of the window to the sun. 'About ten o'clock?'

Sam took a pocketwatch from his shirt and flicked the small instrument open. 'A quarter after.'

'I'm getting better,' she said with a tiny smile and sipped her tea again. 'When do you think...'

'I don't know.'

'Would you let me ask my question?'

He waited to hear her question.

'When may I have my bath?'

Bath? What'd she want a bath for? 'I can get you some water.'

'No, Sam. A bath. A proper bath. In the tub that's outside.'

'Oh. That tub. Can you wait for Alice?'

'No. I need a bath now.'

'I can't smell you.'

'Please, Sam? A bath isn't too much to ask considering there's one lying idle outside.'

'Wait for Alice, huh?'

She could feel the beginnings of the initial weakening and forged ahead. Quietly. 'Does the thought embarrass you?'

Sam couldn't look at her for very long.

'Really, Sam. Don't pretend you haven't seen me naked. Isn't that how you found me?'

But he couldn't be cornered easily. 'Wait for Alice. She'll probably bring stuff for you to wear and then I can have my clothes back.'

'Alice must be the one you gave my baby to.'

94

'Why can't we just say she borrowed her for a while?'

'Perhaps I shall believe that if she comes. I do know one thing.'

'Seems you know it all, Ma'am.'

Anna ignored him. 'I shan't last another hour without a bath.'

Sam studied her for quite some time.

'And even you declared you had no idea when these people would come. There wasn't that much rain to stop them. It's all a paradox, really.'

'A what?'

'You once told me no one knew where you lived and yet you wait for people to visit.'

'All right, I lied. You want a bath? You get a bath. Just stop nagging me.'

Sam picked up the tin bucket and went out, mumbling to himself.

Anna smiled. For the first time in her life, she'd been able to manipulate a man other than her father with a sad look, a quiet question, persistence. It was also easier to get out of bed today and toddle to the door. Sam was taking great long strides towards the creek. Anna made it down the porch step, refusing to fall this time.

When Sam hauled the bucket out of the water and turned, she was right behind him. 'You look awfully tired,' she said quietly, stepping out of his way. 'I suppose I could wait for Alice if that's what you really want.'

'Would you make up your mind?'

'You're angry with me.' And she looked down at her hands.

With a sigh, Sam put the bucket down. 'No, I'm not angry. Just tell me if you want a damned bath or not.'

'I shall wait for Alice to arrive.'

'You sure?

Anna nodded.

'You're right. I am tired. When I'm tired I get edgy. It's hard to sleep through a lot of screaming. All I know, the sooner you talk about what happened, the sooner we'll both get some sleep.'

She turned away, ignoring him.

'If you talk, it doesn't come back to haunt you quite as bad.'

'Wisdom from someone who knows, perhaps?' she asked.

'Maybe.'

95

'You will never know what haunts me or why. And as for not being able to sleep, you may have your bed back at any time. I never asked for it.' Anna walked off in a huff.

'You're not as tough as you think you are, lady.'

There was no reply.

'Where are you going?' Sam called.

'In search of paradise!' she yelled and slammed the outhouse door.

By the time Anna reappeared, the tub had been emptied of its wooden cargo. She followed the drag marks in the dirt, across the porch and into the shack. Sam was heating water over the fire.

'They're coming,' was all he said.

Anna listened and heard nothing unusual. 'How do you know they're coming?'

'I just do.'

Anna lowered herself into the only available chair, an ancient, fragile-looking rocker. 'Tom knew of things to happen before they happened.'

'Like I said, they're on their way.'

'You're a lot like your father.'

He cast her a glance that could have cooled a boiling stream.

'I know you want to know what happened but I can't tell you, Sam. I can't tell anyone. No one would believe me.'

'You could always try.'

'I can't!'

Two simple words overflowing with hate and anger. She tried to hide the fear in her eyes. Impossible. Tears never lied, either.

'Anna, all I'm saying is I'm here. I want you to remember that. And if Alice sees you've been crying, you'll never forgive me.'

'I'll never forgive you?'

'Dry your eyes or you'll find out.'

And they arrived. Cormac, Alice and Leonie Newberry. Rattling buggy, screeching Irishwoman. Anna winced as the door opened and Alice swept in. All she saw was the red flame of windswept hair, the fierce, hot face and Susan, wearing pretty, unfamiliar clothing. Before Anna could speak:

'Here she is and I didn't want to give her back, mind, but Cormac was adamant and … why are you crying, pet?'

Sam was trying to sneak out of his own house.

96

'What's this you've been doing to the girl, now, Sam!'

'Please,' Anna begged. 'Give me my baby?'

And while Alice handed the child over, Sam made his exit and Alice followed. Hands on hips, she watched the goings-on at the buggy. One man to load the trunk, yet two to get it off? 'What's this you've been doing to the lass, Sam!'

'Shit,' Sam whispered. 'I told her not to cry.'

'So she's improving then?' Cormac asked with a grin.

Anna was reminded of her grandmother—a huge, overbearing woman who tended to take control of any situation. Where Grandmother had been forceful and intimidating to the unwary, she also lacked an ounce of warmth. Somewhere, she knew, Alice was lit by not just warmth, but a flame. Anna had never seen her baby as happy or as pretty and she felt a curious mixture of jealousy and gratitude. Alice was the opposite of her husband, a short, wiry Irishman with mischief in his eyes. It wasn't hard to realise why he and Sam were such good friends. They carried the trunk in and set it down, heavily.

'Out with you and stay away. Leonie, close the door and stand guard.'

'Yes, Ma.'

Once the door closed, Alice warmed. She took the baby again and set her in what looked like a cot. Sam must have made it. 'Good Lord,' she said. 'He expects a child to sleep in it?'

'She does. She likes it, Mrs Newberry.'

'There'll be none of this Mrs Newberry. You'll call me Alice.'

'Do you know Sam well?'

'Does anyone know Sam well? Of course I do. You had him worried sick. Never seen him as flustered and worried. But he's fine now. And so's the little one. She'll be drinking from a cup now and you're welcome to have Marigold as long as you need her.'

'Marigold?'

'The goat. She's outside. Just you watch Sam's vegetables. She's already seen them.'

'Oh.'

'There's no need to be frightened, pet.'

Anna looked up into Alice's eyes and a thick silence hung in the air. Even Leonie wondered what was going on. And ever so slowly, Anna's face contorted. 'I just want a bath, Alice. I have to be clean again. It's been days. It's been so long. Sam wants to know what happened but I can't tell him. I can't tell him because he's a man. Just a bath, Alice, please? That's all I want for now.'

Alice, lost for words, reached for Anna's hand and held it tightly. 'I brought you some clothes and some lavender water, pet. That will help.'

Another woman's presence was all the help she needed—for a little while, at least.

And still, Leonie didn't understand what was going on. God forbid she ever would.

'An inch was all I wanted.'

'Come again?'

'An inch. I'll be in trouble if there's no rain by Christmas.'

Not being a farmer, Sam wasn't preoccupied with the weather. Nor did the weather play much of a role in Sam's chosen occupation of harassing the law, breaking it on occasion.

'Tell me something,' Sam said after a thoughtful swig from Cormac's bottle. 'You ever heard of blacks murdering for gold?'

'Can't say I have, Sam.'

'Something's not right.'

'Bejesus, I'll give you a medal.'

'She knows who's responsible and she's not saying.'

'And would you if the boot be on the other foot, like?'

'Depends what the circumstances were.'

'So you're thinking it weren't blacks at all, then?'

'I don't know. I'm hoping she might say something to Alice.'

'I'll let you know if she does.'

Silence ruled again.

'She's a pretty one, no doubt about it. What is it you plan to do now?'

'I don't know.'

'Is there anything at all you do know?'

'Maybe I'll wait until she gets a little better and decide then.'

'I see why you're worried.'

Sam laughed—he wished there was something funny happening to prompt it.

'One day, there you be, a free rover and now a sudden family man.'

'Bullshit.'

'No. Punishment. You can't look me in the eye and tell me she's not the one you told me about weeks ago, now? The married one?'

'Give me some peace, Cormac.'

'Now can you not see what you've done?'

'No, but you'll tell me anyway.' Sam grabbed the bottle from Cormac's hands.

'I don't think I have to. So I'll just tell you what I thought the first time I laid my eyes on Alice. Know what I thought?'

Sam rolled his eyes and took an almighty swig.

'I thought, I'd like to be tryin' a bit of that. And look where that thought got me.'

'You couldn't survive without her.'

'True. But the fact of it's this. You say everyone was dead at Bitter Creek. What I'd be thinking of, but you're not me, of course—I'd be thinking about whoever it was shot her, he'd be expecting her as dead as the others, too.'

'And when he finds she's not dead? Yes, it's crossed my mind.'

'If it were me, Sam, I'd not be wanting any witnesses.'

Silence hung in a heavy cloud.

'We could safely assume it was well planned but I'm beginning to wonder what use blacks would have for white man's gold.'

'Unless they were led by a white.'

'Ah, but who?'

Sam studied the closed door.

'Seems to me it would have been easier to leave her where she was. Turned a blind eye, so to speak.

Sam glanced at Cormac. 'And could you have done that?'

'No,' Cormac said with a smile. 'This is what you get for wanting another man's wife.'

'You're asking for a punch in the nose, Cormac.'

'So I'll be keeping my ear to the ground instead.'

'Thanks,' Sam said absently.

99

Tranquillity arrived moments after the Newberry's buggy departed. The silence was so loud it was almost deafening. Susan was sleeping on her stomach, thumb in mouth. She seemed so much bigger, fatter, her hair was longer and starting to curl. Anna touched the soft, fine hair. Whole again now the baby was home.

Anna didn't bother to turn when she heard the footsteps.

'I missed her too, you know.'

'I see that now, Sam. I tried, but Alice wouldn't let me thank her.'

'She's like that.'

'You were right. She brought me clothes, gave me all of her baby clothes.'

'And a goat.'

'And a goat. But something's missing, Sam. Something is still missing. I don't know what it is.'

Sam had the overwhelming urge to touch her, hold her, tell her everything would work out fine. But she didn't need lies. He reached out and touched her cheek, anyway. Anna flinched and moved away.

'The dresses she gave me are big but at least you shall have your own shirts back now. After I wash them of course.'

'Anna?'

On his lips the silent question: Who was it?

But something in her eyes prevented him from breathing for a little while. He turned away. 'Why don't you get some sleep while you can? You know, while Suzie's sleeping.'

'Her name is Susan.'

'Yeah, right. Susan. I'm taking a walk.' And he took his rifle for company.

For supper they shared the last of Alice's baking. Anna seemed to eat a lot now and never complained very much. How could she complain if she didn't talk? No matter how hard he tried, Sam couldn't deny it was good to have company. Especially Anna's company. And to think he'd fantasized about this sort of thing.

Sam poured out the last of his whiskey. A slug before bed always helped him sleep. So went the excuse.

'Tom and I used to pretend it was tea we shared in the afternoons. No one realised what it was we were really drinking.'

'Sounds like Tom.'

100

Anna watched Sam sit. Perhaps he thought ladies didn't drink whiskey?

'I'd only have a little, of course. I found it helped me sleep.'

'You too, huh?' Sam asked but it wasn't really a question. His face creased with a smile. 'All you have to do is ask, you know.' He gave her half of his whiskey. Anna caught his eye and an unfamiliar shyness leapt inside him.

'I dare not ask any more.'

'How come?'

'Denials. My life's been full of them. Yours too, I expect.'

And there they were, two strangers trying to find conversation to fill the gaps. Sam said nothing. This was going to be tortuous. Now she was clean and looking half alive, she was very, very attractive. The whiskey was helping him feel it in more ways than one. The baby squeaked in her sleep and while she slept she was no excuse. Sooner or later, Anna would have to face the onslaught. Sam glanced at her, at the way she sat, holding the mug and staring into the crackling fireplace and he couldn't tell what was happening inside her.

'Anna, why are you protecting him?'

The question was out. Finally.

'Protecting who?'

Anger rose. Sam fought it. 'The one who tried to kill you. You're protecting him.'

'Perhaps I'll go to bed now.'

'I think you'd better sit here and talk to me, girl.'

'No.'

'Yes.'

'No! It's none of your business! It's over!'

Sam made a hasty grab for her arm and he wasn't expecting her reaction. He'd never hit a woman in his life and he probably never would but to see her cower away from the inevitable she thought was coming stunned him senseless for a moment. But he didn't let go. 'It is my business because you're here with me and it's not over. What if he finds you survived? Huh? What then? He sure as hell won't want witnesses. So don't you tell me it's over. It hasn't even started yet.'

Her face contorted. Tears blurred the room. 'Please don't say that.'

'Maybe it's not what you wanna hear but I can't help it, Anna. Who is he?'

101

'Everyone is dead, why can't we just…'

'My old man died out there too and you know who's responsible!'

'No, I don't!' She tried to loosen the grip from her arm but it was futile. She had to sit down again and tears wouldn't work now.

'Have you thought about when he comes looking for you?'

Terror touched every fibre of her being. 'Don't say that!'

'You're the only one who can hang him, Anna.'

'Them!' she spat. 'It wasn't just one. They all…'

'You think I don't know what they did to you? Who is he?'

'Which one!'

'The one that shot you.'

'None of the others are important?'

'Anna, I'm trying to help you. I know it mightn't feel like it or even sound like it but…'

'If you wanted to help me you should have left me to die!'

And he wondered if it was the whiskey talking. She couldn't mean it.

'I just want to forget.'

'You won't unless you talk about it.'

'To a stranger? I barely know you.'

'Does it matter? Sometimes it's easier to talk to somebody you don't know, someone who don't know you. Hardy ever get judged that way.'

Anna knew he'd never relent. Perhaps a lie would serve a good purpose? 'I don't know who he was and I don't remember his face. Now please, Sam. Let go of me.'

Sam released his grip, stared into the fire and heard the sounds of the woman getting into his bed: the creaks, the covers moving, her quiet breathing.

'Give me time, Sam. Just some time.'

'I would if it was mine to give,' he whispered.

He slept soundly that night, feeling more than hearing her wake, unconsciously reaching out to touch, knowing the touch would calm her back into her safe, dreamless void. He caught two words:

Sergeant.

Sergeant.

That filtered into his brain and lay there below the surface. Just like yesterday, he was back at Lambing Flat, sitting on his horse, Luke there

102

on the ground, searching one of the many bodies. A white this time. 'Luke, what the hell are you doing now?'

'He won't be needing it. Better me than someone else. Help me, Sam. Come on.'

'Split the proceeds?'

'Of course.'

Sam rode off.

The memory returned to haunt him in full, living colour.

Ten men volunteered to help with the mass burials—Harry Ryan couldn't accommodate fourteen at once. Not to mention the Chinese as well.

Before dawn, Billy Dingo rode in.

Luke was waiting. He could smell the fear. For a while he thought it was his own. He'd had a restless night, blaming it on the heat of course. He'd spent hours fighting off the vision of the baby dying slowly amid the already dead. Or dogs taking it. Fighting over it.

'She's not there, Sarge.'

'What?'

'I counted fourteen, same as Daniel did. She wasn't with them. No woman, no baby.'

The sergeant's mouth went dry.

'Hear me, Sarge? She's not there.' Billy spat the words as he dismounted and began to unsaddle his horse. 'You said she was dead but you wouldn't let me make sure of it.'

'Shut up!'

Billy Dingo balanced his saddle over the railing and hung his bridle after stabling, watering and throwing his horse some hay.

'Get back out there before the burial party arrives.'

'Oh, Sarge!'

'I want two graves, Dingo. You hear me? One for her, one for the baby. This woman is dead, do you understand me?'

Dingo said nothing. He was too weary for anger.

'Do as you're told. When I get there, I want to see two graves. Understood?'

With a quick nod, Billy took Daniel's horse and as he tiredly swung on, he said, 'Too bad they'll be empty.'

'I'll find her if she's alive. She can't have got far.'

'Yeah? I spent all day searchin' and if I can't find her, how can you?'

Daniel, still shaky from his ordeal, was miffed to discover his horse gone. It had a soft mouth and by the time Dingo was finished with it … thoughts soon passed. The sergeant told him to organise the burial party.

'Mr Michaels, are you sure you want to come?' Daniel asked as he gave the seventy year old blacksmith a leg up. The old man wouldn't be denied, even if he looked too frail to walk across the street on his own. But the more hands, the quicker the mess would be buried. Daniel didn't want to face it again. He'd rather be involved in the daunting task of apprehending those responsible, even if he didn't know where to begin. With any luck, the news would reach Brisbane within the week and the Sub-Inspector would return.

Daniel, leading the pack for the five hour journey, saw Maddy standing on her verandah, cat in arms. Watching. Always watching. Daniel looked away before she waved. Even the sergeant was abnormally quiet. Maybe he was preparing himself, too. No one, not even old Luke, was made of iron. 'You right there, Mr Michaels?'

Daniel received a grunt in return.

Damn the goat, Anna thought. I want my baby back. 'She's too small to be drinking like that.'

'It's not whiskey.'

'She needs me, not you.'

'She's not complaining and you need to rest.' Sam went back to concentrating on Susan, balanced precariously on his knee. He was showing Anna how Alice had taught him to feed the baby and Alice had a knack of making hard things appear easy. More goat's milk was lost down the dress and on to his lap than was ingested. Sam had strict orders not to allow Anna to attempt anything for at least another week.

As usual, he was caught in the middle—used to tending the kid now and vice versa, something which forced Anna's teeth to grind, jaw to ache. Susan was far happier with Sam.

Betrayal.

Jealousy assisted a rapid recovery.

104

Anna refused to stay in bed and refused to admit a short walk to the outhouse and back was exhausting. Worse, Sam followed her everywhere. His innocence and helpfulness was aggravating.

'You better start taking this in with you,' he said, holding Susan under his arm, indicating the long stick leaning against the outhouse door.

'Thank you, no. If your black snake intends swallowing me, he asks for all he gets. Now leave me alone. Go away.'

'You really want me to go away?' Sam asked.

'Yes!' came the snap from behind closed door.

'Okay.'

Anna heard the receding footsteps and she didn't see Sam or her baby for over an hour. As the minutes passed, each seemed infinite. Panic, floating in the shallows, soon surfaced and it gasped for air.

Where had he gone? Why would he leave her alone for so long? Imagination needed no assistance. He didn't answer her frantic calls, either.

Sam eventually returned when the baby grew restless and hungry. Anna was sitting on the porch step, weeping. He didn't know why. She'd told him to leave her alone, he had.

'What're you crying for?'

'Where have you been!'

Sam looked suitably innocent and stricken. 'We were looking for paradise.'

'Don't ever do that to me again! If you want to get lost, fine, but don't take my baby with you!'

'Here, she's all yours.' Sam thrust the wet, crying child at her and loped away. Then, as if remembering something important, he stopped and turned. 'Make a deal with you, Anna-ma'am.'

She studied him cautiously.

'Tomorrow's Tuesday, right? You prove you can manage all day on your own, I'll go to town on Wednesday.'

'That is a deal?'

'We need supplies. I'm gettin' mighty sick of rabbit stew. Besides, I need some news.'

'You won't tell anyone I'm here, will you?'

'Anna, who am I? What am I?' He walked back to her and the baby reached for him. He tried to ignore it. 'I thought you'd be begging to come with me.'

'I never beg.'

'Someone in town you don't want to see?'

'You won't corner me, Sam Manning. Stop trying. And don't lie to me, either.'

'Lie? Me?'

Anna rose up off the porch. 'I know which days the mail coach runs.'

'Oh.'

'I know what you do on Wednesdays, Sam Manning.'

She walked inside and Sam smiled to himself. Before she closed the door in his face, she said, 'There is no need to make me the centre of your excuses.'

His smile faded.

Bitter Creek was cleared. Decaying residues of humanity were wrapped in canvas as quickly as possible and rolled into one long, narrow hole after another.

'Who were these?'

Brannigan heard the sergeant ask Billy Dingo the question. Dingo, true to name the day before yesterday, had had a sudden change of mind and belief. Now he was with the others burying the dead.

'Who was what, Sarge?'

'Here. Who were they?'

'The Hall woman and her baby.'

Daniel stopped shovelling. If he opened his mouth to voice his immediate question of: 'Where was she?' he'd probably taste the rotting meat and throw up again. There was nothing left in his stomach to lose except perhaps his stomach itself. He hadn't been the only one which was a slight comfort. The Hall woman and her baby? Why hadn't he seen them? And as if to answer his silent question:

'They was over there, Sarge. In them trees.'

Daniel looked to where Dingo was pointing. North. Nothing else was said. Daniel's partially covered body received another load of dirt. Spent their lives digging in it and in the end it always claimed them.

The sergeant was calm throughout, expressionless, thoughtful, busy with his monotonous chant of the same Biblical verse he'd be hearing in

106

his sleep. No one said very much. What was there to say that was appropriate?

Still the doubts remained. Something's very wrong, Daniel thought.

Chapter Eight

'I SHALL MISS YOU, PAPA,' Maddy said quietly from her seat on the coach. Luke was too busy calming Jane to say any more than, 'And I shall miss you, Maddy. Take care of your mother.'

She glanced at her mother's dramatics and wanted to say:

If I see her.

She could imagine her with Aunt Rachel already. Never home. If it wasn't shopping in the city, it would be a succession of luncheons and garden parties to which Maddy wouldn't be invited. She'd be made stay at home with Ronald the Rat, her fourteen year old cousin. If he dared mince another frog and put the remains in her underwear drawer again, she'd mash him to a pulp.

Still, being in Brisbane for a while would give her plenty of time to finish her tablecloth. There'd be nothing else to do but embroidery. And she'd have some water to look at, too. Rachel lived close to the river but not as close to the Governor's house as everyone, including Mother, liked to think.

Maddy expected the dramatic change to take place at any moment now. Ten years would instantly peel from her mother's face. It always happened when her father wasn't about. At home being a martyr, she looked and acted her age. Forty three. But with Aunt Rachel ... just the thought was embarrassing.

Maddy didn't want to go. If she was a boy, she'd be allowed to stay. She could shoot better than any boy she knew, anyway, but no, her father had decided it best they leave until the mess was cleared up and danger, whatever that was, had passed.

Lady Jane's departing performance was admired by the two gentlemen on the coach. The sergeant was embarrassed at the way his wife's nails almost drew blood on his arm. 'Be careful, darling,' she moaned. 'For me, please be careful?'

She looked at him like she'd never see him again. She was probably planning how not to return, anyway. It was all a lie. Maddy knew Mother spent half her life hoping for news that Lucas had died on duty. It was the only chance she had to escape back to the city where she belonged.

Maddy wanted to jump out of the window and she would have, too, if Daniel hadn't been there watching, ready to wave her goodbye.

108

The coach finally pulled out. The seats were hard, uncomfortable. The ride was already rough and jarring and they hadn't reached the end of the street yet. Maddy looked out. Her father wasn't watching. It was no use waving. He was talking to Daniel and the other trooper who'd been sent when the news of the massacre at Bitter Creek had been made public.

His name was Dennis. He wasn't even handsome. What help was one extra man?

And home for Christmas? It was another lie, another broken promise which amounted to the same thing.

Maddy sighed. Lady Jane was already in full conversation with both male passengers. Something about how dangerous it was to be married to a senior trooper. Senior? Oh Lord, Papa's only a sergeant. Recriminations, retaliations, Manning was not to be played with. He's a murderer you know.

Maddy groaned and wanted to scream out to leave Sam alone but no one would hear her. No one ever did. Ahead lay a long, boring journey unless Sam Manning decided to adjourn the proceedings. The thought cheered Maddy. She even smiled to herself:

'Everyone out! Move!'

Maddy wasn't dressed in grey, nor did she have on thick socks under her boots. She wasn't the Maddy she saw in the mirror. No, she was beautiful, slim. Fragile. She was the last to step down. Mother, crying, being comforted by the bearded gorilla she seemed to fancy. Everyone was terrified but not Maddy. Brave in the face of scintillating danger. Her heart skipped a few beats when Manning gazed directly into her eyes. Then he went about robbing everyone else first. He took Mother's wedding ring from her finger but she didn't really care. It meant nothing to her.

'And you,' the bushranger said, smiling. Adrenalin surged so heavily Maddy almost floated away. 'What have you got for me?'

'Nothing, sir, nothing at all.'

Warm hands lifted Maddy's new, pretty face. His breath was sweet.

'Maddy!'

The daydream sprang a-leak. The sweetness was Mother's perfume, there was no handsome bushranger's lips about to touch hers, just three faces, peering curiously at her.

Maddy felt flames ignite her face.

'Maddy! What do you say? Mr Morris has asked you a question!'

Sam watched the coach rattle down Mitchell's Hill. He swore to himself. Since he'd found Anna he'd lost track of the days. It wasn't Wednesday at all. It was Thursday, dammit. The coach was going, not coming.

'Shit', he muttered.

Just as Maddy had given up hope, she thought she saw Manning's black scarfed figure high on the hilltop, watching. Her heart skipped and fell into her boots when the figure turned the horse and rode away. The wrong way! Oh no, no, no! Prove to them you're not a monster, Sam!

The coach continued on its rough journey.

Maddy rearranged her daydream. No, she wouldn't want Daniel to rescue her. She'd spend the rest of her days roaming the mountains with the bushranger, living a life of excitement with the man of her dreams.

Sam crept into the Establishment via the back door—he'd seen the troopers still in town. As he slunk down the carpeted hallway the floorboards creaked in protest. Ginger-Lee's door was open, welcoming. He peered in. Empty. She'd acquired new curtains, nauseating pink, and apart from that, nothing had changed. Sam felt no sudden anticipating heat, his mind kept seeing Anna with the baby in her arms as she waved him goodbye. Though nothing had shown on her face, Sam felt she was pleased to see him go.

He didn't like that, he wanted to get back, quickly. But it meant a wait. He couldn't venture downstairs, not now. More later than sooner, he recognised Ginger-Lee's approaching footfalls. As she wandered in, humming a song under her breath, Sam grabbed her from behind and covered her mouth with his huge hand. 'It's me', he said. Under ordinary circumstances, 'me' could have been anyone. Her struggles ceased and Sam let go, finger to mouth now, closing the door quietly.

'What're you doing, Sam? Trying to scare me to death?' she growled in a whisper. Before he had time to reply: 'What're you doing here? Haven't you heard?'

'Heard what?' he asked as he scanned his favourite whore from dyed red hair to painted toenails. All thoughts of Anna disintegrated.

'Sam, you shouldn't be here. There's traps looking everywhere for you.'

'Yes, I know', he replied, nuzzling her neck, slipping his hand into her dress for a delicious feel.

She pulled away, surprising him. 'It's true?' she asked, wide eyed. Sam pulled her back to him and tried to slip her dress off her shoulders. 'Sam, no!'

110

No?

'What's wrong?' he asked, shocked, dwindling at her rejection. Ginger-Lee turned away and realigned her clothing.

'Have you ever lied to me?' she asked.

'You're my only girl, Ginger-Lee. You know that. I never want anyone but you.'

'I don't mean that.'

Sam looked dazed.

'You once said you'd never killed anyone. Is it true? Is it still true?'

Sam reached out and turned her. He liked to see eyes in situations like this, but he saw only fear and affection in hers. His blood chilled. 'Is what true?'

'They're saying it was you, you the ringleader.'

'Ringleader for what?'

'All those miners at Bitter Creek. Tell me it's not true. Tell me it's a lie, that you didn't murder men you knew for their gold?'

'Jesus Christ,' he whispered and had the sudden need to sit. 'They're saying it was *me*?'

'The whites, the Chinese, the woman and child. Everyone.'

Sam looked up into the woman's pale eyes and saw the tears emerging but his own shock was now a cold, sick feeling. 'I didn't kill anybody.'

Ginger-Lee sat with a thump beside him on the bed they'd shared so often. This time she only groped for his hand and strong fingers curled over hers. 'Lucas is saying it was you. Says he has evidence of it, enough to hang you. By God he will. I never thought I'd hear myself say this, but you have to go back wherever it is you came from, Sam. Go away and don't come here anymore. If Lucas finds you've been here, I'm the one to suffer. No friendship is worth fifty pounds.'

'Reward, huh?'

She nodded. Sam made no move to go. Not yet. 'Tell me what they're saying.'

'Most popular story is how you got together a pack of blacks and took to the Chinese diggings first before you raided your own father's camp.'

'That's different,' he whispered.

'Don't you see it's because you've been seen there at Bitter Creek, Sam?'

'Yeah, taking my old man his tobacco.' Sam rubbed at his eyes and didn't let go of her hand. 'You said a woman and a child?'

111

'A team went out there not two days ago and buried them all.'

'Did they … you don't believe it?'

'Lucas is doing a mighty fine job of convincing half the district you're dangerous now. Go Sam. Go as far as you can away from here. I don't want you to hang.'

He held her tight and planted a small kiss on her forehead. She knew it would be the last time she'd feel his touch, smell him, see him. Then he was on his feet. His face had drained of color but his eyes were still summer blue and bright.

'If I never see you again, you remember one thing, girl. I'm no murderer and I never have been.'

'God be with you.'

'No, God forgot me a long time ago.'

And he was gone.

'Psst. Ryan.'

Harry Ryan thought he was hearing things as he was tucking into his sandwiches during a lull in trading.

'Psst, Harry, you there?'

The ageing storekeeper and undertaker went to investigate the source of the sounds coming from the back of his shop. He found Sam Manning crouched behind a display coffin. The face was pale, the eyes wild. 'Sam, what the hell are you doing here?'

'I need supplies. Sugar, flour, tea, tinned meat and ah.' There was a pause as Sam pulled a tattered list from his breast pocket. Coins and notes soon followed. 'Bandages and a hairbrush if you've got one.'

'Sam, there's no need to whisper. You can come in. No one's about.'

For the first time in two years, Sam wondered if he should trust old Harry Ryan.

'Come on, Sam. If the traps find you here I'll be measuring you for one of the finest and no one wants that. Do you not trust me?'

One of the finest? He was surrounded by coffins and had hardly noticed. He followed Harry, watched him turn is Open sign to Closed. He even offered Sam one of his sandwiches. Harry attended to the list and Sam's gaze stayed mainly on the door.

'And so you should be scared.'

112

'I'm innocent, for Christ's sakes.'

'I know that. Even Elsie doesn't believe it, as does most of the town.'

Sam dived for cover when footsteps were heard on the verandah and a glimpse of uniform appeared. It was Daniel wondering why the door was locked. 'Get on out to the wagon and hide under the canvas. I've to take an order out to Mrs Sellar. Get off with you, quickly.'

When Sam departed, the door was unlocked. 'Morning, Harry.'

Harry consulted his timepiece. 'You're behind yourself, Daniel.'

The young constable pushed his cap back on his head and fished in one of Harry's huge glass jars for a peppermint. 'No one's been in for bandages or infant things?'

'No one injured or newly birthed, no. Why?'

'No reason. Thanks for the sweet.' With a smile, Daniel left, duty done. The doorbell jangled on closing and Harry looked at the scrawled list. Bandages. Small cup. Hairbrush. For a moment the old storekeeper wondered just what was going on.

'Elsie?'

After a soft incoherent mumble, Elsie Ryan appeared at the top of the stairs. She was up to her elbows in bread dough. 'What?' she snapped.

'Mind the store for me, dear.'

'You said two o'clock.'

'Elsie, don't argue.'

'Two o'clock and not a moment before,' she snapped and Harry sighed. Sam could wait another half hour. He'd send a boy to fetch Sam's horse and ride it to Sellar's, no questions asked or answered for a pocketful of mints.

The baby slept. Boredom rose in copious amounts. Anna soon tired of chatting to the staring, comatose goat and had tried to sweep the floor. After a great deal of exhausting effort she discovered the floor was wooden. Sam was right, she wasn't that strong. She tired quickly.

And Susan slept on, thumb in mouth, dreaming whatever it was babies dreamed of. Anna tried to sleep and soon tired of waiting for it to come.

So she sat by the clear sandy creek, half listening for the baby to wake and give her something to do. Perhaps Susan knew it, perhaps that was why she slept so deeply. Memories drifted back as she watched the myriad of smooth river stones toss and tumble down the tiny waterfalls.

Michael's beard, already gray. His voice, one she once found comforting, now replayed in her mind as curses. Tom was there too, so close she could almost smell him. Tobacco and sweat and old age. 'No, no, you're tippin' it out the … dish.' Funny how he never cursed when she was nearby. And his gnarled, arthritic hands snatching the pan from hers, picking leeches from her arms and ankles. 'No, no, when I say shake it, I mean like this!' Cranky, impatient old man. But how she loved him.

But now there was nothing but the clear water, rippling, foaming, bubbling. She looked around her, a complete circle of mountains. A lifetime in distance from the mud and blood of Bitter Creek. Aptly named. No place for a woman. Or a man. Let its gold lie unclaimed for all the good it would do; no amount was ever enough. Gold. It turned a placid creature into an hysterical monster. A Fool's Gold. Let it rot in the hell it causes. It's over, it's gone.

'It never happened,' she told the water and it didn't want to listen. 'I've nothing now. Nothing at all. No husband, no home. Not a penny to my name.'

Nothing now, except for Sam. A thief. You take it easy, he'd ordered. I shall try, she'd replied. And off he went—if stories were true—to relieve the mail coach of its burden.

'This is what I get for envying another man, for wanting something I couldn't have. I had forty-three ounces of gold, not including two nuggets, and now I wear someone else's boots and even *they* are too big.'

She rarely felt silly talking to herself; at times it was the only voice she managed to hear. A voice couldn't emerge as quickly as thoughts. Thoughts took all manner of shapes and directions and lately, Anna felt her mind had a better chance of killing her than that bullet ever had. Sam had swept her away from death when it was close enough, so close she could feel its icy touch.

Anna looked up into the afternoon sun. Boredom tasted very sour. Susan slept on, there was no sound at all except the bubbling water. Anna dipped her fingers into it. Neither warm nor cold. Fresh scabs stuck the bandaging to her wound and it itched. She needed to feel water caressing every conceivable part of her body and why not? Sam had said he'd probably be late and there was no reason to doubt him.

Sunshine would only aid the healing.

Anna decided to sit in the creek. She peeled off the dress Alice had lent. It was far too big, the bloomers, too. The bandage though was sticky from congealed blood and pus and wouldn't come off easily. Persistence won. It brought a sharp, hot sting and the warmth of fresh blood tickled.

114

Anna stifled a curse—Lord knew, she'd learnt a few good ones of late, and she concentrated on the ugly black circle high on her chest. It was healing, but very slowly. Raw, red, tender and weeping pus. Scabbing, well, it used to have a scab. She'd just torn it off.

Don't get it wet, Alice had said, holding up Anna's arm and washing her as best she could.

'Get it wet indeed,' Anna said quietly. The damage is done inside. She could feel its scorching heat with every breath she took.

I won't give in, Alice. I won't give in.

So it takes more'n a bullet to kill you, does it, pet?

Anna tried the rocks, slippery under tender feet. She almost fell four times. With impeccable timing, just as she'd sat, naked, enjoying her newfound freedom, she heard the sound of the approaching horse.

She clambered back to where her clothes lay. She'd time to don Alice's dress and nothing else when Sam came into view.

'There's leeches in the creek,' was all he said, giving her an odd look as he went by while Anna tried to hide the bloomers and bandages, and tried, too, to pretend she wasn't wet while her hair dripped in her eyes.

'I thought you said you'd be late?'

'And I thought Alice told you not to get wet. You're bleeding again.' Sam dismounted and sent her a look that proved just how crazy she was. He unsaddled the gray. He seemed to rattle when he walked, too.

'What did you get?' she asked.

'A headache,' he replied and removed the bridle. Sam put the saddle on the porch. The horse followed Anna's lead into the shack. 'Close the door or she'll come in, too.'

Anna closed the door on the curious horse and while Sam's back was turned, she put her bloomers on. Sam was emptying the pockets of his coat, one thing after another was put on the small table. Flour, tea, sugar, bully beef, potatoes already sprouting. (He put those aside.) Matches. A bottle of whiskey. A small enamel cup and a brown paper bag.

'Goodness, you rode home with all of that?'

She expected him to say something funny in return, something witty perhaps. Sam wiped his forehead and took off his coat. Anna stepped aside as he hung it on a nail behind the door. He poured himself a whiskey from the new bottle. Something was wrong. She could sense if not see the dark cloud hovering over his head.

'You all right?' he asked, standing by the window, looking out at nothing.

'Yes, I'm fine.'

'I told you to take it easy. You promised me you would.'

'I did.'

When he turned, the bored look in his eyes belied any innocence she could have mustered, or any excuse for that matter.

'I had nothing to do.'

'So you swept the floor.'

'Sam, what's wrong?' she asked. He finished his drink in reply and took a hairbrush from his trouser pocket.

'Here, I thought you'd be needing this.'

She took the brush. 'Thank you.'

'Any time.'

'Did you steal it?'

'No. I didn't steal it,' he snapped and went outside. Yes, something was indeed wrong. Was he ill? He didn't look ill. Anna was concerned more than curious. He returned with water and then again with kindling. Though he appeared to be relaxed now, something intangible betrayed the image.

'Are you feeling yourself?'

'Huh?'

'You seem preoccupied.'

'I'm tired. Don't fuss, all right?'

'I'm not fussing. Yet.' she added.

Of course not. That's what they always said. One way or another they poked and prodded till they hit bottom. Women were all the same. Let her try. See how far she gets.

Anna began to brush out her tangled hair. Wincing, ouching.

Sam wondered why she wasn't asking question; being a smartass again.

'I got some new bandages,' he said.

'Oh. Good.'

He walked out again. Anna pretended she didn't know he'd gone. But she went to the window and watched as he loped off towards the mountains at the back of the hut. Not mountains exactly, but boulders of granite as big as mansions balanced upon little rocks half the size of a wagon wheel. Sam disappeared behind one such mansion. Swallowed whole it seemed, like the Pied Piper disappearing into rock.

116

The story had given her nightmares as a child.

He took no gun therefore he wasn't hunting.

She waited to see him again. Nothing. Alice's dress fell off her shoulders. Wearily, she rectified it. The other side fell. Anna sighed and wondered if he had a needle and thread. Susan slept on, she'd be awake half the night, demanding entertainment other than hitting two spoons together.

Still no sign of Sam.

Anna turned to the purchases and looked up at the dusty cobwebbed shelves along the wall. Tins, empty bottles. Rags. Three dishes, two mugs. Knives. Knives not meant for polite culinary usage, these were knives with one purpose—to kill.

Michael had a Bowie knife like this one. He kept it under his pillow at night, in case…

In case of what? She asked him once. He abused her for being brainless and naive. She knew what he meant now. Anna put the knife down. She could tell by sight alone it was razor sharp. Sam used it to peel vegetables, not to disembowel prospective thieves.

She looked into the brown paper bag. Bandages. She thought of Dinny; Tom holding him down while Anna wrapped up his foot. The screams were only strengthened by the rum someone poured down his unwilling throat. Late at night she was still there, whispering to him to let her go because his fingers sent her arm numb. *Don't leave me.*

She hadn't. She'd endured the same terrifying loneliness when giving birth to Susan. Three long days of agonizing labour.

Anna rubbed at her arm where in her mind, she could still feel Dinny Masterson's touch.

Where on earth had Sam gone?

The silence was oppressive after the ceaseless noise of Bitter Creek. Quiet terrified her. Death crept in with the stillness, death was silent.

In Dublin's fair city, where the girls are

Her voice came as a whisper, shaky, barely a song at all. Tears burned at her eyes and she didn't know why. From the window she glimpsed Sam. Wiping her eyes, she saw he was dragging something.

Bright. She must be bright. Happy. Cheerful. It would be the only way to find out what was wrong with him. Anna built up the fire into a neat A shape so that when all was alight and crumbling, the small log on top would collapse and ignite fully. Michael used to laugh at her fires but they rarely failed, even after rain when the kindling was wet.

Sam dragged the chest in and threw his shirt over the rocking chair.

117

'Some stuff here might fit you. I remembered it a bit late. The things Alice gave you don't fit. Don't suit you much, either.' He chose a key from one of many on a ring in his pocket. There were keys of all shapes and sizes and one he knew well. It instantly opened the rusty padlock on the battered chest. 'There you go, it's all yours if you want it.'

Sam stood back.

Anna opened the chest and couldn't believe what she was seeing. The first dress was a dark maroon colour, heavy, thick. The next was a deep yellow, almost golden. It was a ball gown with lacy frills on the sleeves and the bodice. It was something a princess would wear. She felt like Cinderella for a moment. Anna rose from her knees unsteadily and held the dress against her. Lost for words, she looked at Sam. He was having another drink and his face was expressionless until he held the bottle out to her and asked, 'Want one?'

Anna shook her head. He turned away, dismissing the question on her lips. Whose was it? Anna carefully folded the ball gown and put it on the bed. A faded blue and white checked cotton dress appeared next. It was lighter and would definitely fit better than Alice's heavy green monster.

There were five dresses in all. Anna kept the gingham aside. There were no shoes, but there was a full length cotton petticoat and a bottle of rose scent, rancid with age. It made her eyes water, or was she crying again?

'Would you help me?' she asked too soon because she had seen the uniform. Dark blue with red braid epaulettes. Under the coat, once white breeches, now gray. The dresses lost their magic. 'What on earth is this?'

Sam turned to find her holding up the uniform jacket. So there it was, he thought he'd burnt it years ago. 'It's a trooper's uniform, what's it look like.'

'This is yours? Or did you steal it?'

'It was mine.'

'You were a trooper? *You*?' She was full to the brim with curiosity and disbelief. The 'you' was almost a giggle.

'Yes, I was a trooper.'

'But you're a thief. A bushranger.'

Sam pulled a face. 'Bushranger, outlaw, trooper, just names for convenience. What'd you want help with?' he asked, changing the subject, aware of her deep, dark interest. She was itching for more information and he'd never give any.

118

As if reading his mind, Anna put the coat back. What happened today, Sam, she silently pleaded. Instead, she said, 'My wounds need dressing. Sergeant.'

So she knew the rank. Sam put his whiskey down.

'Use the spirits.'

'It'll hurt.'

Anna let Alice's huge dress fall, catching it at her breasts. She waited for the alcohol's burn and when it hit, she bit her lip hard enough to taste blood. Sweat popped to her face. She fought dizziness and sudden weakness.

'Maybe you better sit down.'

'Don't fuss, Sam. I'm not an invalid.'

'Why are you so stubborn?' he asked.

As she formed the response he tipped the bottle directly into the blackened bullet wound and was ready to catch her when she fell.

For Jane Hannaford the overnight stay in the coach house was as unavoidable and as horrid as the heat and the incessant flies. She relieved the situation by extolling her virtues as a trooper's wife and waking everyone with her news of how she'd be invited to meet the Duke of Edinburgh when he visited next year—after all, her husband was a good friend to Commissioner Seymour.

It was certainly news to Maddy. Her father didn't know Commissioner Seymour although Aunt Rachel probably did.

Maddy kept eating. Mother complained about the food but that was normal. To Maddy, anything she didn't have to cook herself tasted wonderful.

And of course, conversation was detoured to Bitter Creek. Rumour was rife, curiosity bubbling. Everyone was taking precautions against 'hostile blacks': saying things like *the only good black is a dead one…*

Terribly unfair really, Maddy thought. She knew a few white people who were far worse than black ones. What Mother was saying came from her own imagination. Papa always thought her too fragile to be told truths. What Maddy had overheard was the truth—people had died. No, died was not the word. Slaughtered was. Now Papa had evidence enough to hang Sam Manning.

Maddy left the table after finishing her meal and walked out into the darkening air. She gazed out to the mountain range in the distant

119

horizon. It had taken all day to travel over that range. They called it The Great Divide.

Sam lived there, somewhere.

Evidence.

Maddy kicked at a rock.

It was probably her father's way of blaming the one he *thought* was responsible. He did that often enough, guilt or innocence made no difference to him. Why, she'd even cornered Daniel in the stables to ask him. Daniel didn't think Sam was responsible—he said as much. Why, he'd even kissed her but was too much of a gentleman to do anything more.

Maddy kicked at another rock and let her gaze drift to the distant hills, smothered now in rich purple glows. She imagined Sam Manning standing beside her. She imagined so much, it seemed her only happiness of late. So captured by her dream of what would happen should the coach leave her behind, she didn't hear the calls.

The boy who tended the horses while his parents tended the people, tapped her arm. Maddy jumped in fright. 'Hey, Miss? Your mother's stuck in the bath tub and my mother can't get her out. They need you.'

Maddy wanted to strangle her mother for having the audacity to interrupt another brilliant fantasy. She looked down at the skinny, scabby youngster. He reminded her of that Stills boy.

'You really the sergeant's daughter?' the boy asked as they walked back to the coach house.

'Yes, I am. Why?'

'Did Sam Manning really do it?'

'Am I a Police Magistrate?'

'Oh, come on. You can tell me.'

Maddy stopped walking and so did the boy. What she said though, he didn't want to hear. Not many people did, it seemed. 'Sam Manning is not a murderer.'

'How do you know?'

'Perhaps, little boy, I know more than I should. Go away.'

'Make me.'

Maddy stomped her black booted foot and the boy ran off into the night. He wasn't about to hang around and torment her, she was built like an outhouse—twice as big and three times as strong as all his schoolmates joined together.

120

The boy waited in the dark before slinking around to the room that served as a bathroom—a rough shed tacked on to the kitchen. He climbed noiselessly on to a rusty feed bin and peered in through his gouged spy-hole, catching his giggles at what he saw. He liked it better when there was a pretty lady in there, no doubt about it. This memory though would keep him silently smirking for weeks. Mrs Whatsername had her fat beam stuck all right. Grandpa Johnson's favourite sow was pink like that. Not as hairy though. The noises were nearly the same, a lot of grunting and groaning, a tremendous fart, too. He nearly choked trying not to laugh.

'Oh God, Mother, did you have to!'

'Just get me out!'

'I am trying!'

The edges of sanity were slippery. The outhouse door slammed shut as she came out. With the sudden bang came a blaze of memory. It wasn't Sam walking towards her, it was Lucas Hannaford. Screams hit the twilight; frightened parrots added to the uproar.

Sam threw the shotgun to the ground and sprinted after Anna. The galahs screaming above only added to the sudden terror he felt as he heard her screams:

'Don't hurt my baby!'

Sam caught her easily and swung her about. 'Anna, it's me. It's Sam.' She didn't seem to hear. She was stiff, he didn't think eyes could widen so far. For a moment, she was Elizabeth. For a fleeting moment, that too-familiar terror ate right through him. 'Anna, it's me!'

And the animal fear died in her eyes. She whispered his name, still shaking.

'I didn't mean to scare you. Maybe I should wear a bell around my neck.'

If she heard his attempt at humour, there was no reaction.

'Are you all right?'

She tried to nod. Another lie.

'Oh, Anna, talk to me? I'm not gonna hurt you, you know that.'

She slumped against him and hung there, silent. Hesitant at first, he enfolded her in his arms until he felt her muscles relax. 'You're gonna have to talk to someone, girl. This can't go on.' He held her for an eternity.

121

Her breath scorched his bare shoulder. 'You'll think I'm insane.'

'You're just scared.'

'But it's over.' Anna pushed away and searched his eyes.

'No, it's not over. It won't be until you tell me what happened.'

'It was the sergeant. Hannaford,' she eventually whispered, expecting him to walk off, laughing. But he didn't.

'I thought so.'

'You knew?'

'No, but it sure as hell makes sense now.'

Sam ventured back to retrieve the shotgun. This time her mind didn't play with illusions. 'How can anything make sense? Why? Why Michael? Tom? Joshua? Everyone... Why me?'

Sam turned to her and tried to keep his gaze on her face but that damned blue dress made it impossible. His mind, his heart and his gut all seemed volcanic, but as usual, nothing showed on his face, or he hoped, in his voice. 'Why you? Why me? I been asking myself that for most of the day. Trouble is, I never got any answers. But I do know something, Anna. You're dead and they're blaming me for killin' you. For killing everyone at Bitter Creek. So I guess now it's a case of, why us. Suzie's crying,' he added quietly and scratched his nose.

Anna couldn't move. The only sound she heard was the pounding of her heart. Surely he was joking?

'Anna, Suzie's crying.'

'I am dead?' she asked, disbelieving.

'Yep. You're buried at Bitter Creek with everyone else. Suzie's dead, too. That's the story, Ma'am.'

'No, it can't be.'

'Anna, the kid's driving me crazy. I can't stand it when she cries.'

'I am not dead! How can they say that!'

Sam sighed. 'Why don't you get on my horse and gallop off into town and tell em all you're alive? Why don't you walk right in, look Luke in the eye and say, I'm not a ghost no more.' Sam paused while his words were digested. 'Luke'd like that. You shoot someone and it's nice to have them call in and say howdy. Specially when they're supposed to be dead.'

Anna's face, if it were possible, paled even further. Sam touched her arm. She didn't flinch.

'He's looking for you, girl. No witnesses, remember?'

'You know this man?'

122

'Aha.'

'But how could he? Why, for God's sake!'

'Don't go looking for reasons. Just makes it harder to understand.'

'How *dare* he.'

Fire sparked her eyes. Sam let his hand fall from her arm. 'Anna, getting angry is not going to help.'

Slowly she turned those firing eyes to him. His blood iced. 'He won't get away with this,' she said calmly.

'Yeah? And what are you gonna do about it?'

She didn't know, that was obvious. 'God forgive me,' she whispered quietly. 'Forgive me for these thoughts.'

Sam believed if he was God he'd probably forgive her for anything. Unfortunately he wasn't God, just some fool who should have kept his mouth shut and his eyes off someone else's wife.

'Supper will be ready when you are,' Anna said quietly and turned away.

It was a hot summer's evening but he shivered from the sudden cold. It was coming from the woman.

Chapter Nine

UNDER NORMAL CIRCUMSTANCES, THE REALISATION that there was now a woman residing under the same roof would have scared him into a sprint in the opposite direction.

Supper's ready.

Already the roles were being played. The only thing missing was conversation.

Anna stared at the tinned meat and boiled potato as if it were something unmentionable. Sam had finished his and hoped she'd push her plate away so he could have hers, too. She fiddled with the food, rearranged it on the dish while his stomach growled. Finally, her fork clattered down and she held her head in her hand. For too long she'd been in a stony, deep silence filled only by darkening thoughts.

'I wasn't gonna tell you. I thought you'd ... oh, I don't know. Forget it.'

'Is that your solution to everything? Forget it? What do you think I am, Sam? Haven't I endured enough already without this?'

'Why are you angry with me?'

Anna knew from his face that he was suffering, too. Marked. Targeted. Suddenly she wanted to apologise and stopped short. 'I'm not angry with you, Sam. But why's he doing this?'

'He doesn't want to hang.'

'Hanging. Ha. It's too quick for that bastard.'

Bastard? The Lady swore?

'He deserves much more.' she added.

'Like what?'

'Castration,' she snapped as Sam casually stole her plate. 'All I need is a blunt knife.'

'And eight men to hold him down.'

'How can you sit there so calm, Sam Manning?'

'No use getting upset,' he said softly while he picked the skin from the potato.

'No use? My God, I'm witness to what that ... to what he did!'

Susan crawled across the floor, grabbed a handful of Sam's pants and made the effort to stand. Sam put a tiny piece of potato in her mouth and

124

she overbalanced, sat with a thump on the floor and pulled faces at the foreign substance in her mouth.

'And what'd he do?' Sam asked softly.

I couldn't tell a woman, Anna thought. I couldn't tell Alice but I didn't really have to. She seemed to know. But Sam? Anna studied him for a long time as he was distracted by the baby. He gave her some potato again. She ate more than she spat out this time.

'I had a friend at Bitter Creek.'

Sam glanced up.

'Not your father. Lu Sun. She was Chinese. Michael never knew.'

'Oh, one of those friends,' Sam said quietly and lifted Susan to his lap.

'Your father knew though. He'd warn me to be careful. We would meet twice, sometimes three times a week.'

At the water hole, Sam thought.

'We'd swim in the water hole not half a mile from the Chinese diggings.'

She was quiet for a while. Sam dared not breathe too loud in case she stopped talking. He'd learnt the value of listening. If only he'd listened to Elizabeth like this, heard what she was trying to say, things might have been different.

'Lu Sun never came to the water hole that day. I waited and waited, and in the end I went to see what was wrong. I knew something had happened, Sam. I knew. Everything I am warned me, said don't go up there. Don't. I didn't heed it. For the first time in my life, I didn't heed it.'

The baby wetly chewed on his wrist, her incoherent yammering breaking the quiet but not the spell.

'Sam, did you see what they'd done to Lu Sun's family?'

He nodded.

'They were more of a family to me than my own.'

He understood that, too.

'I remember hearing the shooting, so I must have run back to Bitter Creek. I don't know why, perhaps I thought I could stop it all.'

There was another pause. She was reliving too much too soon so she changed direction.

'My scalp crawled when I first saw him. It was as if I knew he was...' She searched vainly for the word. A thousand sprang to Sam's mind. 'Evil? No, it was more than that. You see, I feel the good and the bad and almost everything in between in people I meet, but he was different. He frightened me, Sam. It was the way he looked at me, spoke to me. He was in uniform the first time, but not … oh, Lord, I can still hear them. I can still smell them. I can still…'

Sam knew if he touched her now it'd be over before it started. So he waited.

'They were all dead or dying. I found Michael but he was dead. There'd been no time, no warning.' Anna absently reached for her fork and fondled it while tears welled in her eyes. She looked across the small table and into her outlaw's eyes. 'I know it was him.'

'Who?'

'Lucas Hannaford. The sun was in my eyes and blinding me but I knew who he was and what he wanted.'

This time the silence was complete. Susan chewed the buttons on Sam's shirt and he winced at the handful of chest hair her tiny fist discovered.

'And Billy,' Anna whispered.

Dingo, Sam thought. It has to be Dingo.

'The black trooper he had with him the day he checked the licenses, he was there. His name's Billy.'

'And the young one?'

'No. Just those two I recognised. The sergeant said if I didn't do everything he told me to, Billy would cut my baby's throat.' The fingers touching the fork started to shake. 'I had no choice, Sam. I did what he wanted.'

If he reached out to hold her hand now, she'd be off and running, probably screaming.

'When they had … when it was over, the sergeant stood up from where he'd been watching them, and he took his rifle and he told Billy to leave the baby. To put her down. He dropped her. Just dropped her. How she cried.'

And Sam needed a whiskey, bad. He didn't really want to hear any more. His gut was twisting.

'Michael shot a dog once, Sam. He told it to lie down and it did. Then he shot it. I was just like that dog.'

Fingers went to her mouth. Sam thought she was going to throw up. He was right. Anna jumped to her feet and ran out into the waiting darkness.

126

For a while, he sat where he was, unmoving, listening to her vomiting. He eventually put the baby back into her fortress and didn't hear the protests.

Anna was leaning against the fence which bordered the garden. Her arms were folded against the pain, the obscenity revisited and confronted. At last.

Sam looked up into the brilliant night sky. The stars were close enough to touch. From beside him came the soft, shaking voice: 'He can't say it was you.'

'He has.'

'What will we do?'

Sam put his arm around her and she didn't pull away. 'I'll think of something.'

Her sniffles were liquid, his strength somehow melting, being absorbed by her. He didn't mind, he needed something to hold almost as badly as she did.

'My father used to tell me I was a born survivor,' she whispered.

'He was right.'

'You're so calm.'

Appearances were deceiving. 'Yeah, well, it could be worse.'

'Do you really think so?'

Sam pushed her away and looked down into her eyes. 'We're not dead, yet. Every day above the ground...' And he smiled. In his reassuring squeeze lay an unspoken promise. Anna felt it and took strength from it. And it seemed as if a ton of lead had lifted. Even if the aching remained, it was far less intense.

'Feel better now?' he asked.

'Yes, I think so.'

'I told you so.'

That night, Anna listened to the baby's steady breathing, to the creaks and groans of the old hut, the occasional pop and fizz from the dying fire. Sam was talking in his sleep, nothing she could understand of course. He seemed restless down there on the floor. Was he planning something? She thought she saw it in his eyes, in his tiny smile as he blew out the light. His repeated promise: I'll think of something.

If he'd used past tense, perhaps she would have believed it. He had thought of something. But like any man, he wouldn't tell her until he was ready, if he decided she needed to know. And whatever he was planning or had planned, it was for her, a stranger. She thought she knew how men reasoned. She wondered if he, or any man for that matter, felt the same emotions? The thought processes were certainly different. Women weren't supposed to think or worry, women were supposed to accept and not a question a man's wisdom.

A man's wisdom.

It certainly hadn't felt wise when Michael had sold off most of her things to finance the expedition to Bitter Creek, or 'Paradise' as he'd called it then. No companies to work for, what a man dug from the ground was his and with it he would do ...

With it he would die.

Anna had begged him not to sell the music box. It had been her grandmother's. The pleas were ignored, so were the tears. He'd promised to buy her a hundred music boxes, perhaps her own orchestra. Gold had no use to him now.

Anna rolled to her side and tried to block the image of the little girl who walked down the front path, winding up the small, gold embossed box. Faint tingles of *Fur Elise* faded and so did Anna. She dreamt of nothing and woke to sunlight across her eyes.

Sam was singing in a booming deep voice, *Way, hey and up she rises early in the morning...*

Susan was cackling with laughter. Anna rose from her bed and peered out the door. They were both stark naked in the creek.

'Good morning,' Anna chirped, mainly to Sam's deeply tanned back and very white behind. The sound of her voice alarmed him. He spun around, joyous baby shielding privates. Anna had seen men blush before but nothing was comparable to this. For a moment, she wondered what he would do if she took Susan away. The thought coerced an inward grin, devilish amusement.

'Morning, Ma'am. She was covered in ... yeah, well, this is the easy way of givin' her a bath.'

Anna could have waited there for a long time if she'd wanted to—his embarrassment was extreme. 'Would you show me how to make those things we had yesterday morning?'

'What, flapjacks?' Sam asked.

'Yes. I quite liked them.'

Damn, Sam thought. She's going to stand there all day. Any other lady would blush and run off, but somehow, he didn't think she would. 'I was thinking,' he said and wished he hadn't because she started to close in. The baby was slippery as hell and squirming. 'I've got paper and stuff if you want some.'

128

'Stolen?'

'Not exactly, no.'

'That would be nice, Sam. Thank you. Are you sure you're managing there? I can take her if you like.'

'No, no, fine. No problem. We've done this before, haven't we, kid?'

With a grin, Anna turned and walked away. Relief was overwhelming.

Anna watched from the seclusion of the hut as Sam put the baby on the grass and dried himself. He almost fell over three times while trying to squeeze his pants on to damp flesh and stop Susan crawling away as well. His modesty amused her. Michael had had none at all. Oh, he'd been attractive in a strange way, but Sam? She wondered if all the stories were true. Of course they were. She recognised what she'd felt the day she first saw him—the day he'd stomped her hat into mud—but any woman would have cause to wonder what his touch would be like.

Something about him was very pleasing.

There was nothing of that, now. Not on his part, anyway. She was here because for now, there was nowhere else for her to go and he knew that. When she was well again … what then?

Why is it when I feel some happiness, despair replaces it? she thought.

They were coming inside now. Anna turned away.

'You really want to know how to slap up a flapjack, Ma'am?' he asked. Susan was hanging upside down under his arm, his shirt was around his neck, his feet were bare. His chest glistened from sweat or water, she couldn't tell. What was mirrored in her eyes to make him smile at her like that?

'I only need to be shown once, Sam,' she said and reached for Susan. Damp, heavy, pudgy, naked and dribbling. Always dribbling.

'She bit me,' Sam said as he slipped his shirt on and didn't button it. 'You should have called her Gator.'

'Gator?' Anna asked as she dressed the baby and brushed her wet hair.

'Short for alligator. I nearly got ate by one in the Everglades once.'

It would have spat you out, she thought. 'What on earth is the Everglades?'

'Remind me to tell you one day.' He went about concocting his flapjacks.

Anna watched. He cooked as she did—a handful of this, a bit of that …

Susan loved them, too. In fact, she accepted everything Sam put into her mouth, not so when Anna tried to feed her. A little jealousy rose yet

129

again. Why did this man take more interest in the child than Michael had?

'You look tired,' Sam said quietly as Anna took his empty plate away. He was still fussing.

'I'm fine, really.'

'I'll go get that paper for you. I don't think I got a diary, won't know till I have a look.'

'A diary?'

'Yours got burnt, didn't it?'

'How did you know?'

'Tom told me.'

Before she could say anything more he was gone, disappearing into the rocks again. Not for the first time did Anna wonder just what was up there.

While he was away, she changed her dress and tidied her hair. It still hurt to hold her arm high for any length of time and in the end, she admitted defeat and left her hair down.

Bugger propriety, Anna thought. Who's here to see, anyway?

Sam wondered why he was doing this. Perhaps it'd give her something to do. Stop her nagging him. Sam dragged out the stolen box he'd in turn stolen from Spencer's Brook and he studied the contents in the half light of the entrance to the cave. His stash.

Two years ago, it all looked new, smelled new. Not now though. Two years ago, he'd wondered where Luke had got it and what use this stuff would be to him, and then he'd heard about the wagon that went over the side and ended wheels up in Dun's Gully. It was probably an order going through to the art shop at Callandoon.

People helped themselves in situations like that.

By the look of the stash at Spencer's Brook, Luke was helping himself a lot, lately.

Then again, Sam didn't know why he decided to steal this box instead of the jewellery. He never wrote these days, he had no patience any more for painting. Got it from his mother apparently.

When your mother painted a flower, boy, you could smell it.

Even as a grown man, Sam often wondered what she was really like. Tom wasn't much of a mother. He kept him from starvation; the house had a succession of women in and out depending on the prospector's financial status at the time. And Sam spent most his schooling behind the door or in the hills, trapping and shooting.

130

He looked down at the box of brushes, oils, papers, and inks. He smiled. He used to draw naked women and sell the sketches to his friends for a nickel. When he'd had enough money, he went to the only whore in town who didn't laugh and close the door in his face.

Here, Mary is this enough?

Mary had said it'd do and his education began at thirteen years of age. His sketches suddenly took on new perspectives. He charged more and fell in love with Mary.

If Mary was her real name.

Women had always been his downfall.

Sam carried the box from his stash. Getting down the hill was a hell of a lot easier than climbing up, especially when he slipped and rolled most of the way.

He'd expected her reaction but not his. She was speechless and so was he. All he'd seen was the hair, so dark it was nearly black and it cascaded all the way to her hips. She was wearing Elizabeth's pale green dress and Elizabeth had never worn it as well. He swallowed his heart before it burst.

'Oh, Sam.'

For a minute or two he was sure she'd leap up and kiss him so he retreated to the door and watched as she rummaged through the box like a kid at Christmas.

'What sort of stuff you draw, anyway?' he asked.

'You'll laugh.'

'We could both use a good laugh right now.'

'Michael used to say I was wasting my time.'

'I'm not Michael.'

'Promise me you won't laugh?'

Smiling, Sam promised.

'One day, Sam Manning, I'm going to have my very own shop.'

He didn't see anything funny in that. 'What kind of shop?'

'Annabelle's Millinery.'

'Hats?' he asked.

'Oh yes, hats. Hats and more hats. I see them. I draw them. All I need is someone who can make them, but I shall find that someone one day. Some of my best designs were burnt but they're still in here,' she said and tapped her head.

'Just hats?'

131

'Gloves, purses, parasols… Do you think it's silly?

'Hell, no. Why should I? I never met anyone who wants to make hats.'

'And I've never met a bushranger. Especially one who used to be a trooper.'

Here we go, he thought.

'Why is it no one has found where you live?'

'I'm smart and they're lazy.'

Anna resumed unpacking the box. 'I think it's because you used to be a trooper and you know how they think and what they're likely to do.'

'Yeah?' he asked, hiding a grin.

'Why won't you tell me very much about yourself?'

Sam squatted by the door and studied his hands. 'Maybe you shouldn't know. Maybe it's safer that way.'

'For heaven's sakes, Sam, I'm dead. How much safer do you want?'

'Maybe it's not the first time I've been accused of murder. I used to be married once, you know.'

'Yes, I know. I've seen her photograph. There.' Anna pointed to the mantelpiece.

'That's not Elizabeth, that's my mother.'

'Oh. But these clothes are your wife's, are they not?'

He nodded.

'Where is she now?'

'She's dead, that's why I'm here, doin' what I do.'

'You were accused of murdering your wife?'

'Aha.'

'Did you?'

'Did I what?'

'Kill her?'

'No, she killed herself. Look, it's a long story, Anna.'

'We have nothing left but time, Sam.'

'Maybe not a lot of that, either. It's all happening again. He's doing it again. It's time it was over, girl.'

'How?'

'I'm working on it.'

'You said he's doing it again? Who?'

132

'Luke.'

'How well do you know him?'

'We used to be friends, used to work together.'

'Elizabeth knew him, too?'

'You're better off not knowing.'

Sooner or later, she thought, I shall discover what you refuse to tell me.

'Sam, I've been thinking. Surely there is someone who can help us?'

'An escaped murderer and a dead woman?'

'Perhaps if I sent a letter to the Commissioner in Brisbane.'

'And tell him what?'

'I'd tell him exactly what happened.'

Commissioner Seymour was new to a new position, but what sort of man was he? Anyone's guess. A letter, signed, dated, chances are it wouldn't even arrive before Christmas. Cormac could post it next time he went to Warwick. A miracle might occur and Anna Hall might be believed even if she was never found.

'Sam, what do you think?'

Sam turned to her. 'His name's Seymour. That's all I know. But you better write that letter soon, girl. They'll be gettin' ready for the Duke.'

'Pardon?'

'The Duke of Edinburgh's comin' next year.'

'You live in this isolation yet you know about that?'

'I don't steal the mail for fun.'

'Sam, are you asleep?'

The question filtered in through the murk. 'Aha,' he mumbled.

'Sam, I didn't know what to say.'

'Huh?'

'I tried to write the letter, but all I could manage was, 'My Dear Commissioner Seymour.'

'Oh.'

'Sam, I've never written to someone like that before.'

'First time for everything,' he mumbled and rolled over.

133

'Do you think he'd believe me?'

No. 'Of course he will. It's the truth.'

'But I was thinking, if the Duke of Edinburgh is coming, the Commissioner may be too busy to take much notice. He might think it's a joke. A fallacy. And take no notice at all.'

'At least you'll know you tried.'

'I don't think I have that much faith any more, Sam.'

'Makes two of us, Anna.' There was silence for a long time and Sam was woken again by the soft voice.

'Sam, are you asleep?'

'Aha.'

'Is the floor very hard?'

'Aha.'

'You could sleep here if you want. I can move over.'

His eyes opened wide. Had he heard right? He rolled over and in the dark, he could see her, staring at the ceiling. She turned her head to him. 'I won't mind if you don't. I've already rearranged your life too much, the least I can do is give you your bed back.'

'It's okay, I don't mind.'

A lie of course. His back was breaking.

'Yes, you do. You wish you'd never seen me.'

'That's not true.'

'Doesn't your back ache?'

Against his better judgment, Sam brought his blanket with him. Anna rolled to her side and faced the wall with a sigh. Sam lay on top of the covers and faced the opposite way.

She smelled so good.

'Goodnight, Sam.'

He made a noise that could have meant anything. Sleep eluded him completely. What'd she think he was? Made of steel? What'd she want by this, anyway?

Anna rolled over and flung her arm across his side. He froze. But nothing happened. Time passed slowly. He wasn't game to move at all.

Soft snores now. The snores ended when she changed position yet again and curled into his back. Her body heat was intense. It matched his. Breasts pushed into his back and he was rising to the occasion. But when her hand fell flat on his chest, he'd had enough. Sam fell out of bed,

134

snatched his blanket and slept in the bath tub for what remained of the night.

Even out here, her snoring gave him hell.

Or was the snoring just an excuse?

'Sam, what are you doing out here?'

There was no response from the man curled in the tub, bare feet protruding skywards. His toes moved, that was all. Anna lifted the blanket shielding his face. 'Sam?'

He opened one eye.

'What are you doing in this tub?'

'Tryin' to sleep.'

'No one sleeps in a bath, Sam.'

'Wanna bet on that?'

Anna pulled the blanket away. 'You could have slept in the bed.'

'You were snoring.'

Anna considered his words and decided he was joking. He must have been. 'I beg your pardon, Sam Manning, but I do not snore.'

'Yes, you do.'

Sam tried to move and instantly realised the floor was better to sleep on.

'I do not.'

'Prove it.'

Anna said nothing to that and walked off, mumbling to herself. Sam finally climbed out of the tub and it took two full minutes for him to stretch his spine. Something clicked at the wrong time. 'Ah, shit,' he muttered and hobbled off to relieve himself. He squinted up at the sky. Cloudless. Hot.

The goat stared at him, unblinking. It was the densest thing on four legs he'd ever seen; it hated being milked and he hated milking it. In all, the hatred was mutual.

It stomped its foot, lowered its head.

'Hit me up the ass with them horns once more, I'll be eatin' goat stew for weeks. Hear me?'

The stomp was more aggressive this time. 'Bastard,' Sam whispered, realigning his pants and turning away. Then he saw the damage. It had got through the fence. The potatoes were the only plants it hadn't eaten. 'Anna! I want my rifle!'

'What's wrong?' she asked, coming out, being hit with a full unabridged recitation of the animal's parentage or lack of it. 'There's no need to swear, Sam.'

'Bullshit! Who tied the bastard here anyway!'

'Who do you think!' she yelled in return. 'And I do not bloody snore!'

'Who's cursin' now!'

'Your pitiful weeds will grow again!'

'They wasn't weeds they was carrots!'

'*Were* carrots, Sam, not *was* carrots! Can't you speak English?'

'No, I can't. I speak my own fucking American and I'm gonna eat that bastard! Where's my rifle!'

'If you kill that goat, Susan will starve.'

'You don't care at all, do you.'

'Go for a walk, Sam. Come back when you're calm. I don't like you when you're foul tempered and cursing.'

'And what else don't you like?

'You're a thief.'

'I'm not a fucking thief!'

'You swore again.'

'So do you when no one's around to hear you. Think I don't know? You're not as perfect as you pretend to be. And you sure as hell won't make me perfect, either, lady.'

'Finished?'

Sam said nothing.

'Good. Then breakfast is ready, Mister Manning.'

Her flapjacks looked and tasted better than his did. Even the strong black coffee had cooled to the right temperature for him. Anna threw another dollop of sugar into his mug. 'I didn't want no more sugar.'

'Perhaps, but you certainly need some more sweetness this morning.'

Icy glances met in silence.

'Does backache make you cranky?' she asked.

'No.'

136

Silence again. Sam slurped his coffee, Anna ground her teeth. He was doing it purposely because she hated the sound.

'Just keep that bloody goat outa my garden.'

'I didn't know she'd eat it.'

'Goats eat everything except grass, don't you know that?'

'I'm not a farmer.'

Sam sniffed. That was no excuse.

'I'm also sorry.' She wasn't really, but she had to bite her lip and her smile. The nasty thing refused to stay hidden.

'It's not funny.'

'Of course it isn't.'

'Taken me months to grow them things. Stop smiling.'

'I'm not smiling. Really, I'm not. Think of it, Sam. Here you are, wanted dead or alive for fifty pounds and here am I, already dead. Out there somewhere are troopers who won't rest until they find us, and you just threw a temper tantrum because your goat ate your vegetable garden.'

'It's not my goat. It's for your kid.'

'Let me rub your back?'

'I'm all right.'

'Sam, you can't possibly ride out to pillage and plunder with posture like an old man's.'

'Do you ever give up?'

'Not until I get my own way. I want to rub your back and loosen up those muscles for you. I can make you feel much better. I promise.'

He didn't trust the sparkle in her eyes, or the way she reached high for a bottle of horse liniment so old that ten years of dust had formed a thick crust on the glass. She opened it and turned her face away, the fumes stung her eyes even from a distance.

'You're not touching me with that crap. It stinks.'

'I'm amazed your nose still works after being so close to your armpits for thirty-five years.'

Sam couldn't believe she had the audacity to say that. 'I don't stink that bad and I ain't thirty-five. Not yet, anyway.'

'Next you'll say you don't snore or talk in your sleep or do other horrible things.'

'Yeah like what? Fart?'

137

'Sam Manning, you have lived on your own for far too long. Now put that down, take your shirt off and lie on the bed.'

'No.'

Anna studied him. He smiled at her and sipped his coffee.

'I asked you nicely.'

'Bullshit. That was an order.'

'Please, Sam? I'm overcome with guilt. I hate to see you suffer needlessly. I used to work in a hospital, I know what I'm doing.'

'Oh, for Christ's sake,' he groaned and stood, peeled his shirt off and flopped across the bed.

Anna tipped some of the ripe, powerful ooze on to her hands. It burned. She sat on the bed beside him. 'Put your arms out, please.'

With a groan, he obeyed.

And soon he was almost asleep from her small-handed kneading. She did it well. 'Lower,' he moaned quietly.

'You'll have to loosen your trousers.'

No warning bells sounded in his relaxed brain. He trusted her. A mistake. There was no underwear. Anna smiled and poured the potion across his lower back. A heated trickle happened to course down between his buttocks. She moved before he did.

She'd never heard language quite like it, nor had she seen a person move so quickly. Off came the pants. Gone was any modesty. He was nothing but a naked blur sprinting for the creek, screaming something about asses on fire. She stopped laughing long enough to yell, 'And I do not snore!' before she kicked the door shut.

Sam didn't speak to her for the rest of the day.

One's bloodshot eyes grinning. One holding her arms, the other opening her dress with a knife. Tearing it from her body, standing back, grinning now at the white man. Wiping his mouth proudly. She tries to kick, they're all too quick. The knife settles at her throat.

Kill it, Billy. Let her watch.

No!

Sam woke, heart thudding from the scream in his ear. 'Anna, it's okay. It's all right.' He was used to this by now. She reached blindly for him in

138

the darkness and his arms eased the panic, the shaking. Within moments it had all faded. 'It's okay now, it's gone.' She settled down, felt his arms around her, holding tightly to her hands. He pulled her closer, his body was hot and hard, yet soft and comforting, too. 'S'okay,' he whispered sleepily, hot breath in her hair. 'You're not alone anymore.'

Chapter Ten

IT TOOK A WEEK TO write the letter and Anna tested almost every word of it on Sam. 'But why tell him where I used to live in Brisbane?' she'd asked.

'So it's easy to check.'

'Oh.'

The letter told of the journey to Bitter Creek, the baby's birth date, how much gold they'd recovered. She named most of the diggers, but no, Sam didn't think it necessary to tell the Commissioner in three thousand words how Dinny Masterson died. She had to keep it as short as possible. 'But why?'

'If he's like me, he hates reading and writing's even worse.'

'Oh.'

'Just the facts, Anna.'

But it was all fact and she thought it was all important and relevant, until she had to detail the day of the raid. It took her three silent days of reliving a nightmare that had almost killed her. She hadn't read any of it to Sam—she gave him the letter dated October 28, 1867 and went for a walk. She didn't return for a long time. As he read, he knew why.

He hoped against hope her efforts wouldn't be wasted and burnt along with the rest of the week's garbage.

When Anna returned she asked if he could get material for curtains. He said he already had some. On hearing that she lost interest in curtain-making and took the easel Sam had made for her down to the creek. She spent the rest of the day on her own, drawing.

Mid afternoon, Sam took her a mug of tea. On the paper he saw a mountain. Three hours later when he came to tell her Susan was awake, the mountain had been discarded for a shop. The sign on it read:

Annabelle's Millinery

'Is that it?' Sam asked.

'What?' she asked, concentration broken.

'Your dream.'

Anna looked down at her drawing. It wasn't quite what she could see in her mind when she closed her eyes, but it was near enough. 'I don't know, Sam. Do dreams ever come true?'

140

Sam touched the mass of hair that hung to her hips. It was soft, shiny. He didn't answer her question, he wasn't qualified enough. 'It's getting dark, Ma'am.'

'I won't be much longer.'

Anna watched him walk off; a casual impish walk, neither hurried nor slow. She wasn't used to this, being brought tea, being offered a hint of encouragement, being brought back to reality softly. It felt good. Very good.

When she finally came in, supper was ready and guilt rose automatically. 'You're not angry with me?' she asked when she sat. The sight of the tinned meat didn't whet her appetite.

'Why should I be angry? I figured you needed some time to yourself but…'

'But? I'm wasting my time living in dreams?'

'No, Suzie needs you.'

'It won't happen again.'

'What?'

'I won't do it again. I lost track of time, I'm sorry.'

'If you don't stop this sorry rubbish, I will get angry. It's not for me to tell you what to do. You wanna draw? Go for it. I'm just saying Suzie needs you, too.'

'Does she?' Anna said so quietly he didn't hear.

'You say something?'

'Do *you* need me, Sam?'

Sam looked at her as if she'd hit him with something spiky. 'Well, I'd probably miss you if you wasn't here,' he said after careful consideration. Trouble brewed if a woman didn't feel wanted.

'Really?'

Sam grinned at her. 'You'll have to do without me tomorrow.'

'Is it Wednesday again?' Anna asked, eyes not matching the innocence in the voice.

Sam kept eating. It was best to ignore her little pokes even if they were barbed.

'If you find the material for me, there'll be curtains when you come home.'

'Curtains.'

'Don't you want curtains?' she asked and because of the question he knew she did and come hell or high water, she wouldn't stop nagging until she had curtains.

'I suppose this place needs something.'

A fire, Anna thought, but asked instead, 'Is the material blue?'

He shrugged.

'Is it up the hill there where you go so often?'

He nodded and kept eating.

'Can I come?'

'Huh?'

'When you go to get the material. Can I come?'

He shook his head.

'Why not?'

'You'd break your neck, that's why not.'

'You don't want me to see what you've hidden up there.'

'Exactly.'

'You don't trust me.'

'Anna, no. All right? Are you hearing me? No.'

It sounded so final so she let the silence grow for a while. Unfortunately, Sam didn't notice it.

'Please be careful tomorrow and don't do anything too strenuous.'

'Who, me?'

'Helping beautiful ladies from mail coaches would be strenuous, yes?'

'Where'd you hear things like that?'

Anna smiled, ate and kept silent.

'It's just gossip.' Sam said and couldn't look her in the eye.

'Promise me you'll take care.'

'I'll try.'

'Sam, you may not have as many friends as you think.'

'I'm not used to people fussin' over me. I'm not dead yet.'

'It's not fuss. It's concern. I like you. I always have.'

Her offhand remark was planned to hit hard. It felt like a collision. 'Don't say things like that.'

'Why? You told me to keep it factual.'

142

'Anna, everything I get close to gets hurt or dies. You understand?'

She didn't have to say a word. It was true for her as well.

'I'll be leaving early. I'll try not to wake you.'

'Mama! It's Sam!'

Oh Lord, not another baby, Alice thought and stopped hoeing. Sam swung Leonie up on to the horse and she clung tightly. 'Any sweets for me, Sam?'

'Sorry, sweetheart, not this time. Give me a kiss instead.' Leonie was set back to the ground after a quick peck on the cheek.

'How's the lass, then?' Alice asked.

'She took lessons in nagging from you, Alice.'

His bright smile told her all was well, very well apparently. More than casual interest arose. Before the questions could begin:

'Is Cormac handy?'

'Down by the creek.'

'Good.'

'Sam, you get back here!'

The horse came to a halt.

'Would your lass be feeling like some female company?'

'She's not my lass, Alice.'

'You know what I mean.'

'I think Anna might appreciate a visit. See you later.'

Off the horse walked once more.

'I don't suppose it's wise asking where you'd be heading this fine Wednesday?'

'Is it really Wednesday?' Sam asked and rode on to find Cormac and to ask him to deliver the favour that sat, neatly addressed, in his pocket.

Cormac wasn't 'down by the creek' at all. Cormac was nowhere to be seen. Sam was already late. Far too late. Damn it, he thought. I'll come back on the way home.

143

Daniel glanced at the time and scratched his leg. Damn the mosquitoes. Dennis wasn't getting eaten alive. Daniel had long since lost concentration on the trooper's conversation. He'd have talked if he had company or not. Daniel filled the gaps with noises of appreciation for courageous efforts—secretly he thought most were fantasy or plain stupidity—or he made noises of agreement, never denials. Denials meant explanations. No wonder the sarge didn't come on this wishful escapade. Daniel doubted Manning would show anyway.

Dennis Smith-Johnson had been sent south-west for one reason: perhaps, two, he was a walking disaster and his constant talk gave everyone a headache. Daniel didn't say much, he was a quick learner. Smith-Johnson was a corporal and outranked him marginally.

And Billy kept well clear of them both.

Christ, Daniel thought. He'd rather be out walking with Maddy Hannaford. At least she didn't talk a lot and what she had to say usually made some sense. Daniel wondered how she was as he chewed on a slither of wire grass.

'Daniel, I don't want to go.'

'You'll be all right, Maddy.'

'You've never met my aunt,' she'd pouted. He'd ruffled her hair. 'Will you still go to the dance at Yarrawonga?'

'I'll probably be working.'

He'd wondered why she'd beamed. If he wasn't on duty that night, he'd take Nelly providing Rose set her free for one night.

'Will you miss me, Daniel?'

'Of course I will.' He didn't say why. He'd rather muck out the stables than the cells. She always offered to do it for him. Cleaning up overturned night buckets and drunk's vomit was woman's work anyway. Give him horse shit anytime, at least it had uses. But he did like Maddy. She was like the sister he never had. She knew her place in life, she was easy to talk to and never, as far as he knew, betrayed a confidence. Perhaps the coach carried a letter from her today?

Funny how he missed not having her about.

'What's this Manning bastard really like, Dan?'

Daniel closed his eyes. Nelly called him Danny, acceptable only from Nelly's little mouth during their heated copulations on paydays. No one, but no one called him Dan. It was Brannigan, or Daniel or Constable or 'Where the hell are you, you little snake-eyed bastard!' when the sergeant needed someone to kick.

144

'I don't know what Manning's like,' Daniel lied. True, he'd never spoken to him. Meetings had been from a distance, yet Daniel was sure he knew Manning as a man. He was aggravating and was as harmful to the public as Archibald, the town drunk, sleeping off a three day binge. Manning's destiny in life was to torment the police and with his torment came a mountain of paperwork. Whenever something went missing, Sam was automatically accused, convicted and when caught, the Big When, he'd surely hang.

Especially now.

The sergeant's evidence was closely guarded, under lock and key, which to Daniel meant it was non-existent. He prayed the Sub-Inspector would be coming back very soon.

Sanity might follow.

'You don't think he did it, do you, Dan?'

'Did what?'

'Bitter Creek.'

'No one gives a pig's fart what I think, Corporal.'

Corporal. Ooh. Dennis pulled a face and rolled a cigarette. 'What's Hannaford's problem?'

'Sam Manning.'

'No, it's more than that.'

'Look, Dennis, I gave up trying to understand the sarge. Just gives me a headache and so do you.'

Daniel watched the road for signs of the coach. Usually there was a cloud of white dust first, then the horses were heard.

And Daniel sensed the presence.

Sam was nearby, waiting, too.

His heart thudded. Daniel was torn. The revelation hit. He was getting as bad as the townsfolk and squatters who protected Manning.

'Here it comes.'

Dennis looked up.

'It's late again,' Daniel said.

The Corporal rose quickly and after checking his pistol for the hundredth time, he walked to his horse.

'No, Dennis. If he stops the coach, we wait until he has a mailbag, then we attempt to take him. Those were the orders.'

'Orders be damned. The reward's mine.'

145

'I wouldn't if I was you.'

'You're not me. Get your horse and move. Now.'

'This is a mistake.'

'Bullshit. He's mine.'

Sam covered his face and kicked the gray into a canter the moment he saw the coach crest the hill and slow, squealing brakes, for the rough crossing. There was a new driver, the look-out was armed. The coach must have been carrying something very important indeed.

'Just the mailbag, friend,' Sam called and pointed his pistol at either of the two on the coach. A second would decide which or their reflexes would decide for him.

'And drop the shotgun, too.'

The mailbag hit the ground and so did the shotgun.

Many things happened at once.

Sam was almost dismounting when he heard the calls from behind:

'Manning!' and Daniel's cry, 'For Christ's sake, Dennis, no!'

The driver reached for another weapon as the first bullet hit Sam's left arm. The impact was heavy, hard, burning. He fell forward and the letter dropped from his pocket. Sam kicked the horse into a canter down the creek, turning, firing blindly, pain filling senses. His right side took a second bullet. Volleys fizzed by. Sam kept as low as he could, knowing if he came off now, he was dead—instinct to survive outweighed all terror.

'Is he dead?'

Smith-Johnson's face was shattered. He'd been shot three times in all. Daniel could see the holes in the coat. Knowing it was futile, he tore the uniform coat open and looked, touched. No heartbeat. He hadn't expected to feel any. Daniel looked about for Dingo.

'Jesus, where'd he go!'

'After Manning. He was shot!'

Daniel looked up into the driver's eyes. 'Thank you, Constable, I know he was bloody shot! I have eyes!'

'What the hell did he do that for, anyway. We almost had him.'

'Tell me something I don't know!' Daniel yelled. 'Christ, Luke will have my balls for this. Get going you two. I'll bring this one along shortly.'

146

Daniel waited for the coach to pull out and continue on its way. He picked up the dirty letter, stamped now with the imprint of his boot.

The Commissioner of Police, Headquarters, Brisbane.

There was a small, bright bloodstain on it. So the Phantom of the Mountains did bleed after all. 'Shit,' Daniel cursed and angry tears welled. He sheathed the letter into his coat pocket and called for Dingo. There was no reply except his own echoing voice. There was nothing but silence, total, stark silence. Daniel looked down at Smith-Johnson's body. 'You've done it now, Manning. Now you *will* hang.'

Sam felt the warmth of blood trickling from his hip down into his boot. Still he clung tight to the horse's neck. Blood dripped from his elbow and on to the horse as she weaved her sure-footed way through the dense, rocky scrub.

He heard the shot. Bark splintered inches from his face. He had no energy to return the fire. He almost gave up. Almost. Then came the memory of Anna's voice, her question, *Do you need me Sam?* Her voice so clear in his head. Repeating the question.

He felt the next bullet fizz past his nose. He felt its quick heat. Sam turned, lost his balance and fell, heavily. Eyes closed, he heard the horse's breathing, the squeak of the saddle as his pursuer dismounted. The cock of the pistol, the footsteps drawing nearer.

Nearer.

And as he opened his eyes and lifted the rock at his fingertips, Sam thought of Anna and this black bastard who'd been holding a knife at little Suzie's throat.

It was over in an instant. The rock contacted Dingo's happy yet surprised face. The cheek and nose shattered, blood sprayed and he came down heavily across Sam.

Sam wriggled out from under the weight and lay quietly in wait for the others. But there was no sound at all. The gray and Dingo's horse were both grazing. Sam whistled, the gray obeyed. She nuzzled him.

Sam lay on his side, barely able to move for a little while. He pulled his scarf off and gasped for air. The horse nuzzled at him to get back on. Sam touched his right hip. His belt was torn, holed. The flesh felt cut, scorching. Pain incinerated his entire side as he tried to get up. He couldn't move the fingers on his left hand but somehow, he managed to tie the scarf around his bicep and finally, he reached for the dragging reins. Sam pulled himself to his feet and stumbled. Concentrating all efforts, he slumped into the saddle once more and trying to focus, to get his bearings, he discerned to the north east, the hazy outline of Girraween Mountain. Unmistakeable.

A couple of hours, he'd be home or dead.

Once he started bleeding it didn't stop easily.

Anna didn't hear the buggy or the woman enter. If the baby's rhythmic breathing had altered in any way, she'd have been awake instantly. But she was so tired, lately. She'd only wanted to take a short nap while Susan slept after lunch.

Anna woke with a scream from the hand on her shoulder.

The scream frightened Alice as well.

'Lordy girl, it's only me.'

'Oh, Alice … I must have fallen asleep.'

'With this heat it's no wonder. Sam's been telling me you're fit now?'

'Oh, has he? Yes, it's true. I do feel a lot better. Is Cormac with you? Young Leonie?'

'No, no. Think I'd bring them along to hear them whine and moan about wanting to go home again? I came for a chat and a cup of tea.'

She also came to inspect the healing wound. Sighing, the verdict was given. 'There'll be none of those magnificent ball gowns for you, pet. Tis an ugly thing, for sure. And the cough now?'

'Gone. I'm fine, Alice. Really.'

'So I see,' Alice said, glancing around the interior of the hut. It was easy to see a woman resided here now. 'You'll be doing too much too soon, pet.'

'I can't be doing nothing all day, Alice.'

'Ha, you even sound like Sam.'

Horror crossed Anna's face until she realised it was a joke. She set about making tea. She did have one cake to offer, unless Sam had found it. Anna searched. Sam had found it.

'I brought a basket of baking for you all,' Alice said and looked down on Susan. Sleeping, thumb in mouth, bottom raised high. 'My, she's a pretty little thing.'

'With a will of her own. She has Sam running all the time.'

'And how is he?'

148

'With Sam it's hard to tell. He doesn't say a lot. I fear there's an almighty temper there somewhere.'

'I've not seen it yet,' Alice said.

'And how long have you known him?' Anna asked.

'Long enough,' was the reply. Alice settled into the rocker. Anna hoped it would hold her. 'And what might your plans be, pet?'

'Plans?'

'When you're well. Lord knows you can't stay here.'

Surely that's Sam's decision to make? Anna didn't voice her thoughts. Alice meant no harm. 'I try not to think of tomorrows, Alice. Do you think Susan is fat enough for a baby her age? Should she be trying to walk? She's only eight months old.'

'Baby's fine. It's you I'm concerned about.'

'Please don't be.'

It was becoming harder to stay polite.

'Do you not think it's time to talk?'

'About what?'

'Losing your husband of course. I can't sympathise for I don't know what I'd feel if I lost Cormac.'

'I feel nothing.'

'Oh, you will in time. You will. It happened so quickly, pet, you've had no time to mourn.'

'Mourn? I hated him. He wasn't a husband, he was a tyrant. I hated him for lying and marrying me and bringing me to this Godforsaken place in the first instance. I hate him for forcing me to have a baby I never wanted...'

'You'll never say that! Never!'

'Why shouldn't I! She hates me! She frightens me, Alice. She hates me. She knows!'

'She knows what? She's a baby!'

Anna had already said too much. Too much to a stranger.

'Anna, do you think I don't know what it's like to be young and a mother? I know it's frightening but you mustn't talk like that. She's just a wee baby.'

'She may be just a wee baby but I don't know how to be a mother.'

'But you're a good mother.'

149

'Am I? Sam's a better mother than I am or could ever hope to be. Lord knows, she likes him better anyway. Perhaps I should just go away and leave them. Perhaps he should never have found me. Don't you see? Everything that has happened is because of me.'

'And what has happened?'

'How do you have your tea?'

'However it comes.'

Alice watched as shaking hands poured tea.

'And do you hate the baby as you hated your husband?'

'Of course not. I feel ... useless. Helpless.'

Alice took the tea Anna gave her and gazes locked. 'You worry about the things you can change, pet and only that. You have more than you think. You have Sam.'

'Of course. Sam. Sam who's been accused of the slaughter at Bitter Creek.'

Alice's mouth opened wide.

'You didn't know?'

Alice shook her head.

'Then you wouldn't know that I am dead and so is my baby. For it, we can thank a sergeant called Lucas Hannaford.'

'It's *his* doing?' Alice asked, voice a squeak.

'He's the one who shot me.'

'And Sam knows this?' Alice asked.

'Yes,' Anna whispered quietly. 'Yes, he knows it all now. But how to prove his innocence? It's as if he doesn't care. He tells me not to worry, he'll think of something. And he keeps smiling. How can he? If he's caught, he'll hang.'

Alice sipped her tea and sighed. ''Tis a mess, all right.'

Anna silently agreed.

'So old Luke says you'd be dead, then. I never thought he'd go this far.'

'You know him too?'

'Ah, who about here doesn't? 'Tis the worst criminal who wears a uniform, Anna. Perhaps that's why we love Sam as we do. At least he's an honest thief. My God, you must be special.'

'Me?'

'You're wearing Elizabeth's dress. Has he told you about her?'

'Only that he was accused of her murder.'

150

'Let me tell you something and you'll swear it wasn't me who told you this, mind, but months ago now, Sam came to visit and he told us about the most beautiful woman he'd ever seen. How she was married to a man who beat her and made her wear a man's clothes while she dug in the dirt. Besotted, he was.'

'Sam talked of me?'

'Constantly. He loved you then, he loves you now. And if he could hear you talking about the baby like you've been talking, his heart would break. He's a good man, Anna. Deep down, he's a good man. Confused and perhaps misguided, but good all the same.'

'He's a thief.'

'We all have our ghosts and we all have our reasons. If you're destined to run and hide for the rest of your life, so be it. You'll not be alone if Sam's claimed you and claimed you he has. You're here are you not? He didn't have to take you in. He didn't think twice about it.'

'I feel such a fool, Alice.'

'Don't we all?'

'Do you think he's handsome?'

'Now that's an obvious question with an obvious answer, pet.'

'The first time I saw him I thought my heart would explode. It pounded so hard I was sure he'd hear it.'

'He probably could,' Alice said with a smile. 'Funny, though, he said the same thing to us. Tell me, is he still sleeping on the floor now?'

Anna didn't reply. She smiled into her tea instead and winced when Alice's huge, calloused hand slapped her knee, hard.

'You little devil,' the Irishwoman cackled.

Hannaford was sipping on a watered rum and meaning to have a word to Rose about the quality of her liquor when the coach rattled by and the two loaned troopers jumped down and hurriedly approached. Luke finished his drink, hid the glass in his desk drawer and met them at the door.

'Smith-Johnson's dead, Sergeant.'

Luke closed his eyes. The tale began, disjointed, nervous. Excited and steamy. He held up his hand to halt the bombardment. 'Where's Brannigan?'

'Bringing the body in, sir.'

151

'Right. Get off with you and have a drink or two. When you've calmed, you'll make out your reports and if they don't tally, you'll do them again and again until they do. Understood?'

They understood and as ordered, headed for the pub.

Hannaford sighed and returned to the relative cool of his office. Some time later, Bert Whipps came waddling in. 'Your mail, Sergeant.' A bundle of letters plopped to the desk.

'How's your wife?' came the question which went unanswered. Whipps left. Perhaps the silly young bitch had told him of the touch the day she came to collect her locket. Could he help it if his fingers had slipped and fallen on to a lush, rounded breast? She enjoyed it anyway. It was too bad he couldn't entice her from Bert's bed and into Room Four at Rosie's. Between them, they'd make a fortune.

He sorted through the mail. Official, most of it and divided into two categories—that which could wait, forever if possible, and the rubbish. There was a letter in Maddy's neat hand for him and one in the same hand for Daniel. Luke picked it up. He smelled it. Scent.

Scent?

He turned it over and was almost inclined to tear it open but no. No. There was a simple way to rectify this: kick the little bastard in the arse and threaten to castrate him if he ever laid a finger on Maddy.

Luke threw the letter on to the other table and opened his. Had it been from Jane he wouldn't have read it, not that she'd have time to write, thank God. Rachel would keep her busy enough. The thought of Jane's elder sister made his skin crawl. He could see them sitting on the huge verandah of the house overlooking the river, sipping dry sherry until they were both politely drunk. Rachel would spend every available moment reinforcing the notion that Jane should leave her husband; telling her relentlessly that she was not suited to be a pioneer's wife or a trap's for that matter.

Luke knew exactly what Rachel Long needed. A man, preferably one who was blind, deaf and oversexed to give the haughty bitch what she needed. Give her something else to think about other than her little sister missing the good life.

'Isolated my arse,' he mumbled and unfolded Maddy's letter.

Dear Papa,

I miss you terribly. Mother has told me I should write in case you are worried that we never arrived. The axle broke at Ipswich and we stayed in a wonderful hotel. It was much nicer there than here. Aunt Rachel hasn't

152

changed at all, but we never expected her to, did we? They are rarely home and Ronald is not here to annoy me, either. He is away being taught how to build bridges.

Papa, I am a prisoner here. I want to come home, desperately. Christmas is close now and I don't want to spend it here alone. Lady McTaggart has invited Mother and Aunt Rachel for Christmas dinner and they shall all discuss some new charity. I have not been invited.

I shall ask Mother if she will allow me to travel alone so I can be with you at Christmas. She is so busy I know she will say yes. Please do not worry about me, Papa. I'm almost seventeen, not a child any more.

Until I see you again soon, all my love evermore,

Maddy.

Hannaford folded the letter, put it back into its envelope and shoved the thing into his pocket. He was on his way to Rose's for a double serving of steak and kidney pie when he saw Brannigan coming in.

He was leading a horse and on it was a draped, tied body.

Daniel dismounted tiredly and waited for the inevitable blast. Nothing came. 'It was Manning, sir. But he's wounded. Dingo's out there somewhere tracking the blood, I suppose. Although judging by how things have gone today, I wouldn't be surprised if Dingo's dead, too.'

'Fetch Harry, boy.'

'Yes, sir.' Daniel was relieved there wasn't any more said. 'Sir?'

'What?' Luke asked tiredly, turning back.

'Dennis didn't listen to me, sir. If he had, he'd still be alive.'

'When you're finished there, I want to talk to you. I'll be at Rosie's.'

'Yes, sir.'

And Daniel wondered what would come next.

Anna had felt this before—a dull edged despair which had no reason for existence. It was like an eternal wait, but for what? The sun was setting in bright blood hues, spreading its stain on hilltop, flaming the trees.

153

She sat by the creek on the huge rock she found comfortable, and from there she could, if she wanted, see for a full three hundred and sixty degrees. She would see anyone approaching and the person she needed so badly to see right now was not coming.

'Where are you, Sam?' she whispered. Susan, bouncing up and down on her knee, turned at the words and she chewed on her fist and grinned at her mother. Anna closed her eyes and held the baby tightly. Just as Alice had said, the baby liked it. She still sucked on her hand but she also rested her head against Anna's chest and for a moment, Anna felt almost close to her.

Then the despair welled again. Something had happened, there was no doubting it. Anna waited and waited until the sun was shielded by granite. Tears filled her eyes for no apparent reason and then the reason caught her.

She'd been asleep when he'd left. She hadn't said goodbye. She hadn't said she didn't want him to go, that the precious letter could wait another week. Trust me, Sam, she'd have said. Please don't go. Not today. Something bad is going to happen. Don't go … Instead, she'd woken late to find a roll of moth-eaten blue cotton on the table as well as a jug of goat's milk.

Blue curtains hung on the small window and his favorite food was waiting. Feed him well, Alice had said. Feed him well, he'll come back for more without fail. Look after him, he'll look after you. Most of all, be his friend.

Be his friend.

The table was set.

She'd taken a bath, washed her hair. And waited. She waited so long her imagination went wild. 'Where is he, baby?' she whispered and cuddled the child closer still. Susan was asleep. She'd spent all afternoon awake, trying to walk.

Anna put her baby to bed, lit the lamp, stoked the fire and tidied the small table. It too, was covered in blue cotton. The same blue as his eyes, well, almost. The cotton had faded with age.

'Sam?'

Had she heard something? At last, he's home! She ran to the door and leaped the porch step. And didn't want to believe what she saw. She screamed his name.

The voice came to him from the edges. He tried to reply. She must have seen him because her scream chilled his blood. What was left of it. The cloud surrounding his eyes was gray and red and he tried to relinquish his grip on the horse's mane but his fingers had locked.

154

Anna was running towards him, yelling things he couldn't understand. All he knew, he was home. Safe. Depends how far behind Billy Dingo was. Fingers let go and he slid off the horse.

'Sam, no!'

The strength she needed came from panic alone.

Anna dragged him across the hard ground, up the porch and finally inside. His heavy, limp body left a red smear across her clean floor. Anna didn't notice it. 'Talk to me, Sam, please talk to me!'

His eyes rolled. His sounds were incoherent even to himself. He tried to tell her not to yell.

Anna, on her knees, managed to take the coat off, then his shirt. She looked at his side, the chunk of flesh that had been burnt away by a bullet. So much blood. Anna tried to sit him up, he kept toppling over. 'Forgive me,' she whispered as she pulled his trousers off. He was in too much pain to object.

Anna reached for the spirits bottle and the bandages; one of Susan's clean diapers. She pressed it tightly against his side, the material flowered a bright red. She tipped a liberal amount of spirits into the raw bleeding wound. There was no scream. He caught his breath then passed out. For that Anna was pleased. And she didn't realise she was crying, not for a long time. She packed the wound, and balanced him so that his shoulders rested against the bed. He seemed to be breathing evenly enough.

'I told you to be careful. Why couldn't you be careful?'

She untied the scarf, soaked with blood. Anna peeled it off and closed her eyes momentarily. 'Oh, God.'

Sam mumbled something again. Something about wild dogs. Dingos. Anna took her attentions back to the bullet wound in his arm. It seemed as though the projectile had hit from behind and had passed right through his arm. The hole at the front was twice as big, raw, gaping, black … She felt nauseous as she reached for the spirits again.

When it hit, so did Sam. His right arm came from nowhere and he pushed violently as he screamed. Anna rolled three times and came to rest against the wall. Undeterred—she'd suffered far worse from a man and lived—she crawled back, grabbed his face in her hands. 'Sit still and let me finish this!' she yelled.

He opened his eyes. Anna. He tried to say her name, tried to tell her Dingo was following him, still.

'Sam, please, if I don't stop this bleeding, you'll die!'

155

He quietened. Anna leant across him and grabbed another diaper from the dwindling pile. She folded it and wrapped it tightly around his arm. 'Can you hold this?'

Sam held it. 'Dingo's comin'. Shotgun, get the shotgun.'

Anna secured the makeshift bandage. 'Is that too tight?'

'Get the fucking shotgun!'

Anna ran for the shotgun. 'What's happening, Sam!' she cried.

Sam tried to get up but the most he could do was fall onto the bed.

'Sam, tell me what's happened!'

There was no reply.

'Sam!'

Susan started to talk to herself the moment Anna heard the movement from outside.

She froze.

Chapter Eleven

WITH EFFORT, BILLY DINGO GOT off the horse. The wad of rag he'd pressed to his face wasn't helping. Occasionally he saw double but not now.

There was the gray, still saddled.

From inside the old hut, he could hear a baby crying. It was familiar. He'd heard it before, that cry.

Manning and the woman were here. He saw where she'd dragged him in. Saw the blood.

The sarge'll promote me for sure, he thought.

Billy took his pistol out and moved quietly around the back of the hut. Through a slit in the curtains he could see her in there. Manning was face down on the bed. Bandaged up. Not moving.

Probably dead.

Dingo had never been happier.

Anna felt the stare from behind her. She turned and saw the silhouette. Swinging the shotgun to the window above Sam's head, she closed her eyes and pulled both triggers. The force sent her backwards into the wall. Glass shattered, a bullet cracked into the wall near her face. Time seemed to slow when she saw the wall of blood. The new curtains darkened and dripped red and for an instant she saw surprised eyes. Then a hat rose into the air, followed by two booted feet.

Then there was silence.

Stark and echoing. Time returned to normal.

Her ears rang. She felt as if she'd been kicked by a horse. Anna dropped the shotgun and covered her face with her hands.

Susan had stopped crying. Her eyes were huge, her mouth was open.

And slowly, Anna realised exactly what she had just done. She looked down at Sam. He was covered in glass and blood. Unmoving.

Have to see. Have to see …

157

Anna took one hesitant step after another towards the door and she opened it. Barefooted, she stepped outside, past the bathtub, the woodpile. She peered around the corner.

In the twilight gloom she saw what was left of the aboriginal trooper. His head was at an angle to the rest of his body. The shotgun's blast had caught him in the throat and had almost torn his head off. His eyes were open and staring at her.

Anna gagged. She couldn't even scream.

Something momentarily died inside her, until common sense prevailed.

If one had found them, how many more would be following?

Anna ran back inside, bolted the door and she leaned against it, shaking; crying now, begging forgiveness for the life she'd just taken.

It never occurred that she'd had to kill to survive.

'That was lovely, Mrs Macauley.'

'Did you have enough, Peter? Are you sure now?'

'Positive. Goodnight.'

Daniel, in his dressing gown, left the table and walked down the hall towards the room he rented from the old, senile widow Macauley. Sometimes she thought he was her flash Sydney lawyer son, Peter, the one who never visited but sometimes sent money. Mainly it was Daniel's rent which kept them both eating. So when she called him Peter, he knew it made her old heart happy if he played along pretending to be her son.

'And where's my kiss?'

Daniel turned, walked back and kissed the old woman's forehead. She pinched his cheek in return and with a smile they went separate ways, she to the kitchen to wash dishes, he to his room to read.

It had taken half an hour of fast talking to convince the sergeant he had no romantic notions about Maddy and he stopped short of saying he'd rather kiss a camel's arse than Maddy Hannaford's mouth. It wouldn't have been wise under the circumstances, but the lies calmed the storm before it appeared. Lately, Daniel thought he was becoming a pretty good liar, too.

Since late afternoon, he hadn't time to scratch his nose let alone read his mail.

158

Maddy's letter seemed lighter than the one he'd picked up out of the dirt at Mitchell's Crossing.

He burped. Mrs Macauley's curry was repetitive.

Daniel took off his dressing gown and put the lamp nearer the window. He was sweating again. A breeze caught and cooled wet skin. Daniel opened Maddy's scented letter and quickly read it. He had a quiet smile at her grizzlings about her aunty and life in general and he was glad the sarge hadn't read it, because he'd have chopped his balls off with an axe when he got to the part:

So for Christmas, all I want is another kiss in the stables.

If she said some funny things, she wrote even worse.

And by now, everyone in town would know Maddy Hannaford sent perfumed letters to Daniel Brannigan. The gossips would have them married before much longer.

Daniel put the letter back into its envelope. He'd write back tonight, he decided, and give her something to anticipate when she came home. If she wasn't on her way back already.

He put thoughts of Maddy aside and picked up the letter addressed to the Commissioner. This was the one he'd been wanting to read all damned day.

Curiosity overcame guilt. Manning had dropped it. It could be crucial, he told himself. Crucial to what, exactly?

The handwriting seemed to be a female's. Neat and precise. Daniel swept over the words and frowning, he flicked through the six pages of the letter.

Anna Hall?

Bitter Creek?

The words were digested, sentence by sentence, paragraph by paragraph. In half an hour, his heart was dancing, trying to leap out of his throat.

The light flickered in the breeze and he turned all the digested pages over. He'd had enough reading.

Daniel rubbed at his unshaven face.

He pictured Anna Hall in his mind. He remembered her very well—how could he forget? It was the license check in September. A month before the massacre. She was panning, oblivious to the leech on her wrist. She was sunburnt, dirty but somehow very attractive. Before her confrontation with the sergeant she'd smiled at Daniel shyly and his heart had turned a full circle in his chest. Oh, yes, he remembered Anna Hall.

159

And Bitter Creek.

Dingo? The sarge? Daniel chewed on his thumbnail and stared out into the night. In his mind's eye, he was watching Dingo holding a baby by the legs; a knife at its throat. That's what her letter stated. But he wouldn't do that. Not Dingo. Or would he? So she was raped and shot. That was more than possible. But no, no, it had to be some kind of deception. Anna Hall is dead.

Is she? Did you see the body?

No, but Dingo said…

Daniel's thoughts froze.

Dingo.

It'd been Dingo who'd buried her body before the burial detail even arrived out there. Dingo, who'd acted like a dribbling idiot only two days before when Manning had led them to the Bitter Creek site.

Manning had led them because Manning knew. And Billy had chanted, and Billy had hid himself away. A day later, he was there, burying a body Daniel never saw amid all the others.

Daniel rubbed at his neck. Then he picked up the last page. The writer said that Sam Manning had saved her life and her baby's life and he did not deserve to be accused of wholesale slaughter which he did not commit. She was positive the Commissioner would act immediately on receipt of this letter etc. etc. Justice would be served.

'He'll bloody act all right,' Daniel mumbled.

And he recalled Maddy grabbing him from behind the morning before she left, grabbing him as he saddled his horse in the stables. Her hand was like a claw against his shoulder. 'Jesus, Maddy. Don't scare me like that.'

'You don't think Sam's responsible, do you, Daniel?'

Daniel searched for any eavesdroppers. He shook his head. 'No, it wasn't Sam.'

'You like him, too?'

'Don't tell your father. He'll shoot me for treason.'

Maddy grinned. It faded to become something he'd seen too often of late. 'You like me, don't you, Daniel?' she asked, stroking his hand as he tightened the girth strap.

'Of course I do, what sort of question is that?'

'Prove it, Daniel.'

She stood there, puckering up, eyes closed. Daniel tried hard not to laugh. Maddy with hurt feelings was a volatile commodity.

160

He had two choices, frighten her back to her senses and therefore stop this nonsense or give her what she expected. Both would probably frighten her.

Daniel let go of the girth and grabbed Maddy. He frightened her, too right he did, but she didn't react the way he'd expected. The mouth on hers was not gentle. The hand on breast was not gentle, either. Tables turned too quickly. She was by far the stronger. She tripped him. He went over backwards into the barley straw. Maddy's weight on him was squashing the very breath from his body.

Jesus Christ! he thought, alarmed. If the sarge sees me I'm dead!

'Maddy, no!' he tried to protest but his words were muffled by her mouth. Her fingers were probing roughly for a certain part of his anatomy he treasured. 'No, Maddy, No!' Using the last of his panicked strength, he somehow managed to pin her to her back. Her bright eyes were alight. Terrifying. Her huge breasts were heaving. She was puckering up again for God's sake. 'Maddy, no. Not here. Someone will see.'

'Let them see, I don't care.'

'Maddy, you're too young!'

She opened her eyes, realising he wasn't going to kiss her again. 'How old must I be?' she asked, whining.

'At least… at least seventeen,' came the breathy response.

'Oh. Then there shall be nothing to do but wait for Christmas.'

'Christmas? Why?'

'I turn seventeen at Christmas.'

The glow was back in her eyes. Oh, shit, Daniel had thought.

The terror was gone now, it had died slowly over the past few weeks. Daniel decided he wouldn't write to Maddy that night. He found an envelope in his drawer and re-addressed the letter to the Commissioner. He would slip it into the outgoing mail and no one would ever know of his treason.

To him it was the truth and the truth kept him awake all night long.

So did thoughts of Maddy.

Anna stared past the speckled hen she could not relocate to a new nest, no matter what she tried to do, and she stared into infinity. She knew the pillow of her body was soft, that her heartbeat lulled him into nullity, a

161

nothing she envied. How many more deaths would there be before this was over? she wondered, returning the hen's stare now and holding Sam a little tighter.

He didn't remember sleeping. He didn't know how she held him all night long, the loaded shotgun beside her, hoping she wouldn't have to use it again, ever. Now and then a soft weeping infiltrated and he was as powerless as ever.

At some stage, it was day and her hands were cool and comforting. There was a voice asking how he felt, a moist cloth cooling his body, satisfying the intense fires for a little while only. And somewhere in the haze, he thought she was Ginger-Lee. Her name emerged thickly, choked.

Ginger-Lee?

'I'm here, Sam,' Anna said.

She could make no sense of his ravings. He couldn't hear her anyway. Touch alone was comfort because he'd know he wasn't alone. Hadn't he done the same for her?

Ginger-Lee?

Eyes searched her face and found someone else's. 'Yes, Sam, I'm Ginger-Lee.' If it helped, she'd be anyone whose presence might ease his pain. She knew what it was like, the pain, the need, the emptiness of solitary suffering.

A curious look passed over his face as if something in his mind had registered that this woman wasn't Ginger-Lee or if she was, she sure had changed. A light of recognition flickered in his eyes. He tried to move.

'No. You must lie still.'

Like a child he obeyed, too weak to argue.

After two nights and one day, the expected became a reality. Sam became violent, fevered. Anna found it impossible to hold him any more.

'Don't trust him, girl. You never seen me.'

'Of course,' Anna said, squeezing his hand.

'Don't trust him, Ginger-Lee.'

Who is this Ginger-Lee! her mind screamed. As far as Anna knew, there was only Elizabeth's ghost to haunt him.

'Promise me.'

'You can trust me, Sam.'

He pulled her hand down hard and squeezed it against his chest. Obviously, he didn't want to let go of this Ginger-Lee. An insane jealousy rose. Alice was lying, she thought. I am not the most beautiful woman

162

he's seen. This Ginger woman is. Anna had to wrest her fingers from his hand. Sam opened his eyes and focused on her face.

'Anna?'

'Try to sleep.' She tried to, but couldn't keep the hurt from her voice or her eyes.

'Dingo?'

'He's dead, Sam.'

Lucidity was returning, perhaps those cold words helped.

'How?' he asked, confused.

'I shot him,' Anna said, matter of fact. Inside she felt ice again.

There was no shock. What played across his face was relief. He smiled and Anna ached. She watched him drift away into sleep once more. Free now, fingers aching, she wondered what he'd say when he was better and discovered she'd had to bury the body. She only hoped she'd dug the hole deep enough and that the heavy rocks she'd gathered were enough to stop the wild dogs from digging the body up. She'd even said a prayer over him but to whose God she'd directed her offering she didn't know.

Anna wasn't sure of anything now, except that she'd killed a trooper and Sam Manning loved another woman. A woman he had not told her about.

'Where the hell is that black bastard!'

Daniel turned away, swallowing his doubt. Without looking at the sergeant, he said quietly, 'He's probably dead, sir. At least I think he is. If he was alive, he'd be back by now.'

'You think? You tell me it's possible for you to actually think?'

Daniel chewed on his inner lip, closed his eyes and dared not face the man. He'd never felt hate quite like it and worse, he seemed to enjoy the feeling.

'Where was he last seen?'

'It's in the reports, sergeant.'

'I asked you, Brannigan! You! What the hell's got into you lately, boy?'

'Nothing, sir.' But it'll be a pleasure to watch you swing. Luke. You old prick. A smile touched Daniel's mouth. 'He was last seen chasing Manning south from Mitchell's Crossing. Sir.'

'Into Girraween again.'

163

'Possibly, sir.' And frankly I don't give a shit, either.

'Take Porter with you and find him.'

'Who, sir?'

'Dingo, you idiot!'

'Porter's useless in the bush. I'll probably lose him.'

'You were just given an order, boy.'

'Sergeant, I would like to attend Dennis's funeral. Please?'

Daniel was surprised when his request was granted. He retired to the stables to think and hate a little more. There was no justice. There never had been nor would there ever be. Enforcing the law indeed. It was a joke. A cruel joke.

Sam woke to the baby's 'dad-dads'. He opened his eyes and turned his head. Susan was standing beside the bed, grinning at him. He smiled weakly and lifted his good hand. The baby watched the fingers rise, cackled and fell flat on her behind.

'Oops. Up you get. Try again, Suzie.' Sam offered her his finger, she clutched it and stood up again, knees buckling but better this time. More confident. 'Good on you, kid.'

Sam felt a breeze coming from the wrong way. He looked up. The window above his head was devoid of glass. What happened to her new curtains? He gazed around the familiar room. There was a bullet hole in the wall near the door.

Anna was askew in the rocking chair, a mug of tea at an angle. Spilling.

'Anna?'

She woke quickly and turned. Her smile was instant. She realised her tea had spilled on the floor. Susan was playing in it.

Sam sat up higher. His side hurt like hell, his arm was heavy and useless. One step became two. He looked down. The pants that felt so odd were his old regulation whites.

'I'm sorry but they were all I could find.'

'No problem,' Sam said and shuffled past.

'Sam?'

He turned too quickly and nearly fell.

'Welcome back.'

164

A true smile touched his eyes. 'Good to see you, too, Ma'am. It's real good.'

Outside, the fresh air hit like a Californian wave. The goat bleated at him. 'Watch your mouth, Marigold. You're living on borrowed time.' He realised what he'd said. 'But I guess we all are.'

Sam saw the mound of dirt covered in rocks as he was relieving himself by the woodheap. A grave. Dingo. Soon came the footsteps and Anna appeared. Too late, she noticed what he was doing and she had to look away.

'You shall have to start working your hand, Sam.'

'Can't do eight things at once, Anna. I'm not a woman. The damned thing won't work anyway. Fingers won't bend.'

'That's what I mean. You have to force yourself. You have to try.'

Sam did try and couldn't fasten his fly one handed. He cursed softly. 'Anna?'

She walked to him and looked up into his face as her fingers fumbled with his buttons. 'You realise this embarrasses me more than you?'

'You're not the one blushin', Ma'am.' An attempt at humour. 'Thanks,' he mumbled when she'd finished.

'I shot a rabbit this morning. I'm making up a stew.'

Instead of wanting to throw up, Sam said: 'Great. I could eat a horse.'

'You nearly had to. That gray of yours follows me everywhere. She ruined two perfectly good shots.'

'When did you bury him?' Sam asked. He was in no mood for small talk, not when heavier things lingered unspoken.

'Thursday.'

'How deep?'

'As deep as I could manage, ' Anna replied softly and studied her feet like a schoolgirl in trouble again.

'No others came?'

'No, why?'

'There were three of them. Maybe four. Hard to tell. I think I got one.'

'Got one?'

'Shot him. I just hope it wasn't Daniel.'

'Daniel?'

'Brannigan. He's just a kid. I don't think he'd follow me too far. He's got more brains than to come get lost up here. But Dingo was a tracker, see. He followed my blood. It's rained, right?'

'Yesterday. There was enough falling in the mountains to make the creek rise, though.'

'Good,' Sam said, relieved. 'I think we're safe a little while longer yet. What'd you do with his horse, girl?'

'Pardon?'

'The horse. A big bay. Where's the horse?'

He was referring to Dingo's horse. Anna's face paled. 'Oh. I never thought of the horse.'

'It's all right. You had your mind on keepin' us alive. It's okay, girl. I know.'

Anna glanced up into his face once more and she stopped him as he began to walk off. 'I thought you were going to die. Just like Dinny. I was terrified, Sam.'

He touched her face. There was so much he could have said then, but nothing emerged except a soft, hoarse, 'thankyou'. She looked different, somehow. Weary. Worried. A bit older.

'You haven't slept much, lady. You look worse than I feel.'

'That bad?' Anna asked. Movement caught her attention. She'd come outside and had forgotten to close the door. Susan was crawling off. 'Oh, no. There she goes again!'

Sam turned. The baby was heading for the creek, attention suddenly diverted by the discovery of a stick to chew on. Anna moved quickly to the rescue. Sam grabbed her arm. At that moment he almost told her he thought he loved her but her eyes were too full of questions, so he kissed her instead. Maybe that would tell her more.

Anna stepped back, surprised. She hitched skirts and sprinted. The baby saw her coming and crawled off, fast. Very fast. Sam watched and thought it all a little funny. 'You little horror, Susan Louise!'

The baby laughed as mother saved her from suicide. Again.

Sam had never seen Anna do anything like this before: lifting the baby and swinging her around. She was getting better. A lot better. She'd be wanting to leave soon. There was nothing here for her. She'd want to go back to Brisbane, where she came from, so far away.

He didn't like the thoughts. It wouldn't be the same here without her. Without them both.

166

'Come on, Sam! Let's have something to eat!' Anna called. He made his way back to the house but first he kicked over the makeshift wooden cross. Two sticks tied together, a semblance of a crucifix. He turned and saw Anna, baby on hip, watching. Horrified at what he'd just done.

'They got their own God,' was all Sam said and hoped she'd believe it. Anna said nothing.

He ate so much she thought one more mouthful of stew or bread would see him explode. He finally sat back and groaned. All the while Sam kept glancing at her shoulder—the black and purple bruise extending from her collarbone into her blue dress. 'Shotgun, right?' he asked. She nodded and used a spoon to entice the baby to open her mouth for more broth. The kid was more interested in eating the spoon. 'You never used one before, right?'

'Right.'

'Did it send you through the wall?'

'I don't remember. I suppose it did.'

'Both barrels?' Sam asked cautiously.

'I shot him in the throat, Sam. He was by the window, he was going to kill us all,' she whispered and wouldn't meet his gaze. At least she didn't see the winces. 'It was my birthday, yesterday,' she added softly, more to change the line of conversation than say anything meaningful. Perhaps she hoped he'd say, "happy birthday for yesterday", or perhaps he'd lean across the table if his stomach allowed it, and kiss her again?

He just sat there, lazy, full, a curious expression on his face.

He said nothing except, 'How old are you?'

'Twenty-three.'

There was nothing else. She should have been used to it by now. Birthdays, Anniversaries, Christmases meant nothing to Michael, either. 'When is yours, Sam?'

'My what?' he asked, caught again in daydreams.

'Birthday.'

'Oh, that. June. Thirteenth or fourteenth, can't remember.'

He can't remember his birthday? Perhaps there has never been anyone who cared enough to help him celebrate? Give him space, Alice had said in all her wisdom. So Anna didn't ask where he was going or how long he was likely to be. The door closed and she was alone again.

And there was wood to be cut and brought in, a goat to be milked for the night. When she was busy, Anna didn't think too deeply. Lately, she kept as busy as possible.

She dropped an armload of split logs to the floor and began to stack them. Her face was filthy, sweat clung her hair to the back of her neck and to her face. Her dress was stuck to her body. She looked perfectly horrible, knew it, and couldn't have cared less. As her grandmother used to say, Even a Princess can't feed the pigs wearing her tiara.

The most beautiful woman he'd seen? Besotted? What rot. Why did she want a kiss, anyway? For heaven's sake, he robbed ladies of their jewellery and kissed them in apology. Meant nothing to him at all. Ginger-Lee indeed. Ginger-Lee, Ginger-Lee … she who had stolen a large part of Sam's heart and left her with a slither of it, a slither she had to share with a ghost.

It's not fair!

Anna threw a log down. It smashed into place. The log was Ginger-Lee's head.

He had a choice, the music box that still worked (at least it had the last time he'd wound it up) or a bunch of wildflowers, little paper daisy things, red flowers from gum trees, a stick or two of wattle. So what if it made him sneeze?

Sam chose the flowers. At least with a bunch of flowers in his good hand she couldn't accuse him of being what he was—a thief.

She was stacking wood when he limped in.

Stacking wood and wiping her eyes on her sleeve. 'Anna?'

She spun. She was covered in dirt, sweat. Mud. And still she was lovely. Sam held out the flowers as he limped in. 'I didn't know it was your birthday. I guess it's one we won't forget for a long time, even if I wasn't here for it. Well, I was here, but … you know.'

The sight of him standing there looking lost, apologetic and frankly, quite silly, caused the sudden tidal wave of emotion. It had been building since Wednesday evening and it exploded like a dam bursting its banks. Sam put the flowers down quickly and held her tight. 'It's okay, Ma'am. You're lucky you can cry.'

And as she bawled and clung to him, it was true. She could cry now; it was safe to.

Sam was back. He wasn't going to die. Perhaps if she thought it often enough, she'd begin to believe it.

168

Uh oh. What's going on? Leonie bit her lip. Suddenly, she knew exactly what the horses were planning to do out there. The ram was a fair bugger for it, so was the rooster. Always up the little black hens. Once, she'd tried to fight him off when he was picking on the tiny hen. He'd been smacked with the broom at least twelveteen times and then he'd charged at her. Got her right on the ankle with his spur. Went right through. Mama had chopped his head off and cooked him.

Leonie didn't like him alive or dead. Even roasted.

Bet you can't chop this one's head off, Mama.

Pa said Molly was 'horsing' and couldn't be trusted. Molly was only a pony though. Too little for this big horse.

She sure didn't mind this.

Remembering the rooster, Leonie simply watched, mesmerized by what she was witnessing. After five or so minutes it was all over.

Molly laid her ears flat, a bad sign. Leonie could see the whites of the eyes showing. She chewed on her lip and winced. 'Get away, she's going to...' Too late. Molly caught the big stallion smack in the chest. He retreated from any more kicks and looked quite dazed. Molly tried to chase him, bite him. Beat him up. It wasn't fair. Then he saw Leonie and came cantering straight for her. He had a bridle on, saddle too. Dog barked from behind her legs but the huge bay stopped before he trampled her and just stood there, shaking his head about, snorting, stretching out to sniff her.

Leonie looked at Molly. She was having a gigantic pee. Head down, eating again.

The new horse didn't seem dangerous. Leonie touched his nose and when it was safe, when he let her, she took up the reins. 'You shouldn't have done that. My father's going to yell at you. Come on then.'

The little girl led the big brute away. 'Papa! Come see what I found!'

Cormac appeared. His eyes widened.

'I found him doing you know what to Molly, Pa.'

She couldn't say the word she'd heard him use on occasion, she did once, and couldn't sit for days. Her mother appeared and almost dropped her cake bowl. 'Oh, Lordy, where'd he come from?' she cried.

'I found him back of the yards, Ma.'

'With Molly? Are you sure?' Cormac asked and inspected the weary thoroughbred which, thankfully, seemed uninjured. What a fine specimen of an animal he was.

'He's a bit of a sook, Pa. Molly kicked him and tried to bite him so he came straight to me.'

169

'Typical of a female,' Cormac said. 'Sink the boot in when a man's at his weakest.' He avoided Alice's inevitable slap.

'What do you make of it?' Alice asked when the joke had died.

'Tis a trooper's horse to be sure. Leonie, girl, fetch up a bucket of grain.'

'Oh no, you don't. You can't keep him. He has to go back to town. Right this moment.'

'In good time, wife. Stop your nagging me and let a man think.'

'Think? And what if tomorrow Hannaford comes along and sees one of his horses here? He'll be arrestin' you for horse thievin'. He's after an excuse, man, and it's not you or I who'll give it to him. You hear me?'

'Yes, yes. This one'll go back to town as soon as he's been introduced to Aggie.'

'Aggie?' I thought we were gettin' a service from Doolan's piebald?'

'What? When there's a thoroughbred for free?'

'You're a bloody renegade, Cormac.'

'Tis why you love me,' he said with a grin. It soon faded. 'So there's a trap out there somewhere. Is the horse familiar to you?'

'Looks like the blackie's to me. Daniel's isn't as tall.'

'Dingo?'

'So let him rot. You'll not be off searching for him.'

'Where's your humanity, woman?'

'It abandoned me on Wednesday when I visited with Anna. Don't you talk to me of the law, husband, you'll be in for a fight.'

Next morning, just before dawn, Alice watched as the stallion moved to his waiting target, Aggie. At eighteen, she was still the quickest horse Cormac had and he loved her dearly. The bay stallion siring a foal seemed a dream come true for Cormac. The horse proved quite a lover in fact.

Alice nudged her wiry husband as they stood watching, arms around each's waist. 'Could be you might learn a bit if you care to watch carefully, now, husband.'

'Learn what?'

'How to please a lady.'

Cormac grunted.

Alice teased him for the entire journey to town in the rattling buggy. The bay was bringing up the rear.

170

'Leonie, not a word, you hear me?'

The child pledged her silence. She'd learnt a long time ago how one whisper of Sam's name could cause his death by hanging, and she knew what death was. She was struck dumb anyway. Sam's face adorned the windows of the Post Office, the Store and of course, the Police Station where her father intended to go first. Yes, it was Sam's face but it wasn't the Sam she knew.

The poster said fifty pounds reward for information leading to the apprehension. The word's meaning eluded her but the murder word did not. Fifty pounds? Pa always said people couldn't be valued: some were priceless, some worthless. A person couldn't be bought or sold, well, not normally, and it was far easier to replace an object than it was to replace a person. Fifty pounds? It seemed a fortune and it was.

If she was lucky, Pa would give her threepence and she'd run over to Ryan's and buy sweeties, and when she saw Sam next, she would give him a sweet for a change.

Leonie tried to read the blurred print for other words she didn't understand. There were a lot of them. Her mother jerked her into the station. She hadn't heard her calling.

It was dark, gloomy, smelly. An awful place.

'Answer the sergeant, Leonie.'

'Sir?'

'Where'd you find the horse, girl?'

She glanced at her father and he nodded. 'He was making babies with Molly out behind the yards when Dog and me...'

'Dog and I,' Alice corrected.

'Let the child speak in her own words.'

Alice lifted her gaze to the ceiling. She had to fold her arms so her fists wouldn't show.

'When Dog and I were rounding up the chooks, yesterday.'

'What time was this?'

Leonie shrugged. 'Not late enough for the chooks to come in. A dingo's been getting them.'

Luke remained calm. He even tried to smile at the child. 'You didn't see the direction he came from?'

'No. I just saw him making babies with Molly.'

'The bridle was on?'

'Yes, sir. So was his saddle.'

'Was the animal covered in sweat,. as if he'd come a long distance?'

'I didn't notice.'

'You can go.'

She looked to her father and he nodded. As she walked out, she heard him say, 'I'll be wanting restitution for damages to my fences.'

Leonie had almost made it to the fresh air when she bumped into someone coming in. She looked up as the hand caressed her head. Daniel. Leonie beamed. He winked at her, sidestepped as if they were at a dance, and waited for a break in the fight before he could speak.

'Restitution for damages? He probably served every bloody mare you have, Newberry!'

'Excuse me, sir? It is Dingo's horse. It's a lonely animal by nature, seeks company all the time. It wouldn't wander off without Billy unless something had happened.'

'That'll be all. Get off with you, you're already late by a day.'

Brannigan departed and Leonie followed him out into the bright sunshine. 'And how are you, Miss Newberry?' he asked.

'I'm good, Daniel. Am I getting taller?'

'I'll say you are,' he said as he got on his horse. 'You'll be as tall as me soon.'

'Where are you going, Daniel?'

'I have to find Dingo.'

'Pa says he's probably dead.'

'Well, you can tell your Pa I think he's right.'

Daniel and the other trooper rode off and Daniel didn't wave goodbye.

Leonie patted the bay until someone came out and took him away.

She didn't have much longer to wait for her parents. Her mother smacked her ear because she was "Sitting like an urchin in the gutter". Leonie wondered what an urchin was as she was swept along towards Ryan's store. She couldn't believe her luck when her father gave her four pence. 'Off you go, now.'

'You spoil her. The child'll want everything and not know the value of real work.'

'Alice, stop nagging.'

Chapter Twelve

'DO YOU THINK HE HAD a family?'

'Anna, you did what you had to. Sitting there thinking about it all the time's no good. You're alive, he's dead. Let it be.'

The tone hurt more than his words. Other questions to which she had no answers were silenced. She went back to the blue material in her hands. She was making another curtain.

'I didn't mean it to sound like that.'

Yes you did, she felt like saying.

Lately, their only conversations came in short, curt sentences. Anna would ask how his arm was and he'd say it bloody hurt and it'd never get better. She'd ask if there was anything else he wanted her to do and he'd reply with a snapped denial. She was doing too much because he couldn't even take a pee without help.

Anna wondered if people who had been married a lifetime ended up like this once they'd exhausted their supply of anything worthwhile to say that hadn't already been said.

Oh, she understood he was angry. She'd be worse. She was almost as self reliant and independent as he. Almost. But everything she tried to do was wrong. He didn't like the way she chopped the wood because it wasn't HIS way. She hadn't dismembered herself yet, had she? No, but he could see it coming, or so he'd say and lope off to kick at a rock. Everything he wanted to do required two hands.

Was it her fault he rode out to rob the mail coach and got shot? He should be lucky to be breathing.

'Does this look like a tulip to you?' Anna asked and held up the curtain to show him the embroidered flower she was working on. It was almost finished. Sam grunted and Anna exploded. 'What is wrong with you, Sam!' she bellowed. Sam looked up, shocked. What was she yelling for? What'd he do this time?

'I asked you a relatively simple question and you grunt at me!'

'All right. You want my opinion? I don't want curtains. Why don't I want curtains? Simple. This place is supposed to look like it's falling down for a reason, girl. No one's supposed to live here. So I don't care if I never get glass for that window and I don't want bloody curtains!'

'If no one's supposed to live here, why is there a vegetable patch?'

173

'Why don't I weed it, huh?'

She was undeterred. 'You could have told me about your aversion to curtains.'

'I didn't want to hurt your feelings. Besides, it gives you something to do. At least you've *got* something to do.'

Anna rubbed at her face and threw the material to the floor. She ground it with her foot. 'There! No curtains! Are you happy now? I am not a mind reader, Sam!'

The silence was thick.

'You didn't have to do that, you know,' he said calmly.

Anna grunted at him. It gave her pleasure to do so.

Sam studied the flower she'd been trying to sew. 'What'd you say it was?'

'A tulip.'

'Ain't they yellow? That's white.'

'You're just like Michael!' she snapped and jumped to her feet. 'You're always implying I can't do anything right! Well, I can, Sam Manning. You hear me, I can!'

'I never said it wasn't a tulip.'

'You didn't have to! Don't do it like that, do it like this ... everything has to be *your* way!'

'Where are you going?' he asked.

'I may not be the world's best cook or cleaner or mother and I may not be able to sew very well but there is something I *can* do, something I am *good* at. And I intend going out there and I intend to do it whether you think it's a waste of time or not!'

The door slammed. Sam winced. He'd only asked where she was going.

In closing the door, she'd cut off his breeze. Sam got up and opened the door. He knew where she was off to, but she'd forgotten her paints and the easel. She turned back. Sam sidestepped to let her in the door.

Anna rummaged for an enamel plate. She stomped off again.

'Ain't you gonna draw?' he asked.

'No!'

'What you gonna do?'

'I'm going to find some gold.'

174

Sam leant on the porch rail and watched. She's bored, he thought. That's it. She's bored and I'm bored and we're both waiting for something, but we don't know what we're waiting for.

She waded into the water. Sam waited for the steam to rise. She was taking handfuls of sand from the creekbed and throwing it into the plate until it was full and the old routine of shake swirl and tip began. Not for the first time in his life did he wonder why people enjoyed doing this.

Sam idled over and settled himself comfortably on the lump of rock she always sat on when she wanted to think. Maybe it was the bubbling water that helped her think. Maybe he didn't know her as well as he thought. He watched until the first plate was empty and nothing was found. What'd she expect? A miracle? She started the routine over again. 'What if there's no gold here?'

'There is and I shall find it.'

'Like that?'

'Yes, like this.'

On the fifth plateful, he asked, 'Want a shovel?'

Pride forced her denial. 'I can do this on my own.'

'Be easier if you took your dress off.'

Even he could see that the wet skirts were heavy and restricting movement. It was a good idea. Besides, it wasn't as boring if there was something nice to look at.

Sam grinned to himself when she peeled the dress off. He was disappointed to see the petticoat. Damn. 'Sure you don't want a shovel? If there's any gold there, it's falling quicker than you can catch it.'

'And now you're an expert prospector, too?' Anna asked.

'I grew up in Sutter's Mill.'

'What's Sutter's Mill? Another Everglades with gators?'

'Sutter's Mill is a gold mining town in California.'

'Oh. I suppose I'm not doing this right, either.'

His smile said it all. Anna was tempted to drown him, however, her anger wasn't strong enough. His grin was melting her frustrations. Still, he had a point. All she would find this way was black sand. There'd been traces of a blue stone. Sapphire, she supposed.

'Would you like to use a gold pan, Ma'am?'

'I beg your pardon?'

'A gold pan. It'd be easier than that plate. I also got a pick and shovel somewhere. Maybe a sieve.'

175

Anna watched the enamel plate sink to the bottom of the brook. 'Why didn't you tell me?'

'You never asked. I'm not a mind reader.'

She ignored that. 'You have prospecting tools and you sit there, laughing at me?'

'I suppose so.'

'Why!'

'There's nothing else to do. Besides, it's not often I get to stare at a pretty lady in her underwear. All right, I got equipment but I don't use it. I don't see the sense in prospecting and I never have. Do you want it or not?'

'Is this another of your jokes?' she asked cautiously, not trusting the look in his eyes.

'Do you want the stuff,' he said slowly, emphasizing every word so she'd finally understand.

'Could I?'

'All you gotta say is yes.'

'You're cranky again.'

'Me? Me? You any idea how long I'd be waiting to hear you ask for anything at all? You're too proud, Anna and that's only half your problem. What you tryin' to prove anyway?'

'You can talk of proof and pride? Do you ever listen to yourself?'

'Jesus Christ,' Sam mumbled and limped away.

'Don't you dare walk away from me when I'm angry!'

Sam turned back to see her trying to come out of the creek. The rocks were extremely slippery and at speed, lethal. He almost called out to be careful and next moment, all he saw were her white legs in the air. She came up again, wet. Very wet. Serves her right, he thought. About time the temper got cooled.

She coughed, spluttered and started cursing. He started laughing, he couldn't help it. And he had to walk away.

'Stop laughing at me!' she wailed.

He turned back. There was no more anger in her voice. It was pure despair.

'I'd rather you hit me than laugh at me!'

Sam went back to her when he knew it was safer to keep walking the other way. It had to be safer. She was dripping wet. The petticoat clung to every conceivable part of her body. He swallowed his thoughts but his

176

body wouldn't play along. Hands itched to touch. He started to swell. Ache. His mouth went dry.

'Don't move,' he said quietly, put his finger to tongue and dabbed at her cheek. He held his finger in front of her eyes and stuck to the tip was a thin sliver of gold.

At sight of it, all was forgotten and forgiven. 'I knew there was gold in the creek!' she cried and planted a hungry kiss on his face. 'Don't lose it. I have to get a bottle.' Off she ran, barefooted towards the hut.

Sam stared at the tip of his index finger as if he'd never seen it before and then he shook his head.

Anna sprinted back with a small glass bottle in hand. She ran to the creek and filled the bottle with water, holding it out to him as if he should know what to do next. Sam ceremoniously dipped his finger in and watched her eyes sparkle as the gold dropped quickly and lay unmoving on the bottom. She glanced up into his face. She was smiling, victorious.

'Kiss me again,' he ordered.

Anna rose on tiptoe and pecked his cheek. Sam shook his head. 'Is that the best you can do?'

'I have to change,' she said quickly, taking the bottle and capping it. She went to walk away. He grabbed her hand. 'Don't, Sam. It's not right.'

'It's not wrong, either.'

'But you can't ...'

Sam pulled her close. Very close. She felt the hard bulge against her stomach. 'Can't I?' he asked but it wasn't a question.

Anna didn't know what to do. Hadn't this very feeling touched her mind the moment she first saw him? She closed her eyes as fingers drew invisible lines on her cheek and her throat. The touch made her shiver. She tried to think of a thousand reasons why this shouldn't be happening and none surfaced. Nothing would have been any defense against what she'd seen in his eyes.

'Touch me,' he whispered as he eased the petticoat from her shoulder. One fingertip was all it took. The touch left goosebumps in its wake. 'Please touch me,' he whispered again.

She didn't think she could move. His breath was hot and tickling in her ear. Sam nibbled on her neck, fingers gently touched breasts. A curious feeling. She tingled. Something glowed deep in her belly. Mouth touched hers. Anna held her breath. Her heart was roaring but so was his. She touched the fingers which tickled and tormented her nipples; setting her alight or so it felt.

177

She was suddenly awake and understanding now of the light in Alice's eyes. All this time, it had been envy.

Anna touched Sam's chest. The hair there was soft. It was almost a lie. So was his skin soft and smooth. It was all a lie. Of course this was right. It had to be. But still, she hesitated. She didn't understand why until she heard Sam's voice:

'Let him go, girl. You gotta let him go.'

Was it Michael he was referring to? Michael whose touches yielded nothing but pain?

'I have let him go, Sam.'

Anna caressed the incessant bulge. She set it free and touched it again. Long and hard and soft, it gulped against her hand. Moist. Like she was where he was touching, exploring.

Anna was lost. Sam whispered something to her, his voice was adrift.

Sam eased her back against her rock. He was explosive. Her touches were unsure but magic all the same. If he hurried, she'd take flight. So he slowly discarded the rest of her clothes and looked down on her as if he'd never seen a woman quite like her before. He hadn't.

There was no fear, no right and no wrong.

Sam filled her to overflowing and she held tight to this new experience. There was no grunting. No squashing. No urgency. He seemed to take her weight, as hurt as he was. She made small breathy noises with each thrust of his hips until she put her head back and wanted to scream.

'Tell me to stop and I will.'

She said nothing. She fisted her hands in his hair. The more urgent she became the more intensely he reacted. No words were needed or enough.

When he'd finished—it seemed to take forever—he set her back to her feet and pulled her close, saying something she didn't hear because her heart beat was too loud and his banged against her face. His sweat was salty, his chest heaving. And the liquid of his seed tickled her thighs.

Anna pushed away and looked up at him. Although he was weary, she now recognised what it was there in his eyes. Words were hidden but the implication was intense.

Sam fondled her hair. 'Let's take a swim,' he whispered and kicked his pants off completely. Before she could protest he grabbed her under his good arm and threw her into the deepest part of the creek. He dived in as well and stood up in five feet of water.

Anna clung to his neck.

178

'You could have drowned me! How do you know I can swim?'

'I've seen you swimming with that Chinese friend of yours.'

A look of total disbelief mixed with shame lit her face. 'You were spying on us?'

He didn't answer. He kissed her instead.

Lieutenant John Barton propped his head up with his hand and studied the handwriting on the envelope. There were no similarities at all to the writing on the six pages it contained—six pages he'd just read for the third time.

He started to cough and reached for his water. Air. He needed air. For a little while, he stared down into the city streets below and before he looked back at the mound of files and documents all needing the Commissioner's urgent attention, he sighed. It was the sigh of an impending headache.

Barton coughed again and this time he spat. Illness had heightened his aim to perfection.

'Carmichael?'

A younger lieutenant came in.

'See to all that for me,' Barton said and gestured wildly towards the waiting workload.

Carmichael groaned inwardly. He had enough of his own to do. 'Going somewhere?' he asked as the Lieutenant took his coat and hat from the stand near the door and tucked something into his coat pocket. It looked like a letter.

'Yes,' was all the reply he received.

Millie Blackburn was weeding her roses when the carriage pulled up next door. A uniformed lieutenant emerged, coughing so much Millie thought he would drop to his knees and cough his life away into the overgrown footpath. But he didn't. He recovered and studied the house next door for some time, consulting papers, tucking them away again. The gate creaked open. Millie walked to the fence.

'No one's lived there for nearly two years,' she said.

The Lieutenant turned to her. 'I see that, Mrs...'

179

'Blackburn. Millie Blackburn. I suppose it's Michael Hall you're after? If so, you're two years too late.'

'Do you know where he might be?'

'Him? He's off chasing gold. Somewhere down Warwick way, I think. Knowing Michael he'd have changed his mind a dozen times on the way and he's probably in Victoria by now.'

'So you know the family well?'

'Not a family. Just Michael and poor wee Anna. She's his poor, long-suffering wife. Quite the beauty, too. I'm afraid there's no forwarding address for a man chasing dreams, Lieutenant.'

After a few more moments of idle conversation about the lack of rain and the heat, Barton thanked her for her time, climbed into the carriage and the driver moved it on.

Millie went back to her garden.

Barton returned to his thoughts: thoughts that itched and ached.

Anna, sitting far enough away to avoid any flying wood chips, suddenly said, 'Something's happening, Sam.'

Sam split the log and turned to her while he picked up the next. 'What do you mean?'

'Someone's reading my letter.'

Sam went back to his work. With any luck, if he kept quiet she'd never discover he'd lost the damned thing. He wasn't courageous enough to admit it.

'Someone really is reading my letter. I can feel it.'

'If you say so, Ma'am.'

'Troopers will come.'

'Yep, just what we need. A whole army of traps.'

'Don't you see? It will soon be over, Sam.'

If he looked at her now, he'd see eagerness and innocence, a lethal combination. 'The good guys always win, right?'

'There is a chance. Even you said there was a chance.'

'I lost the letter, Anna. I don't know where it is. I think I dropped it when I got shot.'

There was the silence he expected. It was pin drop quiet for a little while.

180

'Then perhaps someone found it and posted it anyway.'

She was as undeterred as always. Sometimes her optimism about the impossible was ferocious.

'Don't, Anna. Believe me, the letter's gone.'

'Why didn't you tell me?'

'I couldn't.'

'I've been waiting for nothing? You expect me to spend the rest of my life hiding from the law? I can't, Sam. I've too much left to do.'

'Making hats, I suppose.'

'Yes!'

'What you gonna do that with? Opening up shops takes money, girl. Money you don't have.'

'I shall get my gold back. All that is rightfully mine.'

Sam didn't want to laugh, it just happened as if by reflex. 'How you gonna do that?'

'You know where it is. You shall get it for me.'

If her dark eyes were the knife, he was the apple. He was being cored again. 'You assume too much, you know that?'

'It's not an assumption. I know that you know where my gold is. I know that you're waiting.'

'Yeah? What am I waiting for?'

'Justice.'

Sam nearly choked. That word hadn't been in his vocabulary for five years.

'You're not interested in helping me at all, Sam Manning.'

Best to play along with her ravings. It made her happy.

'You think that if it's fine for you, it should be fine for everyone. Is that not the case? You may be able to live in isolation, perpetual boredom and utter squalor for the rest of your life, however long that may be, but I am not.'

'Fair enough,' he said. When he split the next block, he felt something rip in his side. He sat down before he fell. Damn her, she was right. She'd warned him, he hadn't taken any notice. 'How do you know someone's readin' your letter anyway?' he asked while the sweat of pain stung his eyes.

'I just do.'

'Like you knew something had happened to me that day, right?'

181

'Yes.'

The look on his face told her she belonged in a mental asylum. It was an expression she'd seen countless times before.

'Sam?' she asked quietly and the tone indicated to him she wanted something. 'Why haven't you told me to leave?'

He wondered what she was up to. Sure, at the start he'd said she'd only be staying as long as it took her to heal. He didn't want a woman about. But back then he thought she'd die. Now what do I say, he wondered.

'Maybe I can't. Or maybe I am waiting, just like you said. Maybe I am waiting for this justice of yours and when you've got your gold, then I'll tell you to go.' Because then you won't need me anymore.

'Why don't you say you love me, Sam? Perhaps I wouldn't want to go if you said what's on your mind.'

Sam pretended he was deaf.

If he held her all night, no matter how hot the nights were, she didn't snore. And it sure was hot. It was nearly Christmas. Sam wondered why she never asked very much. And there was a lot he hadn't told her. Like Elizabeth. Maybe she was waiting or not interested. Sometimes it was hard to tell. Sometimes, he'd see the question in her eyes, usually after they'd made love. In the quiet, following hush he'd try to talk but nothing sensible ever emerged.

Once she said it was a like a long dark tunnel.

Life here was nothing but a long, dark tunnel. Occasionally there'd be a flicker of light at the far end but the closer she got to it, the further away it went just before she reached it. Sam seemed to know the flicker of light at the other end wasn't him. It was a combination of freedom, gold and a hat shop.

And he'd never worried about the future like he did when she lay sleeping in his arms. He wanted her to do what she wanted and have what she wanted. But he also wanted her. He always had been a selfish bastard. He couldn't have her and she couldn't have him and that's all there was to it.

Anna woke him before dawn on Christmas Eve. There was no sensuality in her touch. She shook him awake. He was used to her habit of springing out of bed in pitch darkness, fumbling for the light. She'd start drawing. In the morning he'd have to give an opinion on a hat she'd drawn. Lately, there were dresses to match the hats. And so, as he was shaken awake, Sam automatically told her that whatever it was, it was great, wonderful and he tried to go back to sleep.

'Sam!'

Whoever said they thought their best on awakening was lying. He was wide awake now, Anna leaning over him. Something in her eyes chilled his spine.

'What's wrong?' he slurred.

'I have to take the baby to Alice's; I have to get her away from here!'

'You been dreaming again, girl. It's all right. It was only a dream.' He reached out and drew her down.

'Something's going to happen, Sam. It frightens me. I don't want you to get shot, or caught. Or hang.'

'They've tried once, think I'd let it happen again? Trust me. It's all right.'

Anna cuddled into him. There was security in his warmth, so much of it that her dream of an old silver mine and Sam being shot there, faded entirely. Sam gently tangled his fingers in her hair.

'Why won't you tell me about your past?' she asked.

'Maybe later.'

'And if there isn't a later? You don't want me to know.'

'Cos the past is over with. That's why. You start looking backwards all the time, you get in trouble. I've had enough of that to last me another forty years. It's over, Anna.'

'It will never be over. You're wanted because of her. This Elizabeth. Every time you look at me I see her reflection in your eyes. She's staring back at me. She's not haunting you, Sam, she's haunting me. Damn her for not letting you go.'

'Why do you want to know?'

She raised on elbow. 'If I know, perhaps I can understand you. You're a good man, Sam. Why do you live like this?'

He wondered where to begin.

'She blamed me when the boy was born dead.'

Something caught in Anna's throat. She rested her head against his chest and hoped he'd say more.

She blamed me when the boy was born dead. Years of heart breaking confused agony summarized in a few words; words a woman could understand. Sam still couldn't.

'It was like an earthquake. The ground under us sort of split open. I was on one side, Elizabeth was on the other. The more I tried, the bigger the hole got between us. My work kept me away from home a lot. And while I was away she took to drinking. I guess it eased the pain. The day she died, she was drunker than usual. She told me she had nothing left to

183

live for, she wanted to die, just like the boy had died. You know what I said? I said I didn't care cos at the time I didn't damn well care. You can't keep trying on your own, you know? It's futile. Is that the word?

'The day she died, Luke was waiting for me outside. He heard us fighting; I could tell by his eyes when I came out. I remember saying she'd be okay when she'd slept it off. And we went out to this brawl. A couple of squatters arguing over a cow. I got home late. Walked in and saw her there. On the floor near the bed. That's all I remember, Anna. That's all I remember.'

'You were accused of murder?'

'Aha. Next thing I know, I'm sitting in a courtroom and Luke's telling the magistrate how he found me sitting beside Elizabeth and there's this rifle in my hand.'

'Why would he do that, Sam? Wasn't he supposed to be a friend?'

'A friend I outranked. Always had. I could blame it on jealousy. Blame it on something, I don't know. Trouble is, what he was saying wasn't a lie. It mightn't have been the truth but it wasn't a lie. Just words, twisted words. He wanted me out. It was obvious. Elizabeth suicided. The first bullet never killed her so she tried again. No one could believe she'd shoot herself twice, or do it right the second time.'

'And they sentenced you to hang,' Anna whispered.

The silence was now complete.

'No matter what, Suzie stays right here with us.'

He was right of course. What would happen if the traps found Susan at the Newberry's? What price would two squatters' lives be worth when it was realised they knew the truth? 'Perhaps we could find somewhere else to go, somewhere no one would know us or find us or...'

'Fifty pounds is a lot of money, Anna. I been told it's my eyes that people remember. And I can't take you and Suzie along with me, the law'd see you as an accomplice. They'd hang you, too. No, what we have to do is wait a little more. If we can wait long enough, Luke will make the first mistake.'

'Perhaps he's waiting for you to do the same.'

'Maybe. Guilt won't destroy Luke. If he's scared enough, a mistake just might. And when people are scared, they get a little impatient. That's what I'm hoping for, Anna.'

'It seems an odd Christmas present,' she offered.

'Maybe you will get your gold back and go buy that hat shop you want.'

'And what about you, Sam?'

184

'I guess I'll go home.'

'To America?'

He didn't answer.

Chapter Thirteen

IF IT HADN'T BEEN FOR the axle, Maddy would have been home on December twenty-third. She didn't know what was worse, too long at Aunt Rachel's or travelling on the packed coach. Or for that matter, too many ten mile inns, cold porridge, sour milk, beds full of tiny crawling things. It took a day to mend the axle and that one day seemed to take forever.

She knew what would be waiting for her at home. A mess. Her father wouldn't have cleaned the kitchen, or changed his sheets, or washed himself or his clothes. Maddy didn't want to even think about the cells. Still, it would be good to get home again, no matter what state it was in. It would be good to see Daniel again, too.

Over the last fifteen miles, she pretended she didn't want to pee. The road over the ranges was rough, narrow and winding. Each bump and grind almost spelled disaster. The situation grew steadily worse. Maddy lived in hope that another wheel would fall off. After all, the last one to do so had certainly livened up flagging conversation. If this wheel did perchance come off, she would be able to rush off into the bush, find a big enough tree to squat behind, and do the necessary. Bump by bump it was becoming imperative.

She was far too embarrassed to ask for a stop. Her mother wasn't but unfortunately Jane would now be choosing what to wear to Lady McTaggart's Christmas luncheon. Her mother and it seemed everyone else in the world had access to a toilet. Everyone except Maddy.

With eyes watering from the strain, Maddy studied the other people's faces. Most of the seven passengers were sleeping until, and it seemed a minor miracle, Maddy heard the driver exclaim, 'Steady up there!' The driver was first down. Maddy was almost trampled in the rush to disembark and head west or north, south or east.

She galloped towards a huge boulder off the road a way, out of sight of everyone else or so she hoped. She hoisted her heavy skirt, downed her bloomers and relief soon followed. Then came exasperation, which turned to concern, which became fright. No wonder her eyes had been watering. She didn't think she'd ever finish. She was splashing her boots, too.

Voices froze her heart.

'Jesus, Sam. You're running a risk. This isn't the mail coach, lad. Hell, it's not even Wednesday.'

An American voice she vaguely remembered from early childhood replied, 'All you folks have a nice Christmas now.'

And everyone returned the greeting.

'Hey up there!'

And Maddy tried to scream but her voice was caught by shock. Her, 'Don't leave me!' came as a little squeak.

When she was finally able to scamper back to the roadway, all she could see was the coach's dust turning to mud in Mitchell's Crossing.

She waited, praying that someone would notice she wasn't on board.

No one did. All they would notice for half an hour was the sudden comfort. There would seem to be more room. And in half an hour, someone would ask, 'Where's that girl? She didn't get off at Warwick, did she?' They would remember, and the driver would be made aware of his oversight and he would, rather cranky now, turn around and go back to Mitchell's Crossing. But Maddy Hannaford wouldn't be there.

Of all people to lose, it had to be the sergeant's daughter.

Sam was taking aim at a fat scrub turkey and just as his finger began to squeeze he heard the low, animal-like moaning that immediately chilled his spine. He lost interest in Christmas dinner. The moan became a wail. Something like an Irish banshee, but not quite.

What the hell's that? he thought.

He soon tracked the noise to its source—a teenage girl sitting squarely in the middle of the narrow, rocky road.

Sam walked his horse down to where she sat, crying. At least that's what he thought she was doing.

'Hey! You okay?' he called loud enough to cover up the noise. A red, puffed, blotched face looked up and instantly recognised him. Sam had never seen anyone move as fast on their behind as this girl was moving. 'Slow down, I'm not gonna hurt you.'

It must have been his year for strays.

Terror flooded her eyes as he dismounted. 'The coach left you behind, huh?' he asked.

She nodded. Face to face with Sam Manning and Maddy was speechless with terror. What if all the lies were true? What if … Sam reached down and pulled her to her feet.

'Stop it, come on, stop the noise.'

After a few heavings and bubblings, she did. Almost.

'You live in town?' he asked. Maddy nodded and couldn't look into his face. 'Okay, you listening?' Maddy did look up this time and wished she hadn't. Sobs began to surface again, big, huge ones. 'There's no coach for another week. It's thirty miles to town.'

Her chin trembled as she choked on another howl. 'But it's Christmas tomorrow, I have to get home.'

'Maybe the coach'll come back, maybe it won't. You can wait here if you want. Your choice.'

'Would you leave me out here on my own?' she asked.

'That's up to you, like I said.' And for the smallest of moments, Sam wondered where he'd seen her before. Familiarity was a faint itch. Unreachable. 'Trouble is, I can't get you to town now, it's too damned late. And if I help you, girl, you better promise to keep your mouth shut. No one knows, right?'

'I promise.' Her voice was a whisper, her legs were turning to jelly. All her daydreams were dissolving. This wasn't how she'd dreamed of being saved by Sam Manning.

'Turn around, girl.'

Maddy obeyed. Sam took a scarf from his pocket and wrapped it around her eyes. Blindfolded, confused, she was helped on to the horse after some ordeal. Once on, she blindly clung to his waist. If she hadn't been so disturbed, she may have enjoyed it. But this was no dream.

This was reality.

Hadn't she imagined something like this ages ago? Maddy clung tighter as the horse moved off. She was dizzy. It was always the way when she couldn't see where she was going.

'What's your name?' he asked.

'Maddy.'

Maddy? Something registered from memory. His voice was cautious and curious. 'Maddy what?'

He felt her entire body stiffen. He repeated his question. Impatient now.

'Maddy Hannaford, sir.'

His heart turned a complete backflip. Finally, Sam said quite calmly, 'It's been a long time, Maddy Hannaford.'

The truth of course. From a thin, gawky kid with red plaits pinned on her head to this full blown young woman.

A Gift from the Gods.

Anna thought she was hallucinating when Sam dismounted and helped his passenger to the ground. She opened her mouth and was silenced with a gesture of his hand. Sam untied the blindfold.

Maddy squinted into the dying sunset. She didn't know where she was and she turned in a wondrous circle before she finally saw Anna standing on the porch, baby in arms.

'Get yourself inside, girl,' Sam ordered.

Maddy took a few tentative steps towards the woman and glanced back at Sam. He was unsaddling the horse, setting it free.

'Go on,' he said, reinforcing the first order.

The woman had caution in her eyes. The baby studied her eagerly. As Maddy drew closer, the child reached out to touch. 'The coach left me behind,' was all she could think of to say.

'Your name?'

'Maddy.'

'Come inside.'

Anna put the baby down. Susan crawled to Maddy, grasped a handful of skirt and heaved herself to her feet. Maddy thought she was wonderful. 'She is a sweet baby, Madam.'

'Please remember to keep the door closed or the baby crawls off outside. Sit down, Maddy.'

Maddy sat down. Susan tried to crawl up into her lap.

'May I hold her?' Maddy asked.

'If you wish. She may bite, be careful.'

'That's all right, Mrs Manning. I've been bitten by worse than a baby.' Maddy picked the infant up.

'I am not Mrs Manning. My name is Anna Hall.'

Can't be, Maddy thought. She's dead. Maddy had a wonderful mind for names and faces, those she cared to remember of course. The baby tried very hard to chew on her nose. 'You can't be Anna Hall. She's dead.'

189

She'd spoken without thinking again. She suddenly wished she had remained quiet. The cold, officious woman bombarded her with questions—how did she know that and more importantly who was she?

Maddy wasn't a convincing liar, not even to herself.

Sam knew it was only a matter of time now. He'd prepared himself for the inevitable yet he still cringed when he saw the approaching thundercloud—Anna. 'I almost had a turkey. Almost.'

'Instead, you brought the sergeant's daughter home.'

'I couldn't leave her out there. It's Christmas.'

Anna ground her teeth in her attempt to remain calm. 'If she doesn't arrive home, he'll think she's been kidnapped and we know whom he shall blame, don't we, Sam!'

Sam smiled and tore the skin from the rabbit. Anna looked away.

'Do you have any idea at all what you've done now?'

'Uh huh,' he grunted.

'She is *his* daughter.'

Sam's smile enlarged. It almost drowned his entire face.

'You honestly expect me to be civil to her?'

'I expect you to trust me, Anna. She's our ticket to freedom.'

'A ticket to more trouble, Sam Manning.'

'You think you can see past tomorrow but you can't.'

'And you can?' Anna asked, not really a question; more like a shaking enraged whisper. A little hiss before the eruption.

'Luke doesn't value much at all except her. Trust me.'

'Trust you! You'll only be satisfied when we're all dead!'

'Of old age, Ma'am.'

She stifled her scream. As she walked off in a huff, Sam wondered how much Maddy remembered. And most of all, how much Maddy knew.

The girl was so whining and persistent that Anna had to relent and let her help. After a little while, her anger receded. It had been hatred at first

190

knowledge and it shouldn't have been. The girl hadn't chosen her parents, nor had she chosen this situation. Being left behind in the middle of rugged bushland would be enough to daunt anyone—Anna knew how she would feel. But she was still faced with one appalling fact—this girl was the sergeant's daughter. Worse, the girl could sense the antagonism if not understand its cause.

'It would be nice to live here where no one would bother you.'

'It's not from choice, Maddy.'

Maddy studied Anna cautiously. 'You really are the lady from Bitter Creek, aren't you?'

'You're surprised?'

'Not really,' Maddy whispered and went back to peeling the potatoes.

'Sam found us and brought us here. He nursed me back to health.'

Maddy didn't voice what she was thinking. The answer to one question would only prompt another forty questions and somehow, Maddy already knew the answers. The truth was not what she was wanting to hear.

Daniel was right all along. Maddy's heart had also spoken the silent truth. 'Sam did not kill anyone, did he.'

'That's right.'

Maddy reached for the second potato and pretended not to watch the woman cuddling her baby. She couldn't remember ever being hugged or told how good she was and there was this tiny child, trying hard to walk now and being encouraged for it. So many smiles. Maddy was both happy and sad. Even when she'd tried her best at school there was no reaction from Mother or Papa, except perhaps a sad expression in her father's eyes when he studied her report card. Was it her fault she wasn't a genius? Or a boy? Mother kept telling her not to worry, it wasn't important for a girl to do well at anything until she became a wife. And then her Mother would regard her rather sadly, too, as if a wife she would never be.

'I suppose you shall be expected home tonight?' Anna asked, breaking the train of thought. Maddy was glad of the interruption.

'I think so.'

'You think so?'

'It depends if Papa received my letter, Mrs Hall.' Maddy washed the skinned potato until it shone and she took up another. Everything the girl did was accomplished with slow deliberate perfection. 'If Papa isn't waiting, perhaps Daniel will be.'

'Daniel?'

191

'Daniel Brannigan, Ma'am. Daniel is all right. He knows Sam isn't responsible for Bitter Creek. He knows Sam is just a nuisance.'

'Is he?' a deep voice said from the doorway. Maddy dropped the potatoes and had to chase them across the floor. The more she tried to regain a semblance of composure the worse she became.

Sam didn't notice a thing except for a clumsy teenage girl. Only Anna had half an inkling of how Maddy was feeling. She'd been through it herself and then she grew to know the man. With Sam, shyness was simply a word.

Sam put the rabbits down and retreated. Anna knew the signs. He was trying to avoid the inevitable for as long as possible. As soon as he left, Maddy calmed. Her face was still bright crimson.

Over one cup of tea, Anna discovered a lot about Maddy Hannaford. She liked to cook and clean and sew. She had a special beau but was too shy to admit who he was. Anna suspected this was Daniel. She also suspected the admiration wasn't reciprocated. And Maddy was adept at turning conversation, too.

'He cannot use his left arm. Is that where he was shot?' she asked.

'You know?'

'Oh yes. Papa and Daniel both wrote and told me. It seems one of the new troopers died. Sam is in trouble again. But I suspect he is used to it by now.'

Anna told her to find Sam and tell him what she knew. Maddy didn't question. Outside in the encroaching darkness, she began calling for 'Mr Manning!'

Sam stood behind her for some time before she realised he was there. She squealed in fright again and Sam wondered why she was so nervous. 'Mrs Hall said I had to come and tell you straight away.'

'Tell me what?'

'About the new trooper.'

'Who?'

'Daniel said you shot him.'

'Shot who? Daniel?'

'No, no. The new trooper. Do you know Daniel?' Maddy asked.

'Sort of, yeah. Is he dead?'

'Daniel's fine, Mr Manning. At least, I hope he is.'

'Not Daniel! The trooper!'

192

Tears filled her eyes because he'd yelled. Instantly apologetic, Sam touched her arm. 'Just tell me what you know, Maddy.'

'You shot the trooper while you were escaping. Everyone saw you do it.'

There was silence for a little while. Sam walked back to where he'd been pegging out his rabbit skins. Maddy followed him.

'When can you take me home, Mr Manning?'

'I don't think I can now, Maddy.'

'But you said...'

'I know what I said.'

'You promised!'

'Look, I'm sorry, I really am, but you're gonna have to stay here for a while.'

'But I can't stay here! I have to be home for Christmas. I have to tell Papa...'

Words failed very quickly.

Suspicion arose.

'Tell him what?'

More tears formed now but Sam was unmoved. For all he knew this could have been another trap. But no, he hadn't been followed. Not even Luke would plant his own kid like that. Or would he?

'Tell him what!' he yelled, shaking Maddy hard enough to rattle her teeth.

'That Mother's not coming back!" she wailed. 'That she doesn't want me, that she sent me home to Papa but he doesn't want me either because if he did, he wouldn't have sent me away in the first place!'

Sam let her go. He watched her run off, howling.

And his idea of a trade off slowly crumbled.

She had to be coaxed to the table to eat. Once seated, Sam thought he understood Luke's need to steal—maybe he couldn't afford to feed his daughter. The joke was so bad Sam had to smile in spite of himself. 'I want to go home,' she said, sniffling. Sam looked at Anna and wondered when she would start, too, but she stayed quiet.

'I want to go *home*,' the girl repeated in case he hadn't heard.

'I need you here, Maddy.'

193

Anna's eyes flickered to Sam, caught his gaze for an eternal moment and released when she heard the teenager say:

'I don't think Papa would appreciate it if I helped you hold up the mail coach.'

Sam let it ride. 'I didn't kill them miners,' he said.

'Those miners,' Anna corrected.

'I know that, Mr Manning and so does the whole town.'

'But I know who did kill them.'

'Sam, don't you dare!'

Sam glanced at Anna.

'It's all right, Mrs Hall. I can tell Papa who is responsible.'

'You won't have to, girl. I'll tell him when he comes looking for you.'

Silence fell. Maddy glanced at Anna for a hint of understanding but nothing came. The woman continued pushing her food around her plate. She would look at no one now.

'Your old man'll shoot me the minute he sees me, girl. If you're with me, he won't.'

Anna saw it in her mind. How could the sergeant shoot if Sam was holding the girl as a shield? Gun at her head, too, no doubt.

'But Mr Manning, Papa hates you so much, he'd shoot you no matter who was with you. But if you took me home, I could tell Sub-inspector Flannagan who is responsible and I promise I won't say how I found out. Or I could tell Daniel. Daniel keeps secrets perhaps better than anyone else I know.'

'Tell her, Anna.'

Anna glanced up. She was feeling ill. Very ill. 'Tell her what?'

'Who raped you and shot you.'

'You're insane,' she said quietly, trying not to look at Maddy. She felt the sudden grip on her forearm. Anna looked up into Sam's bright eyes and was frightened of what she saw there.

'Tell her, dammit, or I will!'

The threat brought on tears.

Maddy was watching the display calmly. Confusion helped. She had no idea what was going on.

'Tell her.'

'I can't. I can't!'

194

Sam let go of Anna's arm and turned to Maddy. 'Your father was responsible for Bitter Creek, girl.'

Maddy sat there like a fish suddenly beached. Gasping.

He continued: 'Anna here is the only person who can prove it. Why else would they say she's buried at Bitter Creek?'

And all Maddy could say, eyes suddenly brimming, 'Please take me home?'

Sam shook his head.

A supercilious pride shone within the tears. 'Then I shall find my own way home.' The girl rose unsteadily, fright pushing more tears down her face. 'I shall say nothing to anyone. I shall forget this has ever happened and...'

'Sit down.'

'No.'

Defiant eyes met his.

'I said, sit down!'

'No!' she yelled in return. 'How dare you say such a thing about my father! It's lies you hear me! Lies! How dare you! You used to be his friend! Do you think I can't remember you? Well I can! I remember you and your wife who was always drunk, and all this is lies!'

She tossed her chair as if it were made from a sack of feathers. She rushed for the door. Anna screamed at Sam to let her go. He ignored her. Sam was on his feet, picking up his knife, throwing it before Maddy had time to pull the door open. Maddy froze. The blade was a quarter inch from her head. She started to shake.

'She won't believe me so you tell her, Anna. You show her.'

'Let her go, Sam.'

'No way. Luke sent me to hang once and by Christ, if she walks out that door I'll give him something to hang me for!'

'You're insane!' Anna screamed and hit out at him.

Maddy bolted. She made it to the porch before the hand slapped on her shoulder. It was reflex. She brought all her immense strength into giving him a good elbow in the stomach. She heard the breath expire, heard him fall to his knees.

The darkness was hers.

195

He waited patiently on the verandah of the station in the cool, drowsy breeze. His watch said six forty-five. An hour ago, or so it felt, it was six-forty. The cook at the pub was keeping a plate warm for Maddy. He even planned to let her enjoy a glass of red wine as well. He'd missed her quiet unassuming presence about the place. Most of all, he missed her quiet goodnights, good mornings and her never-ending, "Is there anything I can do, Papa?"

The place was like a morgue and had been for the weeks she'd been away.

Six-fifty now. Still no sign of the coach.

'Brannigan?'

Daniel duly appeared, fighting to roll a cigarette. He'd recently taken up smoking and still hadn't acquired the art.

'Are you sure she said today?'

'Yes sir. Maybe the wheel fell off again.'

Hannaford grunted in affirmation.

'Or maybe Manning's decided to branch out into kidnapping as well as murder.'

Luke threw him a cold glance. 'Have you been drinking again?'

'No,' Daniel said. He didn't bother with sir lately. It seemed a waste of breath. A little relieved though, Daniel watched the coach appear. His relief was short lived. His quip of a moment before, born of exasperation and what little humour he had left inside proved … well, he hoped it wasn't true.

It felt odd, though, the sergeant's only daughter going missing minutes after a Manning appearance—to wish them all a Merry Christmas for Christ's sakes. It certainly sounded like Sam.

'But how in God's name could you leave my daughter behind!'

Daniel waited for someone to have the guts to answer.

'We went back, Sarge, but she wasn't there. All of us searched for an hour or more. There wasn't a sign. I'm sorry.'

'You're sorry! Is that all you can say?'

Daniel finally lit his cigarette. You're not sorry yet, mate, he thought. You'd better start looking for a new job. I can guarantee you won't find one in this town now.

196

'Maddy!'

Her heart beat so fast it hurt. She used to like playing hide and seek, she used to enjoy the thrill of the chase and being chased, the adrenalin surge, getting caught. But this was not a game. He'd thrown a knife at her. He was out there now, extremely angry, wanting blood. Her blood. She knew it.

'I don't want to hurt you, Maddy!'

A lie. Of course he did. Everyone wanted to hurt her. Everyone. Mother, Papa, Daniel. Everyone. 'Leave me alone!' she yelled, only then realising she'd led him to her hiding place and it was too late and too dark to find somewhere else.

Footsteps now.

'How the hell did you get in there?' came the question. She was no wilting flower—more like a field of barley in full head and she was crammed into a tiny niche between two granite rocks. 'Come on out, girl. Enough of this. Running away isn't gonna help anyone.'

Maddy refused to budge. She was so squashed she could barely sniff.

'Look, I never said you wouldn't get home. It's just a matter of when. I need your help, Maddy. I need you to cooperate.' Sam crouched. Maddy huddled into a smaller knot. 'All right. I'm sorry if I scared you. Don't do it for me. Do it for Anna. Do it for the baby. Hell, it's the baby I'm thinking of here, you know. Not me. What sort of chance has the kid got if you and me don't help it out just a little?'

'But how?' she sniffed. 'What can I do?'

'I only want to make a swap. That's all.'

'You're going to exchange me for … for what?'

'Anna's freedom. Maybe some justice.'

'But what if I don't want to help you? What if I want to stay right here for the rest of my life? What if I don't want to go back there?'

'One minute you do, next you don't. Look, I'm giving you a choice here. It's up to you whether it'll be easy or hard. Now come on out and stop this bullshit. You weren't stupid when you were little so don't act stupid now.'

After a pause, he offered his hand and she accepted it. He pulled her out.

'Can you write?' he asked as they walked back to the hut.

'Of course I can write,' Maddy snapped.

'Good. You're gonna write to your father. You're gonna write what I tell you to write. No questions, just do it.'

197

Maddy obeyed.

Sam put the letter into his pocket and rode off into the night, alone, armed.

'Papa won't come alone,' Maddy whispered into the darkness.

'Sam knows he won't,' Anna replied, voice sounding as numb as she felt.

'If Papa comes at all. I don't think he loves me enough, Mrs Hall.' The voice was shaking, despairing, confused. Anna didn't know what to say, perhaps nothing was needed. Anna rolled over and took the girl's hand. After a while, Maddy said quietly, 'I know what you've said about my papa is the truth. But no matter what he's done or what he is, I still love him. But there are times when I hate him, too, and sometimes he's nothing more than a stranger. But he's my papa.'

The stillness was loud. Outside a multitude of crickets played a symphony of sound.

'I once saw him kick a man until he confessed to whatever it was he was supposed to have done. I was six years old then and even when I was six, I understood why people hated me. It was because of him. But I still love him. It makes no sense, Mrs Hall.'

'Yes it does, Maddy. It does to me.'

'Do you believe Sam when he said he was doing this for you?'

'Yes.'

'He wouldn't deliberately hurt me, would he?'

'No, of course not,' Anna said.

Daniel was awake on the hour every hour until two am when he finally gave up the idea of trying to sleep and opened his window wide. He sat by the billowing curtain and stared out at the darkness. It's Christmas, he thought.

On the chest by the bed was his present for Maddy—a neatly wrapped box of lace hankies. He'd bought them after her last letter in which she'd written, *I'm sure you shall find your present very useful.* He thought he'd better get a present for her in return.

Her luggage had arrived intact. The present already wrapped and labelled with his name had been thrown to him. Here, the sergeant had said before he rode off to Christ knew where this time. And now the long thin box lay on his dresser, unopened. It was probably an engraved pen.

Yes, it would be useful. Useful for writing reports and signing papers when he was left in charge of the station. Like now for instance. Even though Inspector Flannagan was back in town, he was still off duty. Trouble had loomed once Mrs Flannagan discovered her missing bathtub.

Now Maddy had disappeared.

Oh, what a lovely Christmas this would be.

Daniel reached for his tobacco and took some between his fingers. His concentration was diverted by the sound of a horse on Burns Street. It was interrupting the pin drop quiet. Daniel looked out of the window.

A grey.

Manning.

Shit, Manning! Daniel dropped the tobacco and swooped on his pants. He was still limping into them as he tried to run barefooted into the street. By then he'd lost sight of the rider. Dogs barked at the unexpected presence in the early morning darkness.

Daniel rounded the corner in time to see Manning get off his horse and slip something under the station door.

He was seen.

The bushranger literally jumped on to his horse. Daniel started to run. No! he wanted to scream. Come back, we need to talk!

But silence fell again, as thick and as complete as before. If it hadn't been for the rivulets of sweat tickling his back and icing in the breeze, Daniel would have sworn it was all a dream.

He returned to his house for the station keys and opened up. He tore the letter open; the letter addressed to "Papa". The power of authority swelled for a few seconds. Daniel opened it. 'Spencer's Brook on the 26th?' he whispered to himself. For a moment he wished it was all a dream because he found himself, half naked at three am on Christmas day, knocking on Inspector Flannagan's door.

'Daniel? Is that you?' Mrs Flannagan asked, bleary eyed, rather stunned.

'It's about Maddy Hannaford's disappearance, Ma'am.'

His Ma'am sounded a lot like Mum.

'Come in, boy, no one's about to bite you. It's Christmas.'

So even Mrs Flannagan didn't give a pig's fart about Maddy. Daniel felt anger rising and it rose even more when the Inspector appeared, half asleep and cranky. Daniel wondered what his problem was, at least he could sleep. Before he was castigated for being out of uniform (or was it not quite in?) Daniel thrust the message in Maddy's neat writing under Flannagan's nose. 'It's been delivered by Manning himself, sir.'

'And you didn't try to apprehend him?'

'I'd like to remain breathing, Inspector. I'd like to talk to you, Sir. About Bitter Creek.'

Flannagan sighed and turned to his wife. 'Make us some tea, Florrie.'

Daniel was urged to sit and he did but he wasn't sure where to begin. 'Sir, how many times has Ryan's supply wagon made the trip to Bitter Creek diggings and returned with up to a thousand ounces of gold?'

'What are you getting at?'

'The accusation that Manning is the perpetrator of the Bitter Creek massacre, Sir. It's not right. I know it's not. If he wanted gold, he'd have taken it long ago. Granted, he led me to the diggings. How else could he report it? More to the point, Sir, I counted fourteen bodies and there was no woman or child amongst them.'

'And?' the Inspector asked patiently.

'You've read the report of Smith-Johnson's death, sir?'

There was a nod in reply. Mrs Flannagan brought the tea out and she lingered until she was told nicely to go back to bed.

'It wasn't Manning's bullets which killed Dennis. It was Porter's. I've been over it in my mind a hundred times. Manning fired one shot. It was wide and blind.'

'You tell me this now?'

'I'd not be believed by Sergeant Hannaford, Sir. There's something else I've kept to myself in the hope some kind of justice would prevail.'

'Get on with it.'

'When Manning was shot a letter dropped from his pocket. I recovered it. I told no one. I read it that night.'

'Ah. Now I see.'

'Sir?'

'It was addressed to the Commissioner and written by Anna Hall, was it not?'

'You know, sir?'

Flannagan smiled. 'And just where did Hannaford say he was going when he rode out this evening?'

'He rode out yesterday, when Maddy didn't arrive, sir. And he didn't say where he was going.'

'Show him this, Daniel. You know nothing you understand? If, and I stress, if, he disappears again, I want you to follow him. I also want you at Spencer's Brook on the 26th.'

'Yes sir.'

Daniel took a tentative sip of the sweet tea and from peripheral vision he caught the movement as a shadow appeared in the doorway. A man coughed, loosely.

'Brannigan, this is Lieutenant Barton from the Commissioner's office.'

Daniel was on his feet quickly. Hot tea spilled on his bare chest.

'It was you who forwarded the letter, Constable?'

'Yes, Lieutenant.'

'Good lad. Keep in mind I want Manning alive, son,' the pyjama clad Lieutenant mumbled.

Sam chewed on some grass to alleviate the boredom as he gazed down at the old miner's hut a stone's throw from the deserted silver mine at Spencer's Brook.

He had planned on going down to see what else he could find in Luke's stash, knowing of course that Anna had probably been right all along. Her gold was there. All the gold from Bitter Creek was there. Including Tom's. Sam supposed that was rightfully his, now.

Luke was there too.

Maddy hadn't shown. He'd panicked. He was probably in there now, taking inventory, seeing how much Sam had stolen. From one thief to another. A vicious circle.

As dawn closed in, Sam felt that yes, here seemed a place as good as any to die. No matter how hard he tried, he couldn't see past tomorrow. He wasn't necessarily scared of dying—hell no, he'd started dying the moment he'd found Elizabeth dead all those years ago. He'd started to die long before he was dragged into the courtroom. Luke had got what he wanted back then.

A simple matter your honour. The deceased could not have used this weapon to suicide.

Luke came out of the miner's hut with a heavy satchel over his shoulder. Sam watched him get on his horse and ride away.

Whatever he was carrying was not heavy enough to be a sack of gold. That much he knew.

Sam made his way carefully to the hut. Last thing he needed to do was fall into one of the open shafts—some of them were a thousand feet deep.

Something had been burnt in the fireplace. It wasn't recent, the ashes were cold. Sam guessed the papers had been a stack of mining rights and licences. It was futile to determine what had been reduced to ash, nothing useful or recognizable remained.

Doubts rose. Maybe this wouldn't work. Maybe it was lunatic. Crazy. Maybe Anna was right. Maybe I am insane, he thought. He pulled up the floorboards anyway and climbed down into the deep, dark, stinking abyss.

Match struck boot. The sulphur smelled fragrant compared to this tomb of riches. He was nearly as familiar with Luke's stash as he was with his own.

Sam opened a heavy metal chest he hadn't noticed on his last visit six months before. Inside lay what everyone had died for.

Gold.

And some of it was Anna's.

Chapter Fourteen

DANIEL WATCHED AND KNEW WHY he was a Constable and Flannagan was a Sub-Inspector. There were no such things as hunches now—it was simply a case of twenty years more experience with human nature, such as it was. Twenty years of learning which Daniel was trying to digest in a few weeks.

As he lay on his gut trying to blend in with the bush, the truth rolled over him in clear concise waves. He felt no elation that his intuitive feelings were proven correct. He felt nothing really. He simply wondered what lunacy prompted his decision to leave farming for this: a uniform that didn't fit, a few shillings in his pocket each month and living amid the antagonism that being a trooper seemed to generate.

You're mad, Daniel, Rose had once told him. You're mad. It's the worst criminal who wears a uniform.

He hadn't believed her then but he always was a gullible lad. For some idiotic reason, Daniel had always thought there was an ounce of good in everyone.

Ha.

Flannagan and Barton had been right in their predictions. Hannaford would most likely (Daniel liked that, most likely; it was always so safe) enlist his coloured friends once more for the confrontation at Spencer's Brook. And of course when the sergeant and his small troupe duly arrived at the appointed place and time, why, there'd be nothing but slaughter to meet their eyes yet again. His daughter though, by some miracle of God, would be left unharmed.

It had sounded wild and unlikely to Daniel but what did make sense at three in the morning when a mind is ajar and imagination runs rampant like a room full of teacherless school children?

It made awful sense now.

If only he knew where in Girraween Manning was living.

He took his attention back to the scene below.

The aboriginal camp consisted of a handful of semi-naked children of varying shades from full-blooded pitch to a pale bronze. Some of the women wore traces of European clothing, some wore nothing. Breasts like razor straps. Bellies huge. Legs thin. All were barefooted. Old men in stringy bark lap laps sat smoking European tobacco in the shade of fragile looking gunyahs.

The younger men sat apart, ignoring the noise of the children, deep in conversation with Lucas Hannaford. Daniel wondered what had been in the satchel until the bottles were withdrawn and a few opened. He watched for well over an hour.

This was where Billy had been recruited of course, from this slither of a meandering tribe. Now that Billy was dead, who would be next to don the uniform?

Of course Billy was dead. He wasn't here. His walkabouts never lasted this long.

So the elders had been right. An educated guess or two unfolded like a Gypsy's prophecy.

Daniel looked ahead into his mind's eye and imagined his own prophecy—Spencer's Brook would be yet another Bitter Creek.

Or was his mind's door opening too far again?

A tired Sam returned to an empty house. 'Anna?' he called without the inflection of urgency in his voice, urgency he certainly felt. 'Anna?' No reply. It was unlike her not to be waiting with a smile of welcome. Not that she had a lot to smile about lately. Who did?

He left the horse saddled and went inside. The place looked cleaner than usual. Apart from that nothing had changed. Suzie's cot was still there. Empty. The kid's clothes were in the chest where they usually were.

Well, she hadn't left home. Something was simmering in a pot. Whatever it was smelled good. They'd probably taken a walk. Anna was always getting bored and taking walks, making him go, too when all he wanted was to sleep.

Sam checked under the bed. Sure enough the easel was gone. So she's drawing hats again, dresses to match too probably. Typical of Anna. We could all be dead tomorrow and she's drawing hats.

Sam uncapped his whiskey bottle, took three wholesome gulps and felt the liquid burn a trail to his toes. He walked off in search.

He was tired and hungry but eating alone and sleeping alone now seemed as alien to him as having permanent company would have felt three months ago. But it had to end. Better now than never.

'It's wonderful!'

'You're not just saying that, Maddy?'

'No, it's beautiful. My mother would wear that to a garden party. She would *love* it.'

'And you?'

Maddy shifted the baby to her other knee. 'Perhaps if these rose-buds here were small feathers? Could you not have removable ornaments? That way one hat could serve many occasions.'

'Would it be hard to make?' Anna asked.

'I don't think so. The design is simple enough…'

Sam listened to the chatter and part of him was elated. He stood back and waited to be noticed.

'Sam! Where on earth have you been?'

'Away.'

Anna was trying to be angry and it wasn't quite working.

'How are you doing, Maddy?' he asked.

'Fine, sir.'

'You helpin' her make em, now are you? Looks like you got yourself a job, girl.'

Maddy didn't know what he was referring to. A full time job minding the baby? Susan began talking, 'Dad, dad, dad' and holding her arms out to Sam. It always made him feel both special and uncomfortable when she did that. He relented and swung her upside down.

'I'm starving. What's cooking?'

'Christmas dinner. You shall have to wait now.'

'Perhaps I can get you a snack?' Maddy offered.

'Thanks.'

When Maddy was out of earshot:

'Where did you go?'

'For a ride.'

Anna resumed her drawing. 'You delivered the ransom note.'

'It's not a ransom note.'

'It may as well be. What if you'd been caught? Captured? Perhaps shot again? What if you'd been killed Sam?'

'I'm here, ain't I?'

'That's not the point. I don't know where I am or even where the nearest civilization is. I know nothing because you won't tell me.'

'You never asked me before. Maybe I have reasons not to say.'

'Like bringing that poor girl in blindfolded? What if Susan takes ill? I wouldn't know how to get to Alice's let alone to a town…'

'Just follow the creek south for ten miles.'

'Now you tell me?'

'Well, you asked.'

He was exasperating to say the least. 'Why couldn't you have left things well enough alone? Why involve that innocent girl in this?'

'It has to be resolved.'

'I don't want it resolved! I want things to be as they were. Just you and me and Susan.'

'Maybe I don't.'

Shock froze any more words.

'Maybe I don't want you here any more.'

'But you don't mean that.'

'Just keep drawing your hats, Ma'am.'

'I thought you loved me!'

'Makes no difference if I do or I don't. You don't belong here.'

'I belong with *you*, Sam.'

It took the best part of what courage he had left to push the baby to its mother. 'You don't belong with me. You belong with Suzie. Suzie and that hat shop you're gonna have someday soon,' he said. 'But you don't belong with me. You never did.'

'You said you loved me! You *made* love to me!'

He couldn't look into her eyes. 'So? You're not the first, you won't be the last. I always lie when I want something. You know that.'

'I don't believe you, Sam.'

'Tomorrow you're outa here. That's all that matters.' He walked away.

Maddy could always sense when she wasn't wanted. After so many years, disappearing on cue seemed to come naturally. It was a simple matter to get Mr Manning something to eat. All he had to do was come in, sit down and tuck in. His food awaited. But it was taking so long … perhaps they'd had no time together lately. It wasn't that she felt unwanted here, just uncomfortable at times, as if she was always in the way.

206

Who would believe she'd spent Christmas day, 1867 with a bushranger? What proof would there be except memories? How could anyone prove a memory?

Christmas. No presents. No turkey.

She wondered if Daniel was worrying about her. They would all know by now, of course. Her luggage would have arrived. Perhaps her father had found the presents she'd already wrapped? Would Daniel have opened his or would he be waiting until he saw her again?

There would be no sixpences in the Christmas pudding this year because she hadn't been home to make it.

Do you miss me, Papa? she wondered. The thought faded when she saw Sam coming.

There had never been a Christmas dinner as quiet or meaningless. No one spoke except Maddy and the baby. Anna was incredibly sad. Maddy supposed she would be, too, in her position. Tomorrow she'd have her freedom. Not Sam though. Freedom he could never have. Perhaps that was why he looked so lost and drank so much whiskey?

'I was nearly killed by a threepence last Christmas,' Maddy said.

Two faces peered at her.

'It is true. I choked on Christmas pudding. Daniel hit me and saved my life.'

A smile almost creased Anna's face.

'Is she supposed to be walking?' Maddy asked.

Susan took three tentative steps towards Sam and collapsed on her behind. She sat on the bare floor, chewed on her fist, dribbled and grinned at him.

Dad-dad-dad-dad

'Can't she say anything else?'

And in the blink of an eye, he was gone.

Lucas kicked the bedcovers off and stared at the fading flowers on the wallpaper. Moonlight rendered them colourless smudges, akin to how he was feeling.

Where were the subtle lies for grieving parents now?

What was left to cling to that would help him believe Maddy would remain unharmed? Nothing but silence and emptiness was left now. Unopened gifts on a dusty dining room table. No one to nag him about a tree to decorate. No wife to complain about pine needles dropping on her floor, no daughter to clean up the messes.

One more month; four more weeks and they would all have been in Sydney. Jane would have had anything she wanted. A finishing school for Maddy.

Now there was no more Jane. He had known she wasn't coming back when she'd said goodbye. And Maddy ...

The three am breeze billowed dusty curtains. Echoes of a drunk's shout drifted in.

Merry Christmas.

Archibald was at it again.

Daniel had no sooner opened the door when Eli Wallis stormed in, fuming. Someone had pinched his prized gander. A wayward goose began a fateful day.

Daniel stepped into Eli's backyard and was instantly bitten by a brown dog. All that remained of the gander was a head, some feathers and two feet. The guts was discovered in Noggy Burn's vegetable patch but of course, Noggy hadn't known anything about a missing goose.

Eli threatened to fix them all and kicked the dog, which was, for Daniel at least, the only enjoyable part of the morning.

The sarge made three trips to the outhouse in half an hour.

'Too much of your own cooking?' Daniel had inquired, his quip falling on deaf ears.

'Be ready to ride at ten, boy,' came the order as the door closed yet again.

Two hours to Spencer's Brook. Arriving on time for once, Daniel

208

thought. But there was an hour to wait, so he took off his boot and inspected the bleeding dog bite on his right calf.

Anna was riding Aggie, the Newberry's old galloper. Maddy clung tight to Sam for the first few miles across the mountains. Only when his legs began to object did he stop for a rest. The women were obviously relieved. Two miles west of Spencer's Brook he eased off his horse and helped Maddy to the ground.

Sam could have sworn the gray mare sighed with relief. He watered her in the shallow creek and looked back. The girls had been on horseback for two and a half hours and there they were, sitting on a log. The baby was crawling off or trying to. Anna had a tight grip on the baby's pants.

'Make the most of it. We won't be here long,' Sam said and walked downstream for a moment of light relief.

'Has he gone?' Maddy asked.

'Yes. Be quick about it. I have to go, too.'

Maddy exited for the nearest tree and listened for the tell tale rustle of goanna or snake. Already today she'd seen two of each. Daniel often said that if you saw a black snake it was a sign of impending rain. Perhaps it's going to flood, Maddy thought as she relieved herself.

But instead of rustles in the grass, she heard voices. Strange voices. Was there no privacy anywhere? Without too much noise, she finished and ran off as quietly as she could to where she'd last seen Sam. He was bent over at the edge of the creek, using cupped hands to drink. 'Mr Manning, I heard people's voices. That way.'

Sam straightened and his gaze followed her pointing hand.

'Men's voices. I couldn't understand the words but they sounded like aboriginals.'

Sam's intense blue eyes fired. 'Show me,' he said, grabbing her arm and hurrying her along the steep grassy slope. At the top he pushed her down. Maddy could see no sign of movement at all, anywhere. 'How many?'

'Two, perhaps three.'

They both heard the movement from below. It was Anna, baby in arms. 'Sam quickly. We have company.'

He grabbed Maddy again and pushed her down the hill. 'Keep that kid quiet,' he said and withdrew his rifle from the gray's saddle. He threw the weapon to Maddy. 'You know how to use this?'

'Yes sir. Papa taught me when I was—'

'Great. Stay here and stay quiet. You see anything you shoot to kill, girl. Just make sure it ain't me.'

He darted off into the bush and as he did he was checking the load in his pistol.

He knew where they were heading. He'd half expected it.

Sam lay on his gut in the grass and waited. Wouldn't be long now.

When the two blacks were finally in sight, he noted they were on foot, armed and making their way along the donkey trail that led to the old mine. He could almost hear them laughing. Probably had orders to kill everyone except Maddy. It'd look good on a report. Sam could even see the written words on the paper: *On arrival at Spencer's Brook ...*

And a shrill girlish scream scared him back to the present.

'You black bastard, get away from him!'

Sam spun.

A young half caste stood not ten feet away, spear raised. In a quick, all-encompassing moment, Sam saw the bright, victorious smile and he heard the crack from the repeater. The youth fell one way, his spear the other.

Maddy was galloping up the hill towards him, the rifle across her body like some professional soldier mid battle. Sam was on his feet, grabbing for the weapon and tackling her to the ground.

'Where's Anna?'

Before Maddy could answer, Anna flashed by on old Aggie. One arm was tight around her baby as down the slope she cantered, across the clearing and into the waiting cover of the thicket.

Sam didn't have time to curse at her. He barely had time to think. Was she drawing them out into the open? One appeared; too far away for the rifle to be deadly accurate. Sam had no choice. The aborigine fell after two shots.

'Come on, let me see you. Where are you ... come on, show me your face.' But there was no movement at all.

Maddy screamed again. The third was almost on top of her. It was reflex action on Sam's part. The third's stomach exploded and Maddy was hit by the full force. Her screams split Sam's eardrums. 'Get him off me! Get him off me!'

210

It took a couple of minutes to calm the girl down and when the noise died, the only sounds were a baby's cries, far off. Distant.

When she saw him coming, she cringed. Anna held the baby a little tighter as Sam slid from his horse. He was shaking with rage. Poor Maddy, covered in blood, was sobbing, dazed.

'You're trying to kill yourself,' he said quite calmly. 'You're trying to kill yourself and you want to take her with you.'

'I took them by surprise! I drew them away from you both and it worked!'

'I told you to stay put!'

'You told me nothing!'

'Stop fighting and tell me what's happening!' Maddy wailed.

Sam glanced back at Maddy and tore the old horse's reins from its tether. He thrust them at Anna. 'Get your fat ass on this horse and follow me. Do as I say for once. Think you can manage that?'

His anger was intimidating. Anna obeyed.

Sam heaved Maddy into place behind him. 'I owe you two, girl.'

'You owe me?'

'You saved my life. Twice. Not bad for one day.'

'That's all right, Mr Manning. I don't mind.'

'Just don't tell your father.'

'Watch your feet. Some of these shafts go all the way to hell and back.'

On foot now, Maddy crept her way up the barren slope towards the abandoned mine. She had heard about Spencer's Brook silver mine but had never seen it or the smelter the Chinese had built. It now stood as a red brick ruin, guarded by jumper ants.

Sam led the way through the warren of uncovered, dangerous shafts. Some were big enough to lose a horse in.

There was no one here of course, it was too early. The less questions Maddy asked the less lies she'd be told. She felt it was better to know little and endure—in a few hours, it would all be over.

The shelter—she wouldn't have called it a house—was built of wood and bricks most likely stolen from the chimney stack of the disused smelter. And once it had a roof. Now it resembled a skeleton—the whole place some old, tired graveyard. It was quiet, eerie. It would have been

211

lifeless were it not for the ants. 'Don't stand still too long,' Sam had warned.

'Who lived here?' she asked.

'Guy called Spencer, I guess.'

Maddy fell quiet. She wondered if she'd been talking too much. She had one question which wouldn't remain idle for long.

'What will happen now, Mr Manning?'

'Your old man'll ride in and expect everyone to be dead. Except for you. I'd bet my life on it.'

'The greatest gamble of all,' Anna said quietly.

'Don't you start on gambling. What you did was the stupidest thing I've ever saw.'

Sam tied the horses and unpacked the two sacks containing Anna's things.

'Is my gold here?' Anna asked.

'Under your feet.'

And even Maddy looked down at the rotting floorboards.

'There's a shaft directly below us.'

'How much gold was stolen, Mrs Hall?'

'We had forty-three ounces, Maddy.'

'Why then, you are rich!'

'Am I?' Anna whispered and rummaged in one of the sacks for a jar of milk. 'Show her, Sam. If this lunatic idea of yours works, the authorities will have to know and who better to inform them than the sergeant's daughter?'

'Please, Mrs Hall. This isn't my fault.'

'Nor is it mine!'And Anna burst into a fit of uncontrollable weeping.

Sam left her crying. Going to her now would be futile. It would void the apathy he'd succeeded in building over the past two days. He heaved up the floorboards exposing the black, smelly hole and he grabbed Maddy's hand.

Anna watched through her blinding tears as they disappeared into the shaft.

'Pooh, it stinks. It's like a grave.'

The shaft was illuminated by the strike of a match. The flame flickered and almost went out. Maddy could barely breathe. Hand over mouth and nose didn't help but the smell was unbearable.

212

Dank, stuffy. Dark. A tomb. Then she saw the treasures Sam displayed. Something hard and heavy was pressed into her hand. 'Here.'

'It's a nugget of gold.'

'It's from Bitter Creek. I know it's hard, girl, but I need you to tell Daniel about this. He'll know what to do. I want you to show him.'

Until now it had all been words: accusations, insinuations. But she loved her father and in the darkness she could see the bushranger's eyes. For a fleeting moment she felt that perhaps Sam had loved him, too, a long time ago. Her memories were faint, but they reeked of a friendship of long ago.

Sam's hand closed over hers. 'This nugget belonged to an Irishman called O'Leary. I was there the day he found it. I got drunk with him. Feel it? Look at it, Maddy. It even looks like Ireland.'

Sam watched her eyes fill with tears as she studied it and nodded in agreement. She repeated 'Ireland' in a whisper.

'God knows what it's worth but this chest here's half full of gold. It's enough to make a man kill.'

'But Papa–'

'Maddy, I never wanted this either but I'm not going to hang for something I didn't do. Forty-three ounces of this gold belongs to Anna. Tell Daniel, girl. I'm trusting you, Maddy. I need you to trust me.'

Maddy dropped the nugget back into the chest and Sam touched her face.

'Do you trust me?'

Forgive me, Papa, she thought. 'Yes. I trust you.'

'It might get rough.'

'I know.'

Sam held her longer than he should have. 'Do something for me when all this is over, girl.'

'If I can, sir.'

'Tell Anna I love her.'

Maddy pulled away and fumbled in the dark for the ladder. She began to climb. 'You should say that yourself, Mr Manning, before it's too late. You may never have the chance again.'

But he didn't tell her because he couldn't. He simply watched her as she held her sleeping baby and he remembered her face, hidden under that hat; how she looked up and a mixture of fright and interest flashed into her eyes. She caught him off guard that day.

He'd loved her then, and he loved her now.

But he couldn't have her then and he couldn't have her now. He'd turned away from too much in his life that running away was now habitual. So he'd leave her with a few months of memories and what had been hers all along, a dream he hoped against hope she'd realise, more sooner than later.

'Annabelle's Millinery,' he said, loud enough for her to hear. Anna glanced up at him, hated what she saw in his eyes and turned away.

'I hate waiting,' Maddy said quietly.

Chapter Fifteen

WITH NO EXPECTATIONS THERE CAN be no disappointments. The sergeant's expectations mirrored the disbelief in his eyes.

Surprised they're alive are you, sarge? Daniel wanted to ask. He remained quiet and wished he wasn't so bloody alone.

'There's shafts everywhere, boy. Watch your step.'

Been here before have you, sarge? he wanted to ask again. Keep it friendly, there'll be no suspicion, he thought. However, being swallowed whole by a shaft seemed more welcoming than this. Daniel wondered if he'd get a bullet in the back, by mistake. Caught in cross fire perhaps? Quartz glittered in the blinding sun.

Shoot on sight.

Yes, sir.

Daniel's stomach rolled over and played dead. He was limping now from that dog bite. His whole leg was paining. Where are you, Inspector? Lieutenant? Porter … they weren't in the vicinity. Barton's ceaseless coughing wasn't heard.

'Here, you go first.'

Gone the resolution to stay behind at all costs. He's going to use me as a shield. Daniel cringed from the forceful yell that seemed to decalcify his entire spine.

'Where's my daughter, Manning!'

The call echoed about the hills.

'Doesn't look like anyone's here,' Daniel weakly offered, trying to fight the instinctive urge to jump on his horse and gallop off, shafts or not. Fear rose.

It was too quiet. Too still.

'I know you're in there, Manning!'

Daniel winced and watched from thirty feet away as two figures appeared in the doorway of the old shack.

'Shoot him,' the sergeant mumbled.

Daniel swallowed his heart. 'I can't. I'll hit Maddy. She's covered in blood.'

215

There was silence for a little while. What looked to be an affectionate embrace was marred by the pistol at Maddy's head.

'Now what, Sarge?' Daniel asked, his voice no more than a squeak. His scalp was crawling. He wished his superior wouldn't hide behind him.

'Get rid of the weaponry, Luke. All of it, down the hole, then we talk. You hear me?'

'Do as he says,' Hannaford said calmly.

'Daniel!' Sam called.

Daniel looked to the bushranger. He knows who I am?

'Down the hole, boy.'

Daniel glanced at the sergeant for confirmation. It came in a fierce nod. Daniel gathered the two rifles, the pistols. Manning called to him again.

'Daniel!'

'What!'

'You interested in stolen goods?'

'Let Miss Hannaford go and then we will talk!'

'Nice try, kid,' was all Sam said, amused.

Daniel threw the guns down the shaft. He listened for six seconds before the final, far-off crash was heard. He stepped away from the hole before it reached out to take him, too.

'I've got somebody here I want you to take back to town, Daniel. You'll take her back alive.'

'Don't listen to him, Brannigan! Let my daughter go, Manning! If you let her go, I'll give you five minutes grace!'

Five minutes grace? Sam thought that was highly amusing. Luke never had much sense of time. Sam tightened his grip on Maddy, more to ease her shaking than to give the impression he'd shoot her at any moment.

'This person I've to take back to town, Manning. Is she Anna Hall?' Daniel called and as he did, Anna appeared. She was holding the baby which was supposed to be dead as well.

'Why did you do it, Papa!' Maddy screamed.

Luke moved so quickly even Sam was taken by surprise. Daniel was pushed aside and he fell at the shaft's gaping, hungry edge. Sam saw the glint of metal, of hidden gun. He should have known.

He pushed Maddy away violently as two bullets sped past. Sam screamed at the girls to get inside. Daniel was screaming too, caught on

216

the crumbling edge of the bottomless hole, arms outstretched to prevent the fall. Overbalancing, terrified.

Luke tried to run. He heard his daughter's screams as the first bullet hit him high in the back. The second shattered kidney. He fell face first into a slag heap of rough, cutting quartz. Traces of silver winked at him.

And Maddy was still screaming but strangely, she wasn't screaming for him. Luke felt Manning's boot crush the hand which still held the small pistol.

'You're not gonna hang me, are you, Luke? You're not gonna hang me again. Your daughter knows, you hear me. She knows now. And she knows where all the gold is. The gold you stole. The gold you killed for!'

Sam kicked Luke to his back. He felt nothing. He didn't want to feel. He didn't want to see the eyes, either. Begging. Sam took the gun. Luke was paralysed, blood foaming from his mouth. He was dying.

'Sam! For God's sake, quickly!'

Sam turned. Anna was on her stomach, one arm around the baby, the other hand clinging to Maddy's ankle. Maddy in turn was clinging with all her might to Daniel's leg.

'Daniel!'

The edges of the shaft were crumbling quickly from the added weight. Both girls were screaming for help. Sam grabbed for Daniel's trousers and heaved but only the trousers moved. 'Help me, Maddy!'

He grabbed for a swollen, injured leg. Maddy's nails were drawing blood around the young trooper's ankle.

'Now!'

Terror added to each's strength.

Daniel slid back from the dark shaft, his pants around his ankles, the flesh from his legs to his chest seared along the broken cutting ground.

Sam rolled him over. The poor boy's face was white. Maddy sat on her behind with a tremendous thump and started to howl.

Sam rose to his feet and bent to help Daniel stand if his legs allowed. Another shot cracked from nowhere.

Or so it seemed.

Sam felt the sudden fire and it thrust him backwards. He landed heavily, the ground whipped out from under him. He couldn't move. He couldn't breathe. Brilliant colors appeared in his mind, reds, yellows, blues, greens. Wheels. Geometric shapes. Damn, he thought. I'm going to die.

217

From the edges he heard Anna screaming, and another's deep throated curse:

'Porter, you bloody idiot! I wanted him alive!'

Is that all they have to say? Sam thought, and then there was nothing.

Maddy was frozen, watching as if separated from herself. She felt nothing. She was numb. Daniel. Sam. Papa? 'Papa!' she screamed and suddenly found her legs able to move. Inspector Flannagan was making her father as comfortable as he could. Papa was trying to talk and each time he tried to take a breath, blood flowed from his mouth. Maddy knew what he was trying to say, even if he couldn't talk.

'Maddy, come away. Please.' Daniel was tugging weakly on her arm.

Maddy pushed him away and knelt close to her father. He tried to hold her hand and say her name but Inspector Flannagan was in the way, talking about murders and robberies and possession of stolen goods.

That was when Daniel did manage to drag her away. He needn't have bothered. Her father was already dead.

Daniel tried to apologise but nothing could take away the empty nothingness which threatened to stay, forever, until Maddy wiped away her tears, stopped her howling, and saw Anna.

'Mrs Hall?'

Anna looked up but her vision was a blur.

'I'm Lieutenant Barton from the Commissioner's office.'

'You're too late,' Anna whispered.

'Come now, my dear. It's over. Come on, with me. We've a lot to discuss. A lot of questions remain unanswered.'

He was holding her baby. Anna didn't notice. Sam was limp and heavy in her arms, his blood hot against her skin. She felt she was drowning in it.

'Anna, my dear, you can't help him now.' The stranger reached out.

'Don't touch me!' she screamed and clung tighter, as if holding Sam close would rekindle the life that was there only a moment ago.

And it took three strong men to disentangle the woman from the dead bushranger.

218

Flannagan and Barton took the women and the baby back to town, leaving Brannigan and Porter to bring the bodies in. Daniel helped Porter with the sergeant, who was more cooperative in death than he had ever been in life. 'I'll be along shortly,' he said and waited for Porter to go.

Daniel sat and rolled a smoke with shaking, bloodied fingers.

It was three in the afternoon on a day he wished to God had never existed. Time had no meaning. What did now? He looked down at Manning again, at the blood seeping from the hole in the chest.

But dead bodies don't bleed, not when the heart has stopped.

'Manning, can you hear me?' There was no reply. 'You saved my life,' Daniel said. 'For that I thank you.' He struck a match against his boot and lit the cigarette, and thought of the Newberrys.

Anna remained in a state of limbo, a direct result of the government doctor's strong medication. She was vaguely aware that life around her continued, vaguely aware of Maddy's presence; the Inspector, the Lieutenant. Over and over they asked her to relate her story, which she did, numbly. She signed papers not knowing what she was putting her name to.

Mrs Flannagan was there constantly, offering a comfort no one alive could give.

Zelda, the Flannagan's housemaid, was caring for Susan.

Sam was dead and part of Anna had died with him.

Maddy was to be escorted to Brisbane after her father's funeral. Anna wondered if she would say goodbye.

She saw little of Daniel—he too, had locked himself away from prying questions, idle curiosity. Anna had no one except well-meaning strangers who would call in to see how the lass from Bitter Creek fared.

After the inquest she would be a very wealthy widow.

But she didn't care.

On December 31st, 1867, the day of Lucas Hannaford's burial, Anna sat alone on the verandah of the Inspector's house. Her thoughts were not her own. Her thoughts were tipping the scales to the side of insanity. For

219

when she dozed in the shade, the breeze cooling her skin, in her mind's eye she still saw Sam's smiling eyes. She could still hear his voice. She could still feel his touch. It was as if he had never died at all. It was as if this had been another of his eternal silly jokes.

Forget me. Go on with your life.

She could almost hear his voice.

It was true. She was insane.

Anna saw the young woman standing by the front gate. By her face, her clothing, her stance, Michael would have called her a whore.

'Don't suppose a lady like you would let the likes of me in?'

'The Inspector is not at home.'

'He's at the funeral. I know. If you're Anna Hall it's you I've come to see.'

'What do you want of me?' Anna asked weakly, tired of these strangers and their curiosity.

'What I've got to say won't take long.'

'Come in then.'

The woman opened the gate and drew her skirts up as she walked. Her hips swayed. Her breasts jiggled.

'My name's Ginger-Lee Cleary and I want you to know that—' Her words failed.

Yes, all those words she'd been saying to herself for three days now, ever since Daniel told Nelly how he'd lost Sam's body, horse too, down a damned mine shaft at Spencer's Brook. The words wouldn't come now.

Something in this woman's eyes swept them away. Ginger-Lee stared at pure grief as if she'd never seen it before, or felt it herself.

'You're Ginger-Lee?' the woman asked.

'You know about me? Sam told you?'

'Go away. Just go away.'

'You didn't know him like I did. No matter what you might say, you didn't know him!' she cried.

Anna rose unsteadily and fumbled her way towards the front door. She closed it behind her but even a closed door couldn't keep out the hysterical voice, the accusations. 'He loved me, not you! He was going to marry me one day! Me, you hear me! *Me!*'

Anna found the bottle of Malt Scotch in the dining room cupboard and she didn't bother reaching for a glass. There was no one about to offend; she was beyond pain now. Physical, mental—it didn't matter.

220

Anna drank until she collapsed. For within that bottle lay a nullity so complete, not even a memory could touch her.

All of the gold had been recovered. Maddy had kept her promise. The place in which Sam Manning had lived for three isolated years was finally discovered. And another cache of stolen goods was reclaimed.

Life continued. It was as if one man's presence and sudden, violent departure made no difference at all.

The episode, although not entirely forgotten, eventually lost its impact on the town and its people. Journalists had travelled from cities to interview her and Anna never read their words.

The newspaper stories though, with assistance from the Queensland Commissioner's Office, prompted a review of a verdict handed down in Castlemaine courthouse in 1861. Lawyers' fees which barely dented Anna's fortune brought about a posthumous pardon.

Had Sam lived, he'd have been reinstated to his former rank.

It was Millie Blackburn's incessant letters which prompted Anna to return to her previous existence in Brisbane. Some six months later, Anna moved, taking the coach with her eighteen month old child.

But time healed nothing. She would have given her wealth to anyone for the chance of having Sam beside her again.

When the coach slowed for the crossing at the bottom of Mitchell's Hill, her wish was almost granted.

'Regular as clockwork he used to be,' one of the male passengers mumbled.

'It's not Wednesday,' Anna said, ending another trail of lies before they began. She knew who the man referred to—he was yet another who claimed to have known Sam Manning personally.

As the coach gathered speed again, Susan woke. Her habit was to kneel on Anna's lap and gaze out of the window. 'Dad-dad,' the child sang, happily.

Anna hadn't heard those words for an eternity. She looked out of the window, too, drawing back the canvas which kept the wind from her face. And for an instant, she thought she saw a man on a gray horse, then the coach turned in another direction. Anna thrust the child to the nearest man and scrambled to the other side of the coach in time to see the figure disappear into the thick bush.

But perhaps there had been nothing there. She asked if anyone else had seen the man on the gray horse? People regarded her strangely. Someone asked if she was feeling quite herself? She'd gone pale, rather suddenly. Her raging heartbeat returned to normal.

She felt as if she'd seen a ghost. But she didn't believe in such nonsense. Or lately, her imagination.

Brisbane. June, 1868.

Susan was tired, cranky. Crying now. Millie had tried her best to make the child see reason. Even a mouthful of lollies hadn't sweetened the temper. It had only made her worse.

Anna felt the child tug on her arm. Millie wanted a cup of tea and scones even though they'd just had lunch. They were at a standstill in Elizabeth Street. Under her feet, cobblestones. To her right, a gas lamplight. The store was a farmer's supply shop; all manner of agricultural things hung amid dusty cobwebs in the window.

'Mind Susan,' she said and pushed the door open. Dust attacked her nose. Anna sneezed in spite of herself. She smelled dusty hay. Leather. The old man behind the tattered counter asked if he could help her.

'I would like to speak to the owner of this establishment,' Anna said.

Outside, holding a naughty child, Millie wondered what on earth was taking so long.

Anna eventually reappeared. 'Don't ask now, Millie. I shall tell you when I'm able.'

Millie, knowing Anna of old, kept quiet. She kept quiet as they walked into the bank and Anna asked to speak to the manager. As always, she was heralded in immediately.

'Anna?' Millie asked later, no longer able to contain curiosity.

'I have just bought a dream, Millie. Didn't you want a cup of tea?'

Maddy saw the carriage approach and the woman who emerged needed no introduction. 'Mrs Hall!' she screamed as she took the stairs two at a time in her rush to meet Anna at the gate. She didn't even care what she looked like, appearances weren't necessary when there was no one to deceive.

222

Anna couldn't believe that this same creature was Maddy. She was bounding to her, arms outstretched. Anna knew the impending hug would shatter her ribs, so she turned back and beckoned Susan to come out. The little girl slowly climbed down from the carriage all by herself. She grinned at Maddy. She remembered her face.

'Yes, it's good to see you, too, Maddy', Anna said, trying to ward off the excited hug.

In a way it was. She looked older, if not wiser. She had lost weight. Her hair wasn't as long. The dress she wore was wet at the knees, her sleeves rolled up.

'Come in. Mother's not home, I'm afraid. Perhaps that's for the best.'

'It's not your mother I've come to speak to, Maddy.'

As they walked up the stairs and inside, Maddy fussed over Susan. 'Mind the floor, Mrs Hall. It's wet.'

Into the house they went.

'Do you have a job, Maddy?'

'No.'

'Would you like to work for me?'

'Oh, yes!' Came the eventual yell of joy when she discovered she would be sewing again, making hats with three other girls upstairs at Annabelle's Millinery in Elizabeth Street.

Maddy began her new job the next day, much to Mother's disgust that her daughter should have to go out to work. It seemed highly unlikely Maddy would ever marry, so she waved her eighteen year old daughter goodbye and wondered who would keep house for them now. Rachel would have to pay for a housemaid, she supposed, as she closed the door with a sigh.

Maddy stopped outside the appointed place in Elizabeth street. Something about it was vaguely familiar. She walked in. The smell was of lavender. There was a woman engaged in polishing a new counter top. 'Yes?' she asked, knowing this young woman was not a prospective customer. How could she be? There were but six items in the display case.

'I'm here to see Mrs Hall.'

'You must be Maddy Hannaford. Upstairs with you. Mind the third step, it's still being repaired.'

Maddy trudged up the stairs and knocked on the door. She remembered why the shop was familiar. Anna had drawn it, almost two years ago, Christmas Day, 1867.

'Do you still think of him?' Maddy asked late one night when the others had left and she and Anna were sipping cups of tea.

'I think of him all the time, Maddy. It's as if he isn't dead at all.'

Oh, but he was. Hadn't she held him, this dead thing that was once the man she loved? Hadn't she felt the warmth of his blood staining her skin?

'Have you heard from Daniel?'

'I received a letter from him last week. He's now in Bowen.'

'That's a fair distance from here.'

'He wants to see me when next he has time off work and can come to Brisbane. Some news he said. News he can't put in a letter. Someone I used to know is working with him. He asked after you. I've not replied to his letter yet.'

'Send him my regards.'

'I always do, Mrs Hall.'

'What are you going to do about James Burnett if you don't mind my asking?'

Anna smiled to herself. James. Dear, how he was persistent. It would be a good merger—he with his fashion house, she with her hats.

A marriage of convenience it would be, if only Susan didn't run and hide each time James came to court Anna. The child just didn't like him.

'I don't know, Maddy. My mind is imagining a good investment for Susan's future but my heart imagines a life of boredom. What would you do?'

'You ask me?' Maddy declared, wide eyed. 'How does he kiss?'

'Like any man who sees me as a lucrative commodity.'

'Don't then,' Maddy said.

She wrote to Daniel that night and told him all about Anna and the business and how every man in the city was after her for her money.

I think she still loves that bushranger, Daniel. I think we all do.

224

During his lunch hour, Daniel took Maddy's letter across to a park by the water and he read her words again as he ate his sandwiches. It was long letter and just what he needed to hear. He ran back to the station and searched everywhere for his superior. 'What's wrong with you? If that smile got any wider you'd swallow your own face.'

'There's something here you should read, Sarge.'

Anna returned from a trip to Sydney with a case full of sketches and photographs of the latest London designs, new fabric samples and colourful accessories. She had two problems—James Burnett who called each day for her decision, and a more daunting one: how to choose five new staff members from a short list of sixteen applicants.

Anna had the distinct feeling of being followed from the moment she stepped off the train and made her way to the office. The feeling dissolved when the door closed behind her and she'd finally been able to kick off her shoes. She called Kathleen to make her a cup of tea and bring the mail.

Millie appeared instead. 'Well?' she asked. 'How was it?'

'I'm glad to be home. How many times has James been in?'

Millie held up both hands and wriggled each finger twice. Anna groaned. 'Have you decided yet?' Millie asked.

'I can't, Millie.'

Millie fell into the chair, folded her arms and sighed. 'But you should marry him, Anna. He's handsome, he's rich—'

'Millie, if you have nothing better to do, I shall find something.'

'It's *him*, isn't it.'

'Millie, not now.'

'It *is* him. You're still hoping a dead man will walk through the door.'

Anna closed her eyes. It was true. Sam Manning may have been dead but he was still very much alive in her mind: the indelible smile, the gleam in his eye. The only photograph she needed lay in her memory. She consulted it regularly. Each time James attempted to embrace her, kiss her, she responded only if she could pretend he was Sam. But Sam's body lay in a mineshaft, two hundred miles southwest of reality, away from the city noises of carriages, buggies, trains, people in a hurry.

And Millie was still carrying on as she always did. 'You have to start living for yourself, Anna. Oh, dear, you look so tired and weary. Shall I call a cab for you?'

225

'No. I have to sort through another mess I've brought upon myself. Thank you, Millie. You can go home now.'

Anna opened the case. The silk rosebuds she'd purchased in Sydney were squashed even though she'd told the porter to be careful with the case. Next time, she would take care of it herself. She sighed and reached for her shortlist of applicants.

Kathleen came in with the tea. 'Ma'am? There's a policeman waiting downstairs and he wants to speak to the manageress. I told him you weren't available but he refuses to leave.'

Anna sighed. 'Tell him I'll be there shortly. Offer a cup of tea, it usually calms them down.'

After a little while, Anna squeezed her shoes back on to her aching feet, adjusted her hair and came downstairs.

The uniformed policeman, a sergeant, was holding a cup of tea which Kathleen had given him. He was staring out of the front window. He was tall. His light brown hair was sun bleached, and something about his bearing seemed vaguely familiar to Anna. For a moment, her heart leapt from recognition, and then common sense prevailed. 'You wished to see me?' Anna asked wearily.

The man turned and his eyes were so terribly blue, intensified by his sudden smile.

'Do you know how many hat shops are in this town, Anna-Ma'am?'